THE ISLAND
AND THE RING

THE ISLAND AND THE RING

Laura C. Stevenson

Houghton Mifflin Company
Boston 1991

This is Meg's book

Library of Congress Cataloging-in-Publication Data

Stevenson, Laura Caroline, date
  The island and the ring / Laura C. Stevenson.
    p. cm.
  Summary: After treachery destroys her kingdom, Princess
Tania discovers that it is her destiny to confront Ascanet, the
ruthless lord enslaving the island of Elyssonne.
  ISBN 0-395-56401-8
  [1. Fantasy.]   I. Title.
PZ7.S84766Is 1991   90-28238
[Fic]—dc20   CIP
                          AC

Printed in the United States of America

VB 10 9 8 7 6 5 4 3 2 1

Prologue: The Island

IN THE BEGINNING, before there were stars, suns, or planets, before there was an earth and a sky, before there was land and water, the universe was a silver void of endless silence. This was the realm of chaos, and it was ruled by Orcus, an unformed spirit who whirled through its breathless confusion, forcing apart any atoms that attempted to end their tumbling, conflicting disorder by combining into form or matter.

The empty strife of chaos ended when the great god Theon harmonized Orcus's discordant elements and formed the earth, the stars that protected it by night, and a sun that warmed it by day. The earth itself he separated into seas and land, adorning it with trees, flowers, and grass, four-footed animals that roamed the continents, fish that swam in the sea, birds that filled the air. Finally, Theon took the purest elements in everything that grew and pressed them together between his palms. When he opened them, a woman stepped from his right hand and a man from his left. These were the parents of mankind; they and their descendants peopled the new earth and lived upon its fruits, without kings, without laws, without wars.

In Theon's new Creation, all were happy except Orcus,

who hated the concord he saw on earth and vowed to return the elements to their former state. Transparent, invisible, disordered, the spirit skulked among the people of Theon, teaching them such words as "mine" and "thine," showing them how a man who hoarded what was given freely to all could become more powerful than his fellows, telling them that vaster riches lay across the seas, waiting to be taken. And after centuries of hearing his whispered counsel, Theon's people began to live as Orcus wished them to. They ripped the earth apart in their search for precious metals, though it had long produced everything they had needed without toil. To protect the wealth they thus gained, they built walled cities and castles, thus forcing themselves to exchange their metals for food that had once been available to all. And to protect their cities, their castles, and their stores, they forged weapons that enabled them to kill the people with whom they had once lived in peace. Soon, the natural affection, love, and harmony Theon had bestowed upon his favored creatures disappeared; no man was safe from his brother's envy, no woman dared walk by herself, no child dared leave his parent's side. Men fought with each other as the elements had warred in Chaos; the sun began to shine less brightly than it had; the earth grew cold and dark.

Seeing the damage Orcus had done, Theon imprisoned the spirit in a cavern far below the earth, decreeing that he could emerge again only in some visible, ordered form. But even Theon could not undo the work of Orcus; once discord had entered the soul of mankind, only the shadow of order could be preserved. Knowing this, Theon wept, and all the clouds in the skies wept with him. Gradually, the lakes, rivers, and oceans rose until at last the people who had destroyed the concord of the world were drowned in the grief of their creator.

In one far-off mountain valley, however, the people of Theon had shunned the temptations of Orcus and lived as the first man and woman had lived. When the skies opened, Theon lifted these people and their mountains out of the earth, holding them in his hands until the waters receded. And when the flood ended, he placed their land in the middle of the sea, protecting it by unnavigable currents and granting to it all the blessings that remained to be given to the earth. Thus was formed the Island of Elyssonne, the last relic of the creation. And for a thousand years, the uncorrupted inhabitants of Elyssonne dwelt peacefully, innocent of the kings, laws, courts, and armies of the reordered world that sprang from the mud of the Mainland.

But one day, Ascanet of Adesh, a Mainland prince famed for his scholarship and skill with the lute, discovered a strange stone while he walked by the sea. That night, he rode to the mountains without his retinue, and in the morning, he announced that he had decided to conquer and rule Elyssonne, the island that lay on the horizon. Lords and generals demurred; sea captains insisted the channel between Elyssonne and the Mainland could not be crossed, but Ascanet waved aside all opposition. When he had defeated Elyssonne, he said, he would be able to rule all the world, and his followers would become kings. Having won his courtiers to his cause, Ascanet journeyed across the mountains and tamed the fierce hippogriffs of the north; within a few months, the great winged creatures had become so obedient to him that they carried him and his army across the channel to Elyssonne.

And so it was that discord and perpetual winter came to the island Theon had blessed with harmony and unending summer. Ascanet made kings of his followers and ordered each king to destroy all those who refused to obey him. He taught the terrified islanders to profit by betraying each other's trust; he taught youths that there was nothing more glorious than war. Within a decade, the island's subjugation seemed complete—and yet Ascanet did not embark upon his promised conquest of the world. Generation after generation passed, and still he stayed, miraculously preserved from old age and death, but never satisfied with his victory, though the island came to resemble not the reordered continent, but the world before the flood, and its inhabitants lived in terror of the Silver Souls, the faceless soldiers who served Ascanet with no thought of disobedience or mercy.

During the five hundred years that passed after Ascanet invaded Elyssonne, only two people dared to defy his power. One of these was Asphodel, a maiden whose brothers were among the first islanders to join Ascanet's forces. Tossing her dark hair, Asphodel called her brothers cowards and swore she would live in the forest before she bent to Ascanet's will. They laughed at her, but Ascanet did not; entranced by her beauty, determined to break her spirit, he asked for her hand. Her brothers gave it willingly, but hearing that, she ran off into the forest as she had threatened and lived among the wolves who made it their home. Ascanet pursued her there, and the Silver Souls hunted the wolves mercilessly, but for months, Asphodel remained free. One day after Ascanet had ridden in search of her, he galloped out of the forest on a horse gone mad with terror, shaking with fear himself. Neither he nor his Silver Souls set foot in the forests of Elyssonne thereafter—but the people who secretly rejoiced in Asphodel's victory soon sorrowed, for she was never seen again.

The other person who braved Ascanet was King Campion of Mazion, whose family was descended from one of the lords Ascanet had brought from the Mainland and made a king. For generations, the kings of Mazion had fought with two rival princes—the kings of Dolc and Fami—for full possession of the island, but nothing had come of their wars but the despair of their subjects. When Campion was young, he saw that despair and grieved for it. Telling his father he wished to learn more of the island before he became a king, he set off, disguised and alone, to explore it. Nobody ever discovered where he had gone, but when he returned, he brought with him a quiet, dark-haired bride, a magnificent gray colt, and the knowledge that Ascanet himself fomented the wars between his subjects, secretly setting them against one another by spreading rumors of attacks and betrayals that had never existed.

And so, when Campion became king, he promised his people that he would never rest until he had unified Elyssonne's kings against their conquerer, defeated him, and brought back the Golden Age in which the islanders had lived as Theon had wished them to. For nearly twenty years, Campion worked to keep that promise, using all the words, treaties, and troops at his disposal. Slowly, his people began to share the vision of the king they came to call Campion the Valiant. And when it was finally whispered from cottage to cottage, from village to village, from city to city that the kings of Dolc and Fami had come to Mazion on a peaceful mission, the men and women who spread the news looked at each other with hope they did not dare express.

CHAPTER

I

TANIA LEANED TOWARD the frozen windowpane and blew a hole in the ice that covered it. Peering through the opening she had made, she saw a flash of black and gold as the royal trumpeters of Mazion marched across the parapet and sounded an elaborate fanfare of welcome. A moment later, a hundred horsemen surged into the courtyard, led by her father, King Campion of Mazion, and her brother, Prince Paran. As the riders dismounted, all was noise and confusion: horses stamped and steamed, brightly cloaked riders tossed their reins to grooms, and stableboys unloaded carts draped with crimson and green livery. The kitchen doors burst open, and thirty pages emerged, bearing steaming wine to all the riders, but serving first three men whose brilliant clothes and circlets proclaimed them to be the King and Crown Prince of Dolc, in crimson, and the King of Fami, in green.

A little to one side of the crowd, King Campion vaulted off his war-horse and laid his hand fondly on its gray crest. Then the two parted, the man to join the visiting kings, the stallion to the stables, both opening the crowd of knights and stableboys without seeming to command, accepting the awe of those about them as natural.

Campion bowed as he reached his visitors and was just beginning to speak, when a single rider on a lathered horse galloped in the gate and pulled up. Several pages shouted the news of his arrival in alarm, but Campion merely nodded to Paran, who had slipped through the crowd to stand beside him. Tania saw her brother hurry to the weary pair and listen to the message the rider had brought. She couldn't see Paran's face well enough to tell whether the news was good or bad, but she saw that he waited to see that horse and man were taken care of before he returned to the other royalty. Tania smiled and looked at the crimson-cloaked Crown Prince of Dolc, who had been watching. Would he have been so thoughtful? He was said to be brilliant in the battlefield, but impatient with subordinates.

She gazed down at the colorful, circling crowd until it dispersed, then walked moodily to the fireplace and sat down, picking up her lute. As her fingers grew warm enough to play, she let them guide her through an exercise that Melibe, her tutor, had taught her. Eight bars of music, then the last four backward; four bars forward, two backward; two bars forward, one backward; one forward. Cadence. An exercise of memory, Melibe had said—and a pattern of harmony and dissonance that reflected the progress of history.

Tania strummed the lute idly, reflecting that she had just witnessed the beginning of a new age of harmony in Elyssonne: the prelude to the alliance of Elyssonne's three kings against their conquerer. She should rejoice—and of course she did. But every whisper of excitement that had preceded the great event had reminded her that her own role in the progress of history consisted merely in watching it pass. And now, having looked down into the crowd of eager men who felt victory was before them, she felt suffocated, not sheltered, by the walls that protected her from the achievements of their alien world.

None of the other women who lived confined in the Ladies' Tower felt as she did, but then, she was the only one among them who had grown up in the world of men. When she was born, Campion had decreed to a shocked court that she was to be treated as her older brother's equal, for women in the Golden Age had had the same education and freedom as men, and for many years, she had been treated as Campion wished. Quiet, black-robed Melibe had taught both royal children first to read, then to love literature, logic, music, and history; Campion's groom had taught them both to ride, then to train young horses. Thus, by the time she and Paran were in their teens, they had acquired enviable skill and knowledge—except the skill of political bargaining and the knowledge of warfare. By some oversight, Melibe had omitted those subjects from their educations.

But then, on Paran's sixteenth birthday, Campion had unaccountably announced that his children had enjoyed the freedom of the Golden Age long enough; now they would have to become true members of the court. Within a day, Paran had moved from the apartments he and she had shared with Melibe to the barracks; subsequently, his days were filled with politics, fortifications, drills, and fencing. And on that same day, she was moved to the Ladies' Tower, the section of the castle set apart from the rough world of men. Henceforth, although she was allowed to keep her books, music, and lute, and although she was allowed to ride three afternoons a week, her days were filled with embroidery, idle talk, and little else. Melibe, who had never loved the ways of the court, quietly left the castle, despite her tearful pleas that he stay. Nobody in Mazion had seen him since.

In the first days she spent in the tower, she'd been convinced that Campion had gone mad, and she'd thought of running away and living in the forest, as Asphodel had centuries earlier. But as her anger changed into reflection, she'd realized that for the past ten years, Melibe had been obliged to excuse Paran from many of his lessons to study swordsmanship and ride in mock charges; she had been sent for herself, to learn to dance, to embroider, and to converse gracefully. She had assumed such interruptions were an inevitable part of growing up, but in retrospect, she could see that Campion had shied away from his determination to fit his children for the Golden Age. Why he had done so, she didn't know; but she suspected the progressive alteration of their lives had been a small reflection of something much larger.

As she sighed and began to play the lute again, the door behind her swung open and one of her attendants hurried breathlessly in. "My lady! Your father wishes you to come to the State Chamber!"

"The *State Chamber?*"

"Indeed, my lady. And as soon as possible."

Tania jumped up and ran to her mirror. Her uncertain, warped reflection looked back at green eyes, at long dark hair neatly coiled around her head, and at a face which, if not quite yet that of a woman, was not that of a girl either. She looked at it thoughtfully for a moment, then handed the attendant the train of her dress and swept down ten frigid, curving flights of steps, hurried through corridors thronged with bowing courtiers, and finally arrived at the heavily guarded entrance to the State Chamber. Nodding at her attendant to leave, she walked through the door and heard it close behind her. In the sudden silence of the great room, she curtsied deeply without looking up.

"You may rise."

She stood and raised her eyes. Twenty feet away from her, Campion was seated on his throne, wearing a gold circlet set with emeralds. Paran stood next to him, taller than she remembered him. She crossed the flagstone floor, trying to

4

think how long it had been since she'd seen either of them at this distance. Six months? No, more than that. At least nine.

She curtsied once more, and they stared at each other in a silence that proclaimed them strangers. At last, Campion spoke. "The Kings of Dolc and Fami have come here to join us in an alliance against Ascanet," he said. "We have labored many years to bring this about."

Tania nodded, vaguely wondering if the "we" were the royal we, referring only to Campion, or if it referred to himself and Paran.

"Fami joined willingly," continued Campion. "But Dolc doubts our power. He has now convinced Fami not to join the alliance without his consent. That being the case, we have found it necessary to make a political sacrifice we had not originally envisioned." His eyes strayed to Tania's face as if seeking her approval.

"Any sacrifice that will cement the alliance is a worthy one," she said, relieved to find that her voice was firm.

"We are delighted to hear you say so," said Campion, "for it touches your welfare." He paused, looking at her steadily. "The King of Dolc will join us only on the condition that you marry Prince Radnor, his son."

Tania stared at her father's face, then at Paran's unyielding profile. "And have you agreed to these terms?" she whispered.

"We have said we would ask you to consider the Prince's suit."

"And if, having considered Prince Radnor, I find him . . . unacceptable?"

Campion turned to her with the expression he had worn the day he had told her she was to move to the Ladies' Tower. "When you have considered the suit, you will find Radnor to be everything a lady could wish for. He's a bold horseman, an intelligent speaker, and a patron of music. I've

5

heard he has the finest lutenist in Elyssonne in his retinue. And, of course," he added, frowning, "if you find him 'unacceptable,' the alliance will fail. We trust we do not need to tell you the probable results of such a failure."

No, he had no need to tell her Ascanet must be defeated, no matter what the cost. But this cost? She looked at Campion pleadingly, hoping that he'd remember he'd married a simple shepherdess for love. His eyes were not devoid of sympathy, but his face told her what she'd feared it would: for reasons she was unlikely ever to know, he'd had no choice. And unless she wanted to live in the knowledge that he had spent endless months preparing to defeat Ascanet, only to see his plans come to naught because of his daughter's refusal to affect history in the only way she could, she had no choice, either. She bowed her head. "Tell . . . tell His Highness the Prince that I will be honored to consider his suit."

There was a brief pause. Surely, they couldn't ask her to agree to marry the Prince before she'd met him. Could they?

"We thank you," said Campion at last. As she looked up, he held out his hand for her to kiss. "You will meet the Prince at the banquet that is to be held tonight. We will hear your decision tomorrow morning."

Tomorrow morning! She kissed his hand dutifully, rose, and would have backed away, but his fingers closed around hers. "I had hoped," he said in a voice she remembered from her childhood, "to spare you the clumsy hands of politics. When you were born, I vowed that by the time you were old enough to marry, you would be as free as the women of the Golden Age. But time has mocked me." He looked at her sadly for a moment, but his face soon hardened. "You may go," he said in his state voice. "Your brother will accompany you to the Tower."

Drained of everything but the habit of obedience, she

6

placed her ice-cold hand on Paran's arm, and they walked out of the State Chamber and through the corridors of whispering courtiers. Neither of them spoke until they'd reached her section of the Tower; then he looked at her.

"I'd like to talk to you," he said. "If I may."

"I'd . . . I'd prefer to be alone."

"I won't keep you long."

She could hardly refuse him, so she stepped through her door as the guard opened it, nodding at him to follow. Inside, she sat down on the settle and picked up her lute. Paran's footsteps crossed the room and halted a few feet from her.

"I wish you'd play something else, Tann," he said after a few minutes.

Startled, she realized she'd been playing Melibe's exercise; *there* was a piece of irony. She laid the lute down. "You don't like the progress of history?"

"Not at the moment." He shot a glance toward her chamber door. "Do your attendants eavesdrop?"

"Why should they? My life isn't interesting enough to be overheard."

Paran half smiled as he strode to the door and opened it; the guard in the empty corridor saluted. Paran returned slowly to the fire and leaned against the mantel, drumming his fingers. "Just after we rode in this morning," he said, "one of Father's scouts rode in with word that Ascanet has assembled a huge army in the Waste. That can mean only one thing: somebody has betrayed the alliance to Ascanet, and he will attack us before we can combine our troops if we don't sign it immediately. And yet, Dolc hesitates and bargains in his old way . . . Do you see?"

Tania nodded. "Is that why Father offered my hand to Radnor?"

"Of course. Dolc has desired the marriage for a long time,

and Father has declined up until now. But . . . well, we have two days, at most, and we don't dare tell Dolc and Fami what the circumstances are until everything is signed. Father wants to make sure Dolc sends his troops to us, not to Ascanet."

Tania tapped her cold fingers together. "I see. And so, if I agreed immediately to marry Prince Radnor instead of merely agreeing to consider his suit . . ."

". . . we could conclude the alliance this afternoon and send off riders to assemble the armies before nightfall. That was what Father had planned to ask you, but he couldn't bear to."

She looked down, remembering Campion's hesitation. "I suppose there's little difference between agreeing to marry a man one has never met and agreeing to marry a man one has met briefly."

"Very little, I should think." He spoke as if he were holding his breath.

"Then . . ." She had to swallow before she could choke out the words. "Then tell Prince Radnor I will marry him. Tomorrow, if he desires."

There was no mistaking the relief in Paran's face. "Not tomorrow," he said. "We'll need him on the battlefield first. He's a brilliant general . . ."

"Spare me," she whispered.

Paran looked at her apologetically. "I'm sorry—I forgot you didn't find military brilliance attractive."

"Neither did you, not so long ago."

Paran sighed. "Nor do I now," he admitted. He stood up and looked around her room, his eyes falling on the books and music that cluttered her shelves. "You aren't the only one whose life has been sacrificed to politics," he said. "I would gladly give up all pretensions of ruling Mazion and live cloistered here with such companions as these."

8

"You'd ache for freedom," she said.

"I doubt it. I never cared for it as much as you did." He looked at her skeptical face and smiled. "Well, we won't argue. I must tell Father of your promise. And I'll ask the Prince to meet you in the Gallery a half hour before the banquet begins. It's not much . . ."

"Thank you," she said, choking a little. "That's very kind of you."

"Tann, if there'd been any other way . . . I . . . look, Tann, I wept when Father told me . . ."

"Please," she said. "Please leave me." She had never cried in front of him in the past; if she could possibly help it, she wouldn't now.

He did leave her; she heard him cross the room, open the door, and instruct the guard to let none of her attendants in until she sent for them. Then his long strides faded into the silence of the corridor.

CHAPTER

II

TANIA DISMISSED HER ATTENDANTS at the foot of the
Gallery stairs and ascended the worn steps alone, holding her
velvet train over her arm and avoiding drafts that threatened
to blow little strands from her crown of braids. As she
opened the Gallery door, she found the long hall lit by a
hundred tapers, transfigured and elegant, as she was, to meet
the Prince of Dolc. She dropped her train, arranged it carefully behind her, then walked slowly past generation after
generation of refined faces framed by blond hair that varied
only in the way it was arranged, each smiling a formal, fixed
court smile. Allowing for the varying abilities of court
painters, all her ancestors looked remarkably alike. All of
them, of course, except one.

She stopped as she came to the last portrait in the row. It
had been painted shortly after her mother had married Campion, and it was not done in court fashion. Campion's bride
leaned gracefully against a tree, holding a shepherd's crook
and gazing at three romping lambs from under a pile of
thick, dark hair that wound around her head in a circlet of
braids. Her smile was like no other in the Gallery: a faraway
smile that suggested she saw beyond what others perceived
and was saddened by her vision. Tania looked at the portrait
wistfully. When she'd been a little girl, she'd assumed the

dreamy face was that of a woman grown, but looking at it now, she realized her mother had been then only a little older than she, Tania, was now. Paran's age, perhaps. And dead in childbirth within months of her twentieth birthday. Tania stood quietly, wondering what her own fate would be.

"I see you're visiting your relatives," said a voice behind her.

Tania started and turned. "Paran?"

A man emerged from the window seat opposite her grandfather's portrait and bowed; he was dressed in the crimson livery of Dolc. "Not Paran," he said. "A friend, sent to meet you in the Gallery because he has been detained. But I fear I have frightened you."

Prince Radnor. Tania curtsied deeply. "I was only startled because I didn't hear you come."

The Prince laughed. "I didn't come. I was here, wondering why men marry women who look so much like themselves."

"My father didn't," she said, smiling. "Have you seen the last portrait in the row?"

"No." He walked toward it; suddenly shy, she lowered her eyes. When she brought herself to look up, she found he was looking at the portrait with an interest she hadn't expected.

"And this is your mother?" he asked. "Where was she born?"

"I don't know," said Tania. "Only Father knows her parentage, and he will say nothing about it. Though he did say," she added sadly, "that he married her for love."

"That's no wonder," he said. "It would be difficult not to love a woman whose face reflects the goodness and innocence of . . ." He stopped abruptly and turned to her. "Ah! You, I think, look very like her."

He stepped into the light, comparing her to the portrait;

she took the opportunity to look at him. What she saw made her step back a pace before she remembered herself. Four parallel scars ran diagonally from the left side of his forehead to the right side of his chin, pulling his eyes and mouth into grotesque parodies of normal features. His dark hair was carefully cut to obscure as much of his countenance as possible, but a line of white slashed raggedly through it, covering some terrible wound. And while he stood gracefully, she could see that he favored one leg and that his left shoulder was hunched forward.

This . . . this gargoyle was to be her husband? Unbidden, memories of tearful tales young wives told their sympathetic older counterparts in the Tower floated before her. She looked desperately at the portrait of Campion that hung beside her mother's, but the young, familiar face returned her gaze without comprehension.

"Very like," said the Prince. A smile crept across his twisted face as he looked at her closely. "I should guess, however," he said, "that you lack your mother's patience. You are not, by your face, a paragon of serenity."

All her horror at his ugliness flooded into her cheeks. "And *I* should guess," she retorted, "that you are hardly in a position to say so until experience has proved you correct."

He laughed, mocking her with his terrible, disfigured eyes. "But you see, experience has just proved me correct."

She had let him score a point, and her humiliation drove two years of training from her tongue. "And who are you," she said, looking at him squarely, "to judge a woman by her face, pray tell?"

He stiffened, and she knew she should stop, but awareness of her cruelty only drove her on. "It may be the prerogative of princes to be candid," she said, "but . . ."

"The prerogative of princes!" he interrupted. "My lady! Surely, you don't think I am . . ."

"His Highness the Prince of Dolc," she said, stopped by the horror in his voice. "Come to meet me in the Gallery, as my brother arranged."

He shook his grotesque head. "I'm a fool to let you think so. My lady, I am not the Prince of Dolc."

Tania's hands jumped to her reddening cheeks. "Who, then?"

"Oh, a man with a mixed history," he said with a shrug. "But presently, a lutenist in Prince Radnor's pay. My name is Eliar; the surname is of so little consequence that you may ignore it. The Prince was detained, and he sent me here to meet you." He looked at her blushing, anguished face and forced his mouth into a smile. "I fear I have done you a grave injustice," he added. "If you thought *I* was to be your husband and uttered no word of protest when you saw me, you are indeed a paragon of serenity."

His smile faded, and his eyes wandered from her to some point at the end of the Gallery. The candlelight fell on his scars, highlighting all their repulsiveness—but also illuminating something behind them that she hadn't seen when she'd looked at him before. In sudden, deep penitence at the thoughts she'd let her tongue express, she touched his crimson sleeve. "You needn't credit me with a virtue I don't possess," she said, surprised by the gentleness of her voice. "You judged my face correctly. But you misjudge your own, if you think a lady would take you for her lord only out of serene, unquestioning obedience. Surely, it takes no extraordinary perception to see that whatever your outward misfortunes have been, they haven't damaged an understanding heart."

He stared at her incredulously. "You have no grounds for saying that."

"That's not true . . ." she began, then stopped, conscious that her judgment had been entirely intuitive. But when she looked at the dark-haired shepherdess, she realized she had

13

grounds she hadn't thought of. She smiled at Eliar. "You see, when you looked at my mother's portrait, you said not that she was beautiful, but that she was innocent and good."

He turned to the picture, and his silence lasted so long that she began to fear she'd spoken too freely. When he finally turned his ugly face back to her, however, the sharpness had gone out of it. "They await you in the Hall," he said.

He wasn't offended, then. She dropped her gaze, shy again in her relief. "I hadn't realized it was so late!" Turning to the window, she looked at her reflection as well as she could and felt her crown of braids. She thought she heard Eliar laugh softly, but when she turned to him, he was looking out into the night.

"Do these open onto the courtyard?" he asked.

"They do, but they're high, so you can see the mountains in the daylight." She peered at the panes, trying to see through their reflections. "Why?"

"I thought I saw a light."

Tania looked again and saw a faint glow flicker, then disappear. "That's peculiar," she said. "I thought the soldiers were all within the outer walls. Perhaps Father posted sentries on the Northern Pass. I don't know . . ." She smiled apologetically. "I'm afraid Father and Paran don't consult me in military matters."

Eliar raised one twisted eyebrow. "They should," he said. "You're a formidable opponent, and you're compassion itself in victory."

Tania wasn't sure whether he was being sarcastic or sincere, so she made no reply, though he seemed to expect one. They stood in awkward silence until he moved uneasily and looked at her. "We really must go."

"Indeed we must," she said gravely. "I was only waiting for you to offer me your arm."

His stunned expression assured her that she had discomfited him successfully, and as she took the arm he offered and adjusted her pace to his limping stride, she felt a little glow of triumph.

The tables in the Hall were filled with laughing courtiers when Eliar left Tania at the door and told the page to announce her presence. As the boy called out her name, the kings at the high table rose and the knights at the lower tables stood with them. Behind the screen that separated the Ladies of the Tower from the men of the court, laughing voices trailed off into the general stillness. Tania gave her arm to Paran, who had crossed the Hall to meet her; he led her to the high table, where she curtsied to Campion and turned to the visiting royalty. The King of Fami held out a plushy hand; she smiled, then curtsied again, this time to the King of Dolc. As he raised her, she saw an expression she'd often seen on the face of Campion's chief groom when he examined a filly newly come to the stable. She smothered a smile, thinking that if he picked up one of her feet and looked at it, she wouldn't be at all surprised. She was curtsying to Prince Radnor now, and her hand was in his. The hand was hard as iron, its long, tapered fingers ornamented with silver rings. Looking up, she saw the same appraising stare she'd seen in his father's face. Hard men, she thought with a twinge of trepidation—men who would never tolerate a temper or a slipping tongue. She smiled at Radnor, wishing he would speak.

But it was Paran who spoke first. "Come sit between Radnor and me, Tania; we've been comparing the merits of our horses, and we need an objective judge."

Radnor's eyebrows rose until they touched his perfectly coiffed bangs. "You are a judge of horseflesh, my lady?" he said. "That's interesting. Tell me—what conformation do you find most fitting in a war-horse?"

Tania ignored the worried glances of the two visiting kings. "Come, my lord," she said graciously, "your question is far different from my brother's. To answer his, I have only to listen to your praise of your horse and his praise of his; my judgment will have more to do with eloquence than with horses. But to answer yours, I must make an abstract judgment about a horse without considering the kind of battles you wish it to fight."

Radnor's eyes opened wide; next to him, his father chuckled. "You've raised a true statesman," he said to Campion.

Radnor looked irritated, and Tania spoke into an uncomfortable silence. "Thank you for sending your minstrel to accompany me to the Hall," she said, addressing the Prince alone. "He was most courteous. I see you are well served."

It had been the right thing to say; Radnor smiled. "Yes," he said, "Eliar is no beauty, but he is also no fool. And he's the finest musician in Elyssonne. We'll have a song from him after we've eaten."

"And one from Tania, too," said Paran. "She plays beautifully."

"So you are a musician?" Radnor looked at Tania curiously. "You have indeed been oddly educated for a lady. What instrument do you play?"

"The lute, my lord."

"Ah—a beautiful instrument if it's played correctly," he said. "Yes, I'll enjoy hearing you play."

"Thank you, my lord." She wondered if she could play at all with his gray eyes watching to see if she played "correctly," and she hoped he would forget his request. But it seemed he forgot nothing; at the end of the seventh and final course, he asked her to send for her instrument. When her page brought it, she tuned it before looking up to ask him what she should play.

He was leaning forward, studying the lute intently. "Was your instrument made in Mazion?"

"No, my lord. It was my mother's lute, and she was not from Mazion." She smiled at him. "Isn't it beautiful?"

"Exquisite. You'll have to show it to Eliar; he'll appear as soon as you've begun. He hates to be looked upon—who can blame him? But music draws him into company." He looked at the instrument once more, then leaned back. "So—play. And sing, too, if you can."

Tania played a few more chords, then, glancing at Campion, she felt her fingers drift into an introduction she hadn't even thought of for two years. He smiled sadly as he heard the opening chord progression; she looked away and began to sing.

> Sleep, sleep, child of man,
> Dreaming of the summer sun.
> When the ring is found alone,
> Winter shall be all undone.
>
> Theon will regain his stone;
> Love to Asphodel will come.
> Sleep, sleep, child of man;
> When you wake, 'twill all be done.

The plaintive tune wandered through the Hall, and Tania played it once more on the lute, without the words. As she caressed the final chords, the court around her sat silent, dreaming.

"Who taught you that song, my lady?" said a soft voice finally.

17

Turning, Tania saw Eliar standing behind Radnor's chair. "My tutor taught me the words," she said. "It's an old prophecy of some sort. But the tune is my own." She glanced at Radnor, hoping he wouldn't ask her to summarize her thoughts on melody and harmony.

But he didn't. Shaking himself out of the reverie that seemed to have enveloped him against his will, he turned to Eliar. "Can you tell me where her instrument was made?"

Eliar limped to Tania's side and bent over the lute. He opened his eyes wide, looked at her—then, seeing her bewilderment, at Campion, who was watching him. The king's eyes met his, and for a fraction of a second, Tania felt some message crackle in the air between them.

Eliar turned back to Radnor. "I can't say, my lord; it's an old instrument, beautifully kept, but that is all I know."

If Radnor suspected, as Tania did, that Eliar had said less than he knew, he made no remark. "Play it anyway," he said. "I don't think I've ever heard a finer tone."

Eliar sat down and played a few chords; Tania ruefully heard a quality of sound she hadn't even dreamed the instrument possessed. Almost in disbelief, she listened as Eliar spun out a single line of notes, added another melody to the first, another—then the complexity of intertwining voices overwhelmed her, and she was lost to everything except his music until he brought all three melodies together in a set of magnificent concluding chords.

"Great Theon!" said Paran when the applause in the Hall had ceased. "What is the enchantment you've played?"

"It's called a fugue, my lord; it's a braid of music with three equal strands plaited into a crown." Eliar's twisted eyes wandered to Tania's crown of braids, and he smiled.

Campion rose and bowed to Eliar. "You have the skills of the Golden Age," he said. "I would be flattered if you'd take the time to instruct my minstrel here"—he extended a fond hand toward Tania—"in your art. That is," he added as an afterthought, "if her future lord approves."

He turned to Radnor's chair, but stepped back, unable to conceal his surprise. It was empty.

The King of Dolc rose. "My son received a message from his groom," he said, embarrassed. "And I couldn't detain him from flying to the stables. You know how these young blades are about their chargers."

That was, Tania reflected, perhaps the only excuse Campion would hear with sympathy, but she could see annoyance behind his stately nod. "No doubt he will return quickly," he said. "In the meantime, we will dance."

At his words, the company began to file out of the Hall. Paran stepped to his father's side, and the King of Dolc took the elbow of the King of Fami as they followed. Left alone at the high table, Tania reflected that she was indeed merely a filly in a royal stable—of no personal importance to kings and of less interest to the intense, critical man she was to marry than his charger. She gathered up her train, preparing to follow them, then saw her lute leaning against a chair. Slowly, she knelt down to put it away, and as her fingers touched its familiar contours, she found that she was crying.

Uneven footsteps drew near her. "It's a magnificent lute," said Eliar's voice.

"Thank you," she said, keeping her eyes fixed on the instrument. To her surprise, he didn't leave; when she shut her case and looked up, she met a quiet gaze of sympathy. He hadn't stopped just to admire the lute, then. He'd seen . . . In unbelieving gratitude, she stood up and tried to smile. "Would you like to play it for a few hours? You could take it to the music room; it's at the foot of the Gallery stairs, at the end I entered this evening."

He hesitated. "You'd trust a stranger with a lute of this quality?"

"No," she said, smiling in earnest now. "But I'd trust a master lutenist to lose his life before he'd let a lute of this quality come to grief."

He bowed and took the lute case gently from her hands. "Thank you," he said. "I'll take great care of it and return it to you in the morning." He turned, and she watched him limp across the Hall to the Gallery door.

"Tania!"

She looked across the heads of the servants who were beginning to clear the tables. Paran was running across the Hall. "Did nobody . . . ?" He leapt up the steps and put an arm around her. "I was sure somebody would take you . . ."

She said nothing; he looked at her penitently for a moment before he gave her his arm. "Let's go through the Gallery," he said. "I'll welcome the silence."

She nodded, and they threaded their way through the tables to the door Eliar had closed behind him. As they reached the portrait of their mother, Paran caught the direction of Tania's gaze and stopped.

"You look very like her, with your hair like that," he said.

She looked at the picture. "I'm afraid I lack her serenity," she said. "She seems to have been able to accept things I find . . ."

Paran cleared his throat. "I'll talk to Radnor in the morning," he muttered. "He has no sister, you know . . ."

"Thank you," she said. In the embarrassed silence that followed, she remembered she'd meant to ask him a question. "Do we have sentries stationed on the Northern Pass?"

"No—all our men are stationed inside the walls; Dolc's are camped a mile south of here, and Fami's are to the east. Have you taken a sudden interest in military matters?"

20

"No, no," she said, laughing. "I saw lights on the Northern Pass when I walked to the banquet, and I wondered why they were there."

"Where?" He stepped to the windows and peered out, cupping his hands on both sides of his face. Tania blew out the taper closest to the window and looked, too. The full moon had just slid out from behind a cloud, turning the mountains black beyond the pale valley. Down the mountainsides, something shimmered like a silver waterfall, rippling light and dark as it passed through invisible trees.

Paran leaned his forehead against the cold pane. "Great Theon . . ." he whispered. He jerked himself up straight, and she saw terror in his face. He covered it in an instant, but she felt herself grow cold.

"It can't be . . ." she whispered. "The guards would have warned you if there had been anything amiss."

Paran tapped his fingers against his sword hilt. "That's true—they've said nothing." He thought for a moment, then turned to her. "Tann . . . if I give you a soldier's order, will you take it?"

She nodded dumbly.

"All right, then . . . go to the storeroom next to the music room. Get some of my old clothes out of the chest against the far wall—do you remember it?"

"I'm not likely to forget it," she said, "if you mean the one we got the flat of Father's sword for playing around when we were little."

"That's the one I mean. And we got the flat of Father's sword because that chest hides a passage that goes under the courtyard and branches: left to the stables, right to an exit outside the walls. Follow it to the stables, find Prince Radnor, and tell him to ride for his troops. After he goes, saddle Pandosto and push the lever in his hayrack. That opens a door through the outside wall of the castle. Go east through the forest until you come to the trail, then ride as hard as you can to the caves. If all goes well, either Radnor or I will find you there tomorrow."

Tania's mind seized the one familiar detail. "Nobody rides Pandosto but Father," she whispered.

"True—but if things go awry, I'll take comfort in knowing you're mounted on the fastest and best-trained war-horse in Elyssonne," said Paran. "Besides, he likes you. I'm sure you can manage him."

Tania swallowed. "All right. Tell Father . . ."

"Of course. And I'll come to you as soon as I can." He looked at her once more, then held her for an instant. Releasing her, he gave her shoulders a little shake. "Take care," he said.

He turned and ran back the way they had come, drawing his sword as he went. She picked up her train and hurried in the opposite direction, down the gallery of smiles that graced the confident, courtly countenances of her ancestors.

CHAPTER
III

HE WASN'T THERE. Tania shivered and blew on her hands, then combed more cobwebs out of her hair while she thought. She'd looked down all four aisles of stalls, in the feed rooms, the lofts, all the tack rooms—Prince Radnor was simply not there. Nor, for that matter, were the night grooms who should have been on duty. There was nobody in the royal stable of Mazion but two hundred horses and herself.

She would have to ride for Radnor's troops, then. If she kept her hair tucked into her hood, they wouldn't know she was a girl, and they would follow her back to the castle. She slipped up the aisle to the main tack room, where she'd emerged from the damp, cobweb-filled tunnel. Groping along the row of bridles, she found Pandosto's and slung it over her shoulder. As she felt along the racks of saddles, she heard . . . voices. They seemed to come from under her feet —but how was that possible? The tunnel was a state secret, and it had clearly not been used for decades. She crouched under the saddle racks, listening. More voices came from the tunnel; then footsteps climbed the ladder. Quickly, she threw a horse blanket over herself and rolled as far back under the saddles as she could.

A few yards away from her, the trapdoor opened and someone stepped out of it. "Oh, the stables. We should have gone straight."

The voice sounded vaguely familiar. Tania peeked out of a hole some horse had rubbed in the blanket. Two men stood in the tack room, wiping cobwebs off their faces in the light of a dark lantern. One of them was dressed in silver that made him seem to waver uncertainly in the dim light.

"Faugh!" he said in a high-pitched voice that made Tania shiver. "Mazion should scour his back entry."

The other laughed. "It certainly is little used. But skillfully hidden, nevertheless. How did you find it?" Tania suddenly recognized the voice—Prince Radnor's. But who was with him?

"The captain of the guards told me about it—most eloquently, may I say—under treatment," said the silver man.

"Your treatment must be very efficient," said Radnor. "Mazion's men are loyal to a fault. I wouldn't have thought the captain would break."

"It took longer than I had anticipated," said the silver man. "But there was time left over to dispense with the other guards while you were at supper." He glanced at Radnor. "They say Mazion's daughter is as beautiful a filly as a man could wish to have in his stable. Did you make no plans to take her with you?"

"No," said Radnor. "It would be difficult, and besides, beautiful or not, she knows nothing—are all Mazion's soldiers dispensed with?"

"Yes. And yours are in the courtyard. If I may say so, my lord, it was a brilliant strategy. There is little for my master's coming army to do."

"Once my men have set the faggots alight, there will be very little to do indeed. So. I would like my payment; I want to admire my handiwork from afar."

24

"My master never pays before he receives a benefit," said the silver man. "The castle still stands, after all."

"I've arranged assaults from within and without; isn't that enough?"

"It's a beginning, a beginning."

"It's a great deal more than that! See here—I've told your master about Mazion's alliance. I've gathered all the royalty in Elyssonne in one place so your master can destroy it. I've given your master the names of all the knights, lords, and soldiers who oppose him. And still he refuses payment? I assure you, I can undo what I have done!"

Tania forced herself to breathe quietly. Radnor had done all that? Her first feeling was a guilty surge of joy: *Paran and Father would never make me marry a traitor. I am free!* But the selfish thought soon lost itself in a myriad of others: *set the faggots alight . . . the destruction of the royalty of Elyssonne.* Unless she could find Paran and Campion, the castle would be lost.

"Calm yourself," said the silver man. "Let's have no talk of undoing. And if you want a guarantee of payment, you may have this. My master rarely parts with it, but he entrusted it to me, in case I found someone who was tempted to defect. I assure you, he values it beyond all things. He will never leave you unrewarded so long as it's in your possession."

Peering through the hole in her blanket, Tania saw Radnor's companion hand him a small, glittering object. Radnor looked at it and exclaimed: "Great Theon! What an exquisite piece!"

"Everything my master owns is exquisiᵤ " said the silver man dryly. "Though Theon has little to do with it."

Radnor glanced up suspiciously. "How can I be sure I can find him and collect my payment?"

"You have only to wear this; it will draw him to you."

"And if I decide not to wear it?"

"Then, were you but virtuous, my lord, you would be free of his influence. But I doubt that is a difficulty in your case." The silver man chuckled, then turned and drew something from his belt. "Now," he said, "if you will hold the trapdoor while I descend . . ."

Radnor complied, his eyes still appraising the gift that shone in his hand. The silver man took one step down the ladder, then turned and struck out. Radnor fell without a sound; the gift spun across the room and came to rest on the edge of Tania's horse blanket. The silver man grunted, wiped his dagger on Radnor's cloak, then forced open the Prince's clenched, twitching hands. Tania choked back nausea and fear. He was looking for the gift. Soon, he'd turn, see it, and . . . she inched her hand from under the blanket and pulled the shining object under its protecting edge.

Suddenly the trapdoor opened wide and fell back with a crash. The silver man turned, drawing his sword, and hurled the lantern at the form that leapt out of the opening. Sounds of sword beating on sword filled the darkness. Tania cringed under her blanket, then realized confusion would let her escape without being seen. Stealthily unrolling the blanket, she shoved the glittering object into her tunic pocket, picked up Pandosto's bridle, and sidled to the door. Once outside, she ran down the aisle between the restive horses, her heart throbbing with fear.

She reached the end of the aisle and opened the main door a couple of inches. It would be a risk, but she had to find her father . . . she stopped, staring: the courtyard was filled with silent men looking up at the Gallery windows in the moonlight. In the Gallery, a light flickered, flickered, flickered— then exploded into huge orange and yellow flames. She stared at the men's fierce, flame-lit smiles in disbelief, insensible of her own danger.

26

A crash behind her made her whirl around. Pandosto was rearing in his stall, pawing at the window that let in a stream of red light from the fire. A few of Radnor's men-at-arms shifted their gazes from the flaming Gallery to the stable. She ducked back inside, but not soon enough—a shrill whistle cut through the roar of the flames, and two men broke from the crowd and strode toward the door.

Shaking in panic that made her hands clumsy, Tania shot the bolts on Pandosto's door and slipped into his stall. He had stopped plunging and was looking out his window, his huge gray body nearly black with sweat. Somehow, his fear calmed hers; she stroked him and slipped the bridle over his head. As she pushed the spring in his hayrack, she heard the crunch of spiked boots on the floor outside the stall. The back of his stall creaked, groaned, then slid slowly open.

The spiked boots stopped. Desperately, Tania vaulted as high as she could, but Pandosto whirled, and she slid off. As she landed in the sawdust, a scream echoed down the aisle. The spiked boots started to run in the direction of the noise; soon Tania heard the sound of scuffling. Clambering up the iron bars of the stall, she slid onto Pandosto's back and urged him toward the outside door. He shot through it, snorting; it clicked shut just as they cleared it.

Outside the walls, everything was still except the terrible roar of the fire. The forest floor was dark and soft, covered with only a dusting of snow. Tania slowed Pandosto to a walk, and they threaded their way between the trees, both of them searching the red-lit darkness for signs of movement. Suddenly, the air filled with the blare of Mazion's trumpets, then a fainter call Tania knew must be Ascanet's. Instantly, the sound of the fire merged with shouts, screams, the neighing of war-horses, and the ring of steel on steel. Pandosto snorted and pranced, turning his head longingly toward the sounds of battle.

"No!" whispered Tania, turning him. "We're going to the caves."

The stallion's muscles coiled in protest, and for one dreadful moment, she felt him hesitate. She set her jaw and drove him forward, bracing herself for one of the explosions that occasionally threatened to land even Campion in the snow. But no explosion came. Pandosto looked back once more, then strode forward in the direction she had told him to go.

At last, Tania saw the moon-drenched road ahead of her and asked Pandosto to trot. He took two hesitant strides and sidestepped into the shelter of a tree, sniffing the wind that blew in their faces. Tania peered over his head and gasped. Fifty yards down the road, a company of silver horsemen shimmered in the moonlight, waiting for some command. Their horses pranced uneasily, but the men were utterly silent, their translucent bodies moving only in response to their fretting mounts. The Silver Souls.

Far down the road, a trumpet called. The rider at the head of the company raised his hand. In an instant, the soldiers grouped themselves into columns of four and cantered past the tree that hid Tania and Pandosto. As they sped by, Tania saw row after row of featureless visages cut only by lidless slits for eyes, lipless crevasses for mouths. Shuddering, she covered her face with her hands.

Pandosto flicked an ear and looked behind him. Tania snatched up her reins as she heard a faint jingle of bridles through the sounds of battle. She urged Pandosto out onto the road, turned him in the direction opposite from the one the Silver Souls had taken, and closed her legs on his flanks. He took off with a speed that left her breathless; trees flashed past her, and the road tilted as he rounded a corner with gigantic strides. She almost missed the trail that led up the mountain because of his speed, then turned him impossibly late, but he whirled to the right without missing a stride and

28

bounded through the deep snow at full speed, hesitating only when they reached a fork near the top. Still shaking in awe of the power underneath her, Tania peered into the trees. The path to the left led to the caves, the path to the right to a cliff from which she could look down at Castle Mazion. She turned to the right.

They reached the cliff after five minutes, and Pandosto pulled up of his own accord. Six hundred dizzy feet below them, Mazion Valley stretched out in the moonlight, and Castle Mazion should have stood proudly at its edge—but where the castle had been, there was only a sea of fire. As Tania watched, one of the great stone towers exploded, sending chunks of masonry cascading into the flames. Another tower leaned to one side, then slid majestically to the ground, sending up a splash of sparks. After it became engulfed in flames, masses of antlike men swarmed toward the outside walls, hurling themselves down into the plain. As they tried to regroup, a company of riders rushed from the forest, drowning them in a silver wave. Those still on the walls hesitated, trapped between the blazing castle behind them and the silver warriors at their faces. Tania buried her head in Pandosto's mane. "Oh, Paran . . . Father . . ."

She hardly noticed when Pandosto turned around and strode back through the forest; it was not until he stopped that she saw he had taken her to the caves. She slid to the ground and ducked into the smaller of the two caves for an armful of hay; as Pandosto began to eat, she slipped off his bridle and leaned miserably against him. He took another bite, then swung his head around and rubbed it on her shoulder. She scratched him behind the ears, but his lack of comprehension made her feel only more desperately alone. She left him with his hay, slipped into the larger cave, and curled up on its stone floor.

*   *   *

She lay all night with her eyes open, seeing the blazing castle in the darkness of the cave and listening to her mind spin plans. She would ride to some lord of her father's . . . unless Radnor had destroyed all of the men loyal to Campion. Could he have done it? She turned over, shaking, as a picture of the faceless Silver Souls flashed across her mind. If she wanted to find one of her father's lords alive, she'd have to ride quickly. Unless . . . relief made her eyelids droop. Paran had known about the tunnel exit from the castle. He must have escaped. And he'd know what to do.

When she opened her eyes, she realized with a shock that she'd slept well into midmorning. Throwing off her cloak, she crawled outside, expecting to see Pandosto waiting reproachfully for hay. But the clearing in front of the cave was empty. Her eyes scanned cliffs, snow-laden trees, the path—no gray stallion. But far worse than that . . . she looked down the path hopefully, then frantically . . . no brother. She sat on a boulder and dropped her head into her hands. *Oh, Paran.* In her heart of hearts, she had known he would never have left Castle Mazion to save himself. Nor would Campion. She had lost them both. She cried then—helplessly, like a little child, choking on her sobs.

Finally, exhausted and dizzy, she leaned back against the cliff and closed her eyes, letting her thoughts float from her grief to her own situation. Within a few minutes, she realized how serious it was. Pandosto was gone. Of course—she hadn't thought to tie him, though she'd used the cave trail to condition horses for years and knew perfectly well that halters and lead ropes lay waiting in the small cave. No doubt he'd trotted back to Castle Mazion and the grain he assumed would be waiting for him in his stall. And the Silver Souls would recognize him, wonder where he'd come from, follow the trail he'd left to the caves . . .

She had no hope, then; she had let her own horse betray her, and she could never escape from Ascanet's mounted troops. Unless . . . she stared at the inhospitable landscape around her, rose reluctantly, and took a few slow paces down the path toward the forest. Since the days of Asphodel, none of Ascanet's followers had set foot in any forests but the ones that, like the forest outside Castle Mazion, had grown up since the Golden Age. But the forest by the caves was not one of those; its looming trees were over a thousand years old. She would be safe there—at least safe from the Silver Souls. But what would happen to her? All the men who had tried to hide from Ascanet among such trees had staggered out after a few days, wide-eyed, stammering, gone mad with visions . . . Tania stopped on the edge of the path, looking up from the huge, moss-covered trunks to the branches that rose a hundred feet above her. They were certainly beyond being friendly, but there was something wonderful about their silent majesty. She took a deep breath, stepped off the path, and walked fifty feet into the trees before she allowed herself to stop.

The forest floor wasn't as clear as the one near the castle. Great trunks lay shattered on the snow-dusted needles, their roots curling in the air. Small trees, starved for the sun, wove the brittle tips of their dead branches together in a translucent tapestry, illuminated here and there by shafts of sunlight. A jay shrieked, its voice accentuating the stillness.

Tania looked over her shoulder one last time, then went on. The tapestry of branches pushed softly against her outstretched hand; as she touched it, light danced across a clearing that opened before her. She blinked and drew back into the protective shadows, staring. *A girl about her own age ran soundlessly into the clearing, her long hair flying out behind her. Stumbling over a hidden log, she fell and lay gasping on the ground. The jay shrieked again; suddenly, a blue-clad rider spurred his horse over the fallen trunks and galloped to the crumpled figure in the snow. Pulling his horse up, he leapt to the ground, drawing his dagger and laughing in triumphant silence. He ran toward the fallen maiden—but stopped, staring in horror. From the ground where the girl had collapsed, a great silver wolf leapt to its feet, its fangs bared and its yellow eyes gleaming fiercely. The man's horse reared in terror; he grabbed its bridle and vaulted on its back as it fled. The wolf sprang after them, snapping at the horse's heels, running alongside it, herding it in panicked circles among the trees. The rider drew his sword, but before he could aim a blow at the wolf, she leapt up and caught its hilt in her teeth, wrenching it from his hand and nearly pulling him from the saddle. Screaming in terror, the horse came upon the path and galloped down it, spurred on needlessly by its rider. The wolf watched them go; then, dropping the man's sword, she lifted her head and howled a long, soundless song of victory. As she sang, huge, shaggy-coated wolves appeared from all corners of the forest, each one bowing as it reached her.*

The branches moved gently, and the clearing disappeared. Tania stood alone, listening to the mysterious, vibrant hum that filled the air about her. Suddenly terrified, she backed toward the caves, wishing to go faster but afraid to run. At last she felt the path under her feet, and the strangeness of the forest unwrapped itself from her shoulders like an invisible cloak. She stared back into the trees, wondering if she'd gone mad.

"You'd do well to keep to the path."

The voice came from behind her. Tania whirled around, her wonder crumbling into terror as she saw a leering, demonic creature emerge from the entrance of her cave. It rose as she watched it and hunched itself crookedly down the path to meet her. No silent vision, this—she could hear its footsteps. Choking back a scream, she started to run.

"What, you don't know me, my lady? I realize our acquaintance has been slight, but even people with poor memories usually remember my face."

The voice was human. Tania hesitated, turned, then stared as the demon looked at her with a dry smile she suddenly recognized. It must be . . . but how could it be? . . . Eliar, Prince Radnor's lutenist.

"Exactly," he said, though she hadn't spoken. "I'm glad to see the forest hasn't deprived you of your sanity. It has that effect on many people. It has grown discourteous to men since men have bowed to Ascanet."

She found she was still staring at him, unable to believe he was real. He seemed to be . . . but then, the vision of Asphodel (Asphodel?—yes, it could have been nobody else) had seemed real, too . . .

He gave her a peculiar stare. "Asphodel? Are you sure?"

She shook her head, trying to clear it. Surely she was mad, was speaking without knowing it.

He limped down the path, his twisted eyebrows drawing together in concern. "Can you not speak, my lady?"

"Yes," she whispered. "Yes, I can speak. I'm just . . . are you real? I thought nobody had escaped the castle but me."

"I'm as real as you are sane, my lady," he said—and smiled as she puzzled over the statement's ambiguities. "But you are very cold. Don't you have a cloak?"

She looked down, aware for the first time that she was shivering. "I had one," she said. "Perhaps I left it in the cave."

"I think I saw it," he said. "Come, let's find it."

He limped to the cave opening and crawled in. She followed him and stopped before the entrance, staring down

33

the path. Presently, she heard a rustle behind her and her cloak dropped onto her shoulders.

"Come inside," said Eliar's voice. "I'll light a fire."

"Won't the Silver Souls see the smoke?"

"All Mazion is filled with smoke at the moment," he said grimly. "They will hardly notice an additional puff."

Tania crawled into the cave and watched Eliar arrange a pile of wood. It burst into flame when he lit it, a tiny replica of the castle that had always been her home. Eliar sat down next to it, his scarred face hideously red in its light.

"You didn't tie your horse last night," he remarked.

"That's true," she said wearily. "Was it his trail that led you to me?"

"No," he said. "It was windy; the trail you left last night was completely covered. I found the path here mostly by luck; then I took a wrong turn and ended up on a cliff above what was left of Castle Mazion. I was tired, and since I wasn't sure where I was, I slept there." He grinned. "And this morning I was awakened by a gray stallion who informed me, courteously but firmly, that my mare was his property. I'm afraid I let them go; I was worried about you. As I'd hoped, your horse's tracks led me to the caves your brother had spoken of."

She stared at him. "You heard Paran tell me . . . ?"

He nodded. "After you gave me your lute, I stopped to look at your mother's portrait. When I saw you and your brother coming, I hid in a window seat—and I heard your conversation. After you left, I followed your brother, intending to help him. But I was too late." He looked at her as gently as his face allowed. "I found him at the foot of the Gallery stairs, with a dagger in his back."

Tania closed her eyes. *Oh, Paran, Paran . . .*

"The dagger was of the type used by Radnor's bodyguard," said Eliar. "When I saw that, I realized you were likely to meet your brother's fate if you found Radnor in the stables. So I took your brother's sword—I was sure he'd forgive me if I used it in your defense—and followed the route he'd told you to take." He pursed his lips. "Unfortunately, I was too late; I came within ten feet of meeting my employer and the Captain of the Silver Souls in the tunnel."

Tania stared at him. "Was it you, then, that jumped out of the trapdoor? And you that met the two men-at-arms who came into the stable?"

He nodded in surprise. "You saw that? I hadn't realized I was so close behind you. You were in even greater danger than I thought. You met no troops in the castle forest?"

She shook her head. "I saw a company of Silver Souls, but they didn't see me. And then Pandosto heard something and galloped here."

"His speed saved you an unpleasant ride," said Eliar. "It took my mare and me several hours to shake Radnor's outriders. I escaped them only when the Silver Souls cut them down from behind."

"Cut them down? Weren't they allies?"

Eliar threw a log onto the fire. "Ascanet has allies only until they've served their purpose," he said. "Radnor was a fool to forget that. There was certainly no reason for Ascanet to spare him and his men once he'd arranged for the destruction of every king, lord, and knight who supported Campion."

"Radnor was successful? The lords, knights, soldiers in the alliance . . . *none* of them survived the attack?"

"None of them but you and I," he said quietly. "Every fighting man in Elyssonne was within range of the castle, and Ascanet had no mercy. The alliance was a great threat to him."

35

Every king, lord, and knight, who supported Campion. The alliance, the hope of the Golden Age . . . everything was gone. It was incomprehensible, unfathomable. Tania looked up and found that Eliar was watching her, his arms clasped around his knees.

"What will I do?" she half whispered. "Where can I go?"

His gaze wandered to the fire. "I could take you to your mother's people. You would be safe with them."

She shook her head. "Father never told us who our mother's people were."

"I'm sure he didn't. Few people know your mother's people exist; those who do are sworn to silence. The oath has never been broken."

"If that is so, how do you know I'm one of them?"

"I saw your mother's portrait. And her lute."

Tania remembered the glance Campion and Eliar had exchanged in the banquet hall. "Do you know my mother's people, then?"

He sighed. "I was once one of them. I have since forfeited that privilege, but I could take you to them. They're kind and very good."

"Who are they? Where do they live?"

"That, I'm not free to tell you."

Tania frowned. "If my mother's people are good," she asked, "why do they keep their existence secret? And why won't they let you go back to them?"

"They keep their existence a secret *because* they are good," he said. "And as for me—I once did a deed that made me unable to rejoin them."

"But if they're as good as you say, wouldn't they forgive you? I would, if you truly regretted what you'd done."

"That," he said, smiling, "is because you're untouched by the world. And because you don't know what I've done."

"I'm not so untouched by the world that I'd trust a man who'd done something terrible and not regretted it," she said uneasily.

He raised one eyebrow. "Surely even an unrepentant criminal can have a good sense of direction," he said. "If you study the matter objectively, you'll see that you need neither beauty nor virtue—simply a guide."

She looked at his sardonic face, then let her eyes stray to the side of the cave. Something was leaning against the wall; it looked strangely familiar. "What's that?" she said, pointing.

"Your lute," he said. "When I came here and saw you'd gotten this far safely, I left it in the corner before I went out to look for you."

"You carried it when Radnor's men were chasing you?"

"It was a little more complicated than that. I had to leave it in the forest and go back for it."

"But the danger!"

He shrugged. "It's a beautiful instrument. And you trusted me to value it more than I valued my life."

For a long time, she said nothing; there seemed to be no words for what she felt. But at last she forced herself to speak. "Thank you for my lute," she whispered. "And, Eliar . . ." She looked up. "I'll go to my mother's people . . . if you'll take me to them."

"What?" he said lightly. "You'll trust an unrepentant criminal?"

"Well, you see," she said, suddenly smiling, "I have very few alternatives, and you claim to have a good sense of direction."

He smiled back at her. "Very well. We'll leave as soon as the Silver Souls decamp."

CHAPTER

IV

IT TOOK THE SILVER SOULS far longer to decamp than either of them had thought it would. Normally, Tania would have chafed at the delay, but she passed the time submerged in memories of Paran and Campion. Eliar didn't intrude upon her grief; he talked to her sometimes, played the lute when she was in a mood to listen, but principally, he left her to herself. She soon found his willingness to do so was rooted not in tact but in an almost unreachable solitude. When she woke at night, she frequently saw his hunched form sitting in the entrance to the cave, gazing out into the starlight. He wasn't standing guard; he'd determined there was no need to. He seemed to stay awake for reasons of his own, secluded in his thoughts, so silent she didn't dare speak to him.

During the daytime, however, he was all activity, supplying them with food, checking on the location of the Silver Souls, and making preparations for their journey. Gradually, she began to see that it would do her good to join him, and one morning as he prepared to leave, she got up.

"May I go with you?"

He hesitated. "I'm going down to the cliff that overlooks the valley."

"I think I'd like to come," she said. "I need to . . . to see it as it is."

"If you wish," he said, turning to leave. "But it's not a pretty sight."

Neither are you, she thought, following him as he ducked out the cave entrance. *And I've grown used to that.*

As she stood up, she saw the sardonic smile she'd rather come to like. "You're flexibility itself," he said.

She blushed. "I'm sorry. I hadn't realized you were . . . listening."

He walked down the path next to her. "Ah, yes—you've been raised in a world in which people listen only to words, not to thoughts."

She remembered her bewilderment when she'd stepped out of the forest and he'd known she'd recognized him. "Are there worlds in which people listen to thoughts, then?"

He nodded. "The world of your mother's people. They find words are clumsy vehicles for thought."

"But words are also screens that hide thoughts," she said. "I'm not sure I'd like to have people know what I'm thinking; it's seldom complimentary."

"I'm sure that's true," he said. "I've lived in courts enough to know what happens to the mind when every word and action is circumscribed. But the world in which words mask thoughts creates an atmosphere which Ascanet can readily use to his advantage. He can, for example, offer ambitious young men like Radnor their hearts' desires in return for a five-year lease on their souls, knowing that their fellows will admire—and emulate—their success without recognizing their corruption."

Tania looked at him. "Did *you* suspect Radnor of corruption?"

"I suspected him enough to ask to come with him to Mazion, but I knew nothing of his plans."

"And yet, you say you can hear people's thoughts . . . ?"

"Not his," said Eliar. "That's why I suspected him. There

39

are some men whose words carry no overtones from thoughts; hearing them converse is like listening to a lute with false strings. The problem is, one can never be sure how the false note one hears will affect events. I could do nothing about Radnor except wait for his actions to reveal his thoughts."

They walked on in silence awhile. Tania's thoughts drifted back to the dark stable, to Radnor, then shied away from the details of his murder to a lesser question. "If Ascanet had a lease on Radnor's soul," she asked, "why did the captain murder him instead of waiting until his term was up and making him a Silver Soul?"

"Perhaps Ascanet thought ambition like Radnor's could cause rebellion among his troops."

"That makes sense," she said. "At least, it makes as much sense as it can. You have to admit, the whole business of selling souls is peculiar. I could never see why a man who knew the penalty for selling his soul to Ascanet would do so, knowing what Ascanet is and what he can do."

Eliar raised one scarred eyebrow. "You have no idea how much Ascanet has to offer," he said. "In the face of his gifts, it's easy to forget what he is and what he can do."

He turned and walked on; she followed him, aware that she'd trespassed in one of his inaccessible inner territories. She'd done it once or twice before, and while she'd never been able to determine exactly what remarks sent him into himself, she'd learned to apologize silently and withdraw.

He rejoined the real world only as they reached the cliff and looked down at the wreck of Castle Mazion that rose out of the snow. Its towers were gone; in their places were heaps of ash-covered ruins. To one side of the piles of black masonry, she saw flashes of light as silver figures moved through the charred remains of what had once been the stables.

"What are they doing?" she asked.

"I wish I knew—whatever it is has delayed their departure. They've been sorting through the ruins for two weeks."

"There can't be much left to steal," she said bitterly.

"They're not looters, even if there were," he said. "Ascanet gives them all they need." He glanced over to the right. "Whatever it is, though, I think they're planning to leave. There were twice as many of them yesterday as there are today. This must be the last company."

"Does that mean we can leave soon?"

"Tomorrow, I'd think. Look—their horses are saddled and waiting."

She looked where he pointed; some hundred horses stood picketed at the edge of the forest. She let her eyes roam from the gutted castle to the birds of prey that circled below her and settled on green, crimson, and black heaps that lay huddled in the plain.

"We should go," said Eliar, after a long silence.

She nodded and followed him back to the cave, grateful that there was so much to do that she had no time to feel.

It was dark by the time everything was ready. Eliar lit a fire, sat down, and picked up the lute; as Tania listened, she let her hair down and began to brush it. He watched her awhile, then reached a cadence and stopped. "You'll have to travel as my apprentice tomorrow," he said.

She nodded; they'd talked about it before.

"I'm afraid," he said regretfully, "that no boy your age has hair that falls to the back of his knees."

Tania raised her hands protectively to the sides of her head. "You mean we'll have to cut it?"

"Just shoulder length," he said. "Nothing really terrible."

Nothing really terrible. She drew a long breath. "Very well."

Eliar set down the lute and rummaged in his pack. She

looked over her shoulder and saw him limping toward her with a pair of scissors.

"Come, now," he said. "I'm not your executioner!"

She stood up and turned her back to him. "No, I suppose not."

Snip, snip, snip. Her hair fell about her feet in long, wavy coils. The hair Melibe had pushed out of her eyes so she could read. The hair Campion had stroked in his rare moments of affection. The hair Paran had said made her look like their mother when she wore it in a crown of braids.

"Now," said Eliar. "Turn around, and I'll cut bangs in front."

She turned; the hateful scissors cut a path through the hair he'd brushed across her face. It was only hair, after all, as useless in her travels as memories of a castle that had once proudly guarded Mazion valley.

"There!" he said, brushing the snippets from her face. "Oh . . ." His hand had touched the damp stream on her cheek.

"It's nothing," she said. "You got hair in my eyes, and they smart." She blinked; two more tears rolled down her face. Stooping quickly so he wouldn't see them, she raked the pile of hair together. "I'll throw it into the forest," she said, trying to smile as she stood up. "Maybe some little creature will make a nest of it."

She took the hair outside and threw it from the path as hard as she could. It was too dark to see it fall.

They set out before it was light the next morning. Eliar set a pace Tania could hardly keep, and as the sky turned from black to gray, she finally asked him to stop. "Life in the Ladies' Tower has made me a poor traveler," she panted. "Must we go so fast?"

"For the next hour we must," he said. "We have to take

the Theda high road, and I want to get well onto it before midmorning. That way, anybody who passes us will see a minstrel and his boy who are journeying from the coast—not two people who have just emerged from Mazion valley." He started off again, a little more slowly. "And as for the valley —I had hoped to cross it in the dark."

She hurried then. And although it was beginning to grow light as they passed the ash-covered snow and the blackened castle, it was still too dark to see the broken bodies she knew were all about them. But Ascanet's vengeance had extended far beyond the castle; the valley was filled with black, drifting snow, and they trudged mile after mile past gutted cottages, villages, and manor houses, inhabited only by thin cats that eyed them warily from inside the ruins.

Suddenly, Eliar pulled up, listened, and touched Tania's arm. "There's a cart coming," he said. "Stand by the side of the road, and if the driver looks important, bow." As he spoke, two dapple-gray horses rounded the corner behind them, pulling a gaily painted wagon. Eliar pulled his hood over his face and bowed as it drew near; Tania imitated him, her hands trembling. She heard the horses stop in front of her and looked up at the red, smiling face of their driver.

"Minstrels, eh?" he said, pointing to the lute. "Well, talk about good signs! You'll be going to Theda for this afternoon's demonstration, I'll warrant." He glanced at the sun. "You'll never make your way there in time on foot. Here— climb in. I'm going most of the way."

Tania glanced at Eliar; he nodded and boosted her over the side of the wagon, then climbed up and sat beside her.

"If you're planning to play in Theda, you'll be rich men tonight," said the driver, clucking to the team. "There's been nary a song to be had in all of Mazion these past weeks. You'll find his lordship's men have open hands, too." He pointed to the two horses in front of them. "Who would've thought old John the Carter would drive a team like this—eh? But one of his lordship's men said to me, 'John, none of the others will drive from Theda to the coast because the way lies by Castle Mazion. They think the ghost of the old king will rise from the ground and haunt them. If you'll do it, there's a fine team and a wagon in our stores for you.' And he brings up this rig. Well, my wife was clear out of her head for joy, and my girls look like princesses now, that they do. So you're going to the right place and the right men—you'll see."

Eliar gave Tania a gentle nudge of warning. "It's a beautiful team," he said. "Any man would be proud to drive it."

"And proud I surely am. This team belonged to the Mayor of Theda—that's what kind of quality it is. Two years ago, Campion ups and gives it to him in return for some sort of favor. Bred out of the king's own stables, these horses are: sons of that big gray stud of his and two fine Percheron mares." His face clouded over. "Between you lads and myself, it's the shame of Orcus Campion's horses got burned along with him. I like a good horse myself, and the old king had the best around."

"You grieve for the King's horses and not for him?" said Tania before Eliar could stop her.

The carter threw her a frown. "It's not safe to talk like that, lad."

"Lads feel more than men who've seen too much of the world," said Eliar quickly. "Don't worry about him—he's as safe as they come. But the old king had style; a youth hates to see that go."

The carter leaned sideways and looked into Tania's hooded face. "You'll be about the age of my youngest girl," he said, nodding. "She wept for the old king, and I didn't stop her. For that matter"—he looked quickly around the empty valley—"I grieved myself when the castle fell. Cam-

44

pion the Valiant, they called him; they don't make better men. But I don't let that get around, lad. Those who loved Campion are dead; there's no point in dying for a man who lies dead in the ashes of his own home. What good would it do him?" He shrugged. "Somebody has to haul the grain, no matter who rules Elyssonne. I don't give trouble to any man who has power over me, so long as he lets my thoughts alone."

And so long as you get the Mayor's team, thought Tania. Eliar frowned and pressed her hand against the seat; while she squirmed in pain, he began to talk with the carter about grain prices and the weather. Slowly, he released the pressure, and she began to feel how tired she was. Sighing, she leaned against Eliar's hunched shoulder, listening to the carter's voice fade away.

She woke when the cart stopped. Looking around her, she saw that it was early afternoon and that the houses near the road were whole. The carter was pointing to a large manor with his whip. "I got deliveries there," he said. "New lord— wants grain for his new horses. He'll probably invite me in for a mug or two, so I'll leave you here. It's only ten miles to Theda; you can make it easily at your age."

Eliar reached into his pouch. "We're grateful for the ride," he said. "Let us buy you a flagon of wine for tonight."

The carter shook his head. "Save your money. Day's over when I have to take advantage of two people who make their way on foot." He watched them climb down, then leaned toward Tania. "You be careful in Theda, lad," he said. "There's men there that got no youngsters of their own. If you speak up the way you did a few miles back, you'll be in trouble."

Tania forced herself to bow. "Thank you," she said. "I appreciate your kindness."

The carter lifted his eyebrows ever so slightly, then smiled.

45

"A good journey to you," he said. He clucked, and the beautiful grays trotted off.

Eliar watched them go. "He's right, you know. You *must* hold your tongue, no matter what you hear. 'I appreciate your kindness,' indeed! As if you were waiting for him to kiss your hand."

"I'd prefer not to grovel before a traitor," she said resentfully.

Eliar raised one eyebrow. "A traitor? You place John the Carter in the same category as Prince Radnor of Dolc?"

"Of course! Prince Radnor betrayed the castle; John the Carter accepted the fruits of Ascanet's victory."

"Then everybody in Elyssonne who wept when your father died but went on with his own life is a traitor?"

"Of course!"

"And where does that leave you and me, pray tell?"

She stared at him for a few seconds before she found her tongue. "But we're not profiting from Father's defeat! Ascanet hasn't bought *our* loyalty."

"Do you really think Ascanet has bought the carter's loyalty? What if the team and the money bought merely his service and his words? Would he still be a traitor?"

"I . . . oh, don't be so difficult, Eliar! How can a man retain his loyalty if everything he does and says undercuts it?"

"By doing the same thing a traitor does, only in reverse: conforming outwardly, but retaining control of what he thinks. It's difficult, but it can be done. And it *is* done. There's virtue enough left in Elyssonne for a Golden Age still, could you but hear it." He turned on his heel and limped off.

Was there, indeed? And who was he, the unrepentant criminal, to preach virtue to her? She stalked after him, thinking of all the things she'd like to say—until she re-

46

membered he could hear the contents of her mind. The thought drew her up. There was no doubting that he heard things she could not; perhaps he *had* heard something in the carter's speech that she'd ignored. She fought with her pride for half a mile, then ran a few steps and caught up with him. "What demonstration are we going to in Theda?" she asked humbly.

He looked at her, then shifted the lute into a more comfortable position. "I daresay we'll find out when we get there," he said.

CHAPTER

V

BY THE TIME they could see the walls and spires of Theda clearly, the road was filled with travelers. Sleek horses trotted past them, pulling sleighs filled with laughing men or gaily dressed women. Nervous country youths waited at crossroads for girls who traveled with their families in two-wheeled carts. Young gallants cantered by on snorting hunters, sending clods of packed snow into the crowds of foot travelers. As they reached the city gates, bells began to ring in a cacophony that covered the shouts and laughter in the snow-covered streets. Tania pulled her hood over her face and held the edge of Eliar's cloak, afraid she'd lose him in the crowd.

"Ho! Minstrels!" A man on a magnificent black mare edged across the square and fell in beside Eliar. "Will you play for my party this evening? I'll pay you well, and I'll lodge you and your boy at my manor—it's a few miles west of the city. You'll not find a bed in all of Theda otherwise."

The bells showered down a tumult of sound that covered Eliar's answer. Tania waited anxiously, wishing she could hear their bargaining. At last, the man nodded and turned to her. "Does your master play well, lad?" he asked teasingly.

"There's no better lutenist in Elyssonne," she said, hoping that was what a minstrel's apprentice was supposed to say.

The man laughed and sprang off the black mare. "He has trained you well, I see." As he swung the horse's reins over her head, his blue hood fell back; Tania saw that he was young—perhaps twenty—and that his handsome face seemed strangely vulnerable. She reminded herself that if he was alive, he was a traitor . . . but still, there was something about him that would have made her like him, if that hadn't been so.

"Come," he said, handing his reins to the groom who had just struggled to him through the crowd. "The demonstration is about to begin, and I must be there. I'm sitting with my family; there's room for two more in our box. If you join us, you'll be able to see much more than you can see from the ground."

Eliar hesitated, then bowed. "We're honored."

They followed their host out of the square into a field ringed with brightly colored pavilions on three sides and packed with standing spectators on the fourth. He strode to the pavilion that stood opposite the center of the field, then leapt gracefully up its stairs to a box draped in the same light blue as his cloak. Two handsome women rushed to meet him.

"Oh, Colin—you're so late!" said the younger one, clinging to him. "We were afraid . . ." She stopped and looked over her shoulder at two men who lounged comfortably in plush seats.

"Yes," drawled one of them. "Your mother and sister have been all atwitter at your absence. But we told them you'd just seen a good-looking horse and lost track of the time."

"I'm sorry you were worried," said Colin, slipping an arm around each woman. "The crowds were thick. But I've found a minstrel and his boy, and I've brought them here with a promise to play for us tonight. Does that make up for

49

your fears?" He turned to Eliar and Tania, who had pulled their hoods well forward.

Eliar bowed. "I'm Wodland of Thawr," he said, "and this is my boy, Nat. We're honored to be called to you."

Colin stepped forward. "This is my mother, Nadia, widow of Sir Colin Lucot; my sister is Flora. And these"—he turned to the two men—"are my mother's brothers, Sir Dolan and Sir Harlan."

Colin Lucot! Tania bowed, glad her face was covered by her hood. That was why she'd felt she'd like him—he looked very much like his father, Sir Colin, the only man who had been truly close to her father. When Sir Colin had been killed in battle three years earlier, Campion had grieved deeply. What would he say now if he saw that the son of his dearest friend had become Ascanet's creature?

She sat down next to Eliar, but to her surprise, Flora plopped down on the seat next to her and giggled. "Do you play the lute, Nat? I always wanted to. Could you show me a little bit tonight?"

Tania edged away. "My master will be playing."

Out of the corner of her eye, she saw Eliar hide a smile. She was spared the necessity of further conversation by three trumpets that sounded in unison. Colin and his uncles rose and walked to the front of the box; as the fanfare ended, they raised their swords together. Colin, Tania noticed, was the only one of the three that handled a sword with any familiarity. His uncles were clearly burghers of Theda, as newly elevated as John the Carter. She wondered bitterly what they'd done to merit the honor.

"That's the salute that starts the demonstration," whispered Flora. "My uncles are important now—and Colin will be too, when he comes of age. His lordship has given us all sorts of money and honors. It's really exciting! See, my father fought on the wrong . . ."

"Flora, come sit down," said Lady Nadia. Watching Flora flounce to the ladies' section of the box, Tania saw tears in her mother's eyes. At least there was one person in Sir Colin's family who knew what loyalty meant.

Trumpets sounded again, and a single rider cantered out from a wide space between the two pavilions directly opposite the Lucots' box. His horse was silvery white, and it snorted at every stride, throwing its head from side to side.

"Who's that?" asked Colin. "I've never seen him before."

"Captain Talus," grunted Sir Dolan. "Just promoted last week. Seems the old captain lost something important and became hippogriff fodder."

Tania glanced at Eliar, but his face was a mask beneath his hood.

The late afternoon sun broke through a gap in the clouds, turning the snowy field to gold and Talus's uniform to silver. Behind him, a company of silver riders trotted out from between the pavilions in four columns, sixteen abreast, their white horses trotting in step. When they reached the center of the field, the riders on the left end of each line halted and wheeled and each column rotated around them in a perfect circle. Sir Harlan nodded. "Brilliant. Beautiful."

It was beautiful, Tania thought reluctantly. She glanced at Eliar; his eyes were shining as he watched.

On the field, Captain Talus raised his banner. Immediately, the soldiers formed their ranks into a single line. As their captain whistled, riders broke off to the right and to the left, forming two companies that trotted to opposite ends of the field, wheeled, and halted. The horses knew what they were to do next; none of them stirred, but Tania could feel their tension rising with the steam from their necks. Talus dropped his banner: the opposing companies moved toward each other at a walk, then a trot, then a canter—then at a shimmering gallop. Halfway across the space that separated

51

them, the riders drew their swords in a simultaneous flash of silver. Tania held her breath as the two companies rushed silently toward each other . . . nearer . . . nearer . . . and galloped between the columns of each other's lines, each man's sword clashing in triumphant unison against the sword of his opposite.

The crowd rose to its feet, yelling, whistling, and stamping. Tania found herself on her feet, too. "They're brilliant!" she shouted to Eliar.

"They are indeed!" He bent down and spoke quietly into her ear. "And have you forgotten Mazion valley so quickly?"

Tania stopped clapping, shocked into silence. It was hard to believe that troops who could perform so beautifully could also . . . She sat down, transfixed by her thoughts.

The Silver Souls drilled for an hour, each of their formations exquisite in its precision. At last, they halted in front of the Lucots' box, their backs to Tania. Every eye in the crowd looked up, scanning the sky. Sir Harlan leaned back in his seat. "And now," he said complacently, "we get the greatest honor of all."

A far-off shriek ripped through the silence, echoed by a gasp from the crowd. Eliar tapped Tania's shoulder and pointed. Looking over the top of the pavilion, she saw a huge shadow come between her and the lowering sun, drawing near with a speed she could hardly comprehend. Before she could believe it was more than a fantasy, it had reached the area above the field. There it paused, beating its wings backward like the kite she and Paran had trained for hawking, the wind from its twenty-foot wingspan bending the sturdy pavilion poles like saplings. After a moment, it soared upward, banking on invisible wind currents, hardly moving its wings as it circled above the awestruck crowd. As it coasted above her, Tania saw it wasn't a bird. It had a horse's body but an eagle's neck and head; a lion's tail and legs but feet that ended in long, cruel talons instead of paws. A hippogriff. And it had not come alone. On its wheeling, soaring back sat a tall man in a blue-gray cloak, riding the monster as if he and it were one.

Colin leaned toward Sir Dolan. "I thought his lordship was mortal—but surely, only a god could ride a creature like that!"

Sir Dolan nodded noncommittally, but Tania was tempted to agree. No mere mortal could control the power and ferocity that circled above them.

As she watched, the hippogriff raised its wings and shot toward the ground, braked at the last conceivable instant, and landed. It furled its wings and trotted toward the troops, arching its eagle's neck, but moving with feline softness. As it reached Captain Talus, his horse shied and plunged. The hippogriff cocked its head; then the end of its tail began to twitch back and forth, and it crouched ever so slightly. The blue-robed rider slapped its feathered neck with a crack that echoed across the field. The tail stopped immediately, and the great beast lowered itself to the ground.

Ascanet sprang off lightly and walked to Talus; Tania watched him stroke the nervous horse's neck as he talked to its rider. Presently, Talus dismounted; Ascanet vaulted onto the horse's back, steadied it, and cantered it toward the silent troops. In the center of the field, Talus looked uneasily over his shoulder at the hippogriff, but it merely yawned, sat up, and began to wash its eagle face with its talons.

Ascanet cantered up and down the ranks of the Silver Souls, then ordered them to part so he could ride between them. He halted directly in front of the Lucots' box, and the Lucots rose. Tania felt Eliar touch her hand; she rose as he did, forcing herself to look at the ruler of Elyssonne from the depths of her hood.

He was not the monster she'd always envisioned at the

sound of his name; there was, in fact, something entirely familiar about him. His easy, commanding seat on Talus's horse reminded her of Campion's magnificence; his face, too, had a look of authority that made her think of her father's. In feature and general aspect, though, it was more like Paran's. The gray hair framed high cheekbones and a sharp chin; the gray-blue eyes were thoughtful and intelligent. It was a face that contrasted with everything she knew him to be, a face that was almost . . . sensitive. Scholarly. How very, very strange.

Ascanet's glance swept across the box, and Tania suddenly found herself looking directly into his eyes. As she shrank back into her hood, she saw him turn to Colin. "Who's the boy yonder, Lucot?" His voice was almost a whisper, the hiss of sleet falling on crusted snow.

"He's the lad of a minstrel I've engaged to sing at my manor tonight, my lord," said Colin, bowing. "His master is beside him."

Ascanet looked briefly at Eliar, then back at Tania. "Come here, lad."

Shaking with fear, Tania stepped slowly forward, her eyes fixed on the immense star sapphire pendant Ascanet wore around his neck on a silver chain of state. Arriving at the designated place, she bowed and stood silently before him.

"Can you not speak, lad?" said Ascanet in his thick whisper. "I'd think you'd need a voice in your profession."

The two uncles laughed as Tania blushed, but Colin stepped to her side. "My lord," he said, "the lad is young. His silence comes from inexperience, not lack of respect. It is unkind to mock him."

Tania's head rose in horror: Colin was rebuking his overlord in public! Did he know nothing of court etiquette—or had he defied it for her sake? She spoke quickly to save him embarrassment.

54

"I can speak, my lord," she said. "But my father taught me never to speak to a man of rank until he spoke to me; I followed his teaching out of habit." She gathered her courage and smiled at his pendant. "And I would think, my lord, that the ruler of Elyssonne would wish to speak many words before he listened with interest to anything *I* could say."

Ascanet raised his eyebrows and turned to Colin. "It seems the lad has no need of your defense, Lucot," he said, smiling. "His tongue is ready enough."

"It is indeed, my lord," said Colin. He had, Tania saw, not the slightest idea that he had been mildly reproved.

But she had no time to think about Colin, for Ascanet had turned back to her. "Your wit is not that of the hinterlands," he observed.

Just as Eliar had said! Tania swallowed hard. "Perhaps not, my lord," she said. "My father hoped my voice and skill would find me a court position, so he gave me what education he could afford."

"You have lived at court, then?"

"How could I, my lord? By the time I was old enough to be trained, the three courts of Elyssonne opposed their true ruler."

Ascanet gazed at her thoughtfully. "Loyally spoken," he whispered. "But I think, not truly." The gray-blue eyes seemed to pierce the darkness of her hood. "Hold out your hands, lad," he said abruptly.

Tania stretched out both her hands, palms down, wondering at the order. They looked very small and feminine—would they betray her? Was that why he'd asked?

Ascanet leaned forward. "You wear no rings," he whispered.

"I have no money for luxuries, my lord."

"Rings," he said, looking at her keenly, "do not have to

be purchased. They can be found. Or stolen."

What did he take her for—a thief? She drew herself up. "They may also be given, my lord, as tokens of trust and affection. Until I am wealthy enough to buy a ring for myself, or old enough to merit trust and affection, my fingers will remain bare."

Ascanet frowned, but in perplexity, not in anger. Finally, he waved his hand. "Your tongue is above your station, lad," he said. "But you're not a fool. You may rejoin your master."

Tania bowed and walked unsteadily back to her place. She glanced up as she passed Eliar; his face was bathed in perspiration.

"And now," Ascanet's whisper addressed Colin, "I have an assignment which will enable you to prove that you are my loyal subject, despite your father's errors."

Colin bowed; Tania could feel the tension in his shoulders radiate through his blue cloak.

"My men," said Ascanet, "have captured two horses that have apparently been roaming the kingdom for some weeks. One of them is a gray mare whose conformation and speed would be the pride of any young man." He paused, fingering his chain. "The other, I am told, is the royal stallion of Mazion."

"That's impossible, my lord," stammered Sir Harlan. "We've been repeatedly assured that nobody escaped . . ."

Ascanet waved him to silence. "Nothing is impossible," he whispered, "except that the stallion unbolted his door and escaped the stables of a besieged castle unassisted."

"Then your lordship is implying that King Campion . . . ?" began Sir Dolan.

Ascanet shook his head. "The King was not a man to save himself while others perished. But we know he learned of the attack before we wished him to; most likely he sent his son off on his own horse." He turned to Colin. "And that is your assignment: to find the Prince of Mazion, to make him your friend, and to bring him to me on some pretext. If you succeed, the horses will be yours. I've sent them to your stables as a token of my trust in your abilities."

Colin bowed his head. "I'm honored, my lord."

Ascanet's smile seemed encrusted in ice. "You may not be honored when you've seen the stallion," he whispered dryly. "It took seven of my men to restrain him. But I'm sure he'll respond to your skill."

Colin bowed again; Tania saw interest kindling in his eyes.

Seeming satisfied, Ascanet backed his horse and raised his right hand from the elbow in a clench-fisted salute. Colin and his uncles returned it. Ascanet nodded, then cantered back to the center of the field. Vaulting to the ground, he handed the reins to Talus and whistled. The hippogriff leapt up and pranced to his side, then crouched to let him spring onto its back. For a long moment, the ruler of Elyssonne looked around the pavilions before he raised his fist once more in salute. Cheers filled the field as the Silver Souls and all the citizens of Theda returned it.

In the midst of the cheer, the hippogriff reared, unfurled its wings, and shot into the air. It circled as the Silver Souls cantered off the field, then turned northward and flew off into the darkening sky. The crowd was silent for a moment, watching it disappear over the horizon. Then everybody spilled onto the field, shouting excited greetings, praising the skill of the Silver Souls, or searching the trampled snow for hippogriff feathers and other souvenirs of the wondrous day.

CHAPTER
VI

"COLIN LUCOT on a horse is like you with a lute," said Tania drowsily from one of the beds in the room she and Eliar were to share. "My principles wither in the face of genius: I know he's a disgrace to his father's memory, but I can't help admiring the way he rides."

"In confusion lies the beginning to wisdom," quipped Eliar from the bed a few feet away. "But your principles will have to stand only a short siege. We're going to leave right after I've played tonight."

She half sat up. "Leave! Are we in danger?"

"You are."

"Do . . . do you think Colin suspects I am who I am?"

"Colin hasn't a suspicious nature," he said, folding his arms behind his head and staring up at the beamed ceiling above them. "It's Ascanet I fear. He picked you out far too readily today, as if something in you attracted him. And you, dear child . . ."

"I told him nothing!"

"True," he acknowledged. "You lied with a grace and ease that does credit to your upbringing. But you also spoke to the undisputed lord of Elyssonne with a supreme consciousness of your own dignity. And since Ascanet is no fool, he'll be back to find out who you are as soon as he has taken the hippogriff to his castle and seen the Silver Souls properly stationed. When he returns, I want to be far away."

Tania lay back miserably. "I'm sorry I spoke to Ascanet as I did. I was frightened, and I suppose . . ."

He turned his ugly head toward her. "If you're going to apologize for the bearing that proclaims you to be a princess, I'll have to apologize for leading you to the pavilion of the most important newly promoted family in Theda," he said. "Perhaps we should leave it at that and save our energies for a hard night's ride."

"We're going to ride?"

"We are indeed. Ascanet has graciously collected our horses and brought them here; we'll accept his bounty."

"But do you know where the horses are?"

"That, as Ascanet would say, is your assignment. After you've bathed, find Colin and ask if he will show you his new stallion. I'm sure he'll be happy to comply. My mare will be somewhere nearby, I daresay."

Tania hesitated. "Couldn't I just go look for our horses? Fine horseman or no, Colin accepted an assignment to kill my brother."

Eliar sat up. "Come, you know he can't possibly find your brother. Don't despise him; pity him, for that impossibility will be his death."

"You mean, if Colin fails, Ascanet will . . . ?"

"Think, my lady. If, as you've told me, Colin is the son of your father's dearest friend, he's the obvious focus of future rebellion. But even Ascanet can't execute a handsome, popular young man without cause; he has to give him a test which, if it's failed, will enable him to say young Lucot is protecting the Prince of Mazion."

Tania sat up slowly and put her chin on her raised knees.

"That's so . . . despicable . . . I can't even fathom . . ."

"You can't? It's standard courtly practice, I believe."

"Not in all courts!"

He stared at the ceiling in a silence she found less than comforting.

"Perhaps we should tell Colin of his danger," she said after a few minutes.

"I thought you felt he deserved anything he got for accepting Ascanet's assignment."

"Not betrayal! Not death!"

"What other fate would you wish on a traitor?"

"Oh, stop it!" she cried. "Maybe he isn't a traitor! I don't know."

"So warn him, if you wish," said Eliar dryly. "But first, consider how you'll tell him you know his assignment is impossible without telling him how you know."

"Oh . . ." She looked up and found Eliar's twisted eyes studying her. "Then I can't warn him, can I?"

"It would be extremely unwise. On the other hand, if it interferes with your finely tuned moral sense to send an innocent man to his death, then you should tell him."

She stared at him in anger and perplexity. "What would *you* do?"

"I? I would find Colin, use his goodwill to enable me to find the horses, and ride off tonight without telling him anything about his impending doom."

"And your own treachery wouldn't . . ."

"Bother me? It would indeed."

A servant knocked, entered, and announced the baths were ready. Eliar sent Tania on ahead, but when she got to the baths, she found his care had been unnecessary; the six baths were separated by walls, and each one had complete privacy. Looking eagerly at the steaming pools, she chose a bath, closed the door, then peeled off her clothes and threw them on the floor, wondering why they hadn't grown to her skin in the past two weeks. As her tunic hit the tiles, she heard an unexpected thump. What could it possibly . . . ? Picking up the tunic, she slid her hand into its pocket and pulled out the smooth object her fingers touched.

It was a ring—a silver ring with an exquisitely wrought band and a star sapphire that glistened in the torchlight. Stunned, she gazed at it for a full minute, sorting back through the past weeks' memories until she finally arrived at the one scene she had shut out of her mind: the dark tack room of Castle Mazion. She tried to shut it out now, but on the backs of her eyelids, she saw the flash of a dagger, heard the thud as a body crumpled to the floor, felt a bolt of terror as a glittering object rolled toward her hiding place. The scene faded as she opened her eyes, but the ring still lay in her hand.

She slipped it back into her tunic and dove into the water, hoping the warmth would drive away her thoughts. For a moment, she forgot everything but the luxurious feeling of the short hair that floated around her face. But suddenly, Ascanet's words floated with it. *Hold out your hands, lad.* And then, *You wear no rings.*

Tania began to wash her hair with the fragrant soap that lay by the side of the bath. Was it possible that . . . ? *He picked you out far too readily,* Eliar had said, *as if something in you attracted him.* He had: it was true. But he couldn't possibly have sensed she was hiding his ring from him; she hadn't known she had it.

She dove again, feeling the soap ripple out of her hair, but seeing the darkness of the tack room loom hazily before her closed eyes. *You have only to wear this, it will draw him to you,* the captain of the Silver Souls had said. But she hadn't

61

worn it . . . *Then, were you but virtuous, my lord, you would be free of his influence.* Was that all that stood between her and discovery: her failure to wear the ring and whatever virtue she possessed? She found she was trembling as she slid out of the water and dressed herself in the tunic and breeches Lady Nadia had found for her.

The main door of the baths swung open. "Nat?" Eliar's voice.

"I'm almost dressed," she said hurriedly.

"I was beginning to think you'd drowned," he said. She heard him limp into the bath next to hers. A splash and a deep breath told her he'd dived and come back to the top. "Ah, magnificent," he murmured.

She was suddenly, uncomfortably aware that he was a few feet from her, unclothed and enjoying the warm water in the same sensuous way she had. For a fraction of a second, she wondered if the rest of his body were as deformed as his face, or if . . . she blushed. Whatever was wrong with her? There were important things to think about.

She picked up Paran's tunic and drew out the ring. It was certainly beautiful—the most intricate piece of jewelry she'd ever seen. "Eliar . . ."

"Wodland." Eliar's voice sounded soapy and irritated. "*Please* watch that tongue of yours, Nat. And will your conscience permit you to carry out your assignment? I have to play in an hour and a half."

Colin. The horses. An hour and a half. Feeling along the seams of her new tunic, Tania found a pocket and slid the ring into it. There would be plenty of time to discuss it with Eliar later. "I'm going right now, Wodland," she said meekly.

As Tania hurried down the stairs, she saw Flora admiring her velvet dress in a full-length mirror. Flora looked up and smiled. "You look very handsome in your new clothes, Nat."

Watch that tongue of yours, Nat. Tania bowed. "Thank you, my lady."

Flora giggled. "I'm not a lady yet," she said. "Though Uncle Harlan is trying to find me a husband who'll make me one."

That would take some doing. "What, my lady? Are you old enough to marry?"

"Of course!" Flora pouted prettily. "Fourteen is *plenty* old enough to marry if your uncles are important."

Tania smiled to herself; Flora could easily have been one of her attendants. "I'm sure you'd have many suitors even if your uncles weren't important, my lady."

Flora blushed, looking very pretty indeed. "You're such a sweetheart, Nat. I'll tell Colin what you said; he always teases me about being vain." A little frown creased her forehead. "He's upset right now—he banged out of Mama's room half an hour ago and stomped off to the stables. That's where he goes when they argue." The blue eyes filled with tears. "And then he gets absolutely *black* . . . oh, you'd never guess if you didn't know him, but I worry so."

So there was a sister under the clothes and the vanity. Tania looked at her with real sympathy. "Tell me where the stables are," she said. "I'll run out and see if he's all right."

"Will you?" Flora's smile had no self-conscious dimples this time. "That's really kind of you, Nat! Look—there's a quick way of getting there without having to go around the front." She looped the train of her dress over her arm and ran across the hall. "Your master will be playing in there," she said as they passed a closed door. "And the door to the wine cellar is right here. Go down the steps and around the first big barrel on the left. There's a little door behind it; go through it and follow the passage to the grain room. Be sure to shut the door behind you, or Colin will be mad."

Tania bowed and slipped through the wine-cellar door, reflecting that innocence seemed to run in Colin's family. She found the grain room easily, but when she stepped out into the main aisle, a groom with a lantern stopped her. "What are you doing here, lad?"

Tania bowed, hoping minstrels' apprentices bowed to grooms. "I have a message for Master Lucot from his sister, sir."

The groom looked dubiously over his shoulder. "He's down the right aisle, there—said he wanted to look at the new stud. But I just looked down that way and . . . well, I'd leave him alone, if I was you."

So Pandosto was down the right aisle. Things were working out very well. "Maybe so, sir, but Master Lucot's sister said it was important."

"Well, don't come to me if you don't like what you see. There's been too much of that, lately. I'm off, myself. I'll leave the lantern—mind you put it out after you've spoken to him."

"Yes, sir. Thank you, sir."

The groom hung up the lantern and shuffled down the main aisle, looking back at her over his shoulder. She turned the other way, and as she reached the right aisle, she heard a low moan. She paused, then peered cautiously around the corner.

A lantern hung in the center of the aisle; in its light, she could see Colin leaning against a stall door, his forehead on one arm. She tiptoed down the short aisle, feeling her heart thump harder and harder. Had he, like Paran, been . . . ? He gave no sign of having heard her, even when she stopped next to him. Shaking, she touched his shoulder. "Master Lucot . . . are you hurt?"

Slowly, slowly, he raised his head and looked at her. "Oh,

hello, Nat," he said tonelessly. "No, I'm not hurt." He lifted a long, beautifully crafted dagger off the stall door and sheathed it in his belt. "I'm not man enough to hurt myself, it seems."

Then he'd been going to . . .

"Don't be alarmed, lad," said Colin. "I'll do nothing, now. Give me a few minutes to prepare a face for men to meet, and we'll walk back to the house together." To her amazement, he shot the bolts on Pandosto's stall and stepped in—something she'd seen nobody but Campion do before. In the silence, she heard a splash in a water bucket, then the sound of a pat. The stall door swung open and Colin stepped out, drying his face on his sleeve. As he bolted the door, Pandosto stuck his head over the top. Colin reached up and rubbed him gently behind the ears. A nicker sounded from the next stall, and a delicate gray head looked out into the aisle. "You, too, eh, my lovely?" crooned Colin. He moved over so he could stroke both horses at once; they nodded their heads up and down, pressing contentedly against his hands. Tania saw him smile the way Eliar smiled when he played the lute.

After a moment, the horses went back to their hay and Colin's smile vanished. "You're pensive, Nat. I'm afraid I've made you so."

Shaken out of her apprentice's role, she wiped her eyes with the back of her hand. "I was just wishing you were a herdsman, not . . ."

". . . the heir of Sir Colin Lucot?" he said sadly. "Your wish is mine—and has been since I was your age. I have no head for politics. I can understand any horse within a minute of meeting it, but men and their beliefs are a mystery to me. And yet, what can I do? If I admit I'm no statesman and retire to my stables, my mother and sister will suffer

65

for my father's sins. If they were sins."

Tania looked over her shoulder. "You mustn't say such things!"

"No doubt," he said bitterly. "I never know what I should or shouldn't say. But that's not the worst of it: I never know what I should or shouldn't believe. Why, I've never even been able to decide if my father's loyalty to King Campion was right or wrong."

Tania remembered herself only a fraction of a second before she spoke. "You . . . haven't . . . what?"

"I know it sounds absurd," he said. "My father was a hero, after all. But you see, he killed as many men for King Campion's cause as my uncles have killed for Ascanet's. My mother insists he was right and they are wrong, but I . . . I see no difference in what they've done."

There was all the difference in the world! Campion's followers had killed men who, by being loyal to Ascanet, tore Elyssonne further and further from the Golden Age. Killing those men had been necessary in order to . . . *Necessary? To bring back the peace of the Golden Age?* She looked up at Colin, her confusion mirroring his.

Colin ran the toe of his elegant boot back and forth in the sawdust. "And now," he said desolately, "I've been assigned a task that involves hideous betrayal of trust. I shouldn't be surprised, I suppose. My father and my uncles have been assigned many such tasks in the past. They've insisted that betrayal, done for a good cause, is a distasteful necessity." He looked down the aisle. "Distasteful! Merely distasteful, if the cause is right? What difference does the cause make to the man who loves his friend and is betrayed, I ask you?"

"Perhaps," said Tania, trying to order her reeling thoughts, "perhaps they merely mean that it is less wrong to betray a man to promote the welfare of all men than it would be to betray him for selfish reasons."

"Yes, but I'd rather not betray a man for any reason at all, if you must know," said Colin. He looked at her bewildered face and smiled sadly. "Don't take my words to heart, Nat; I seem to have a void where other men have convictions. I never know right from wrong—or even honor from self-deception—when it comes to politics. The results of causes men call 'good' and 'bad' look identical to me. Asked to choose between them, I'm like a novice at a horse fair: I have to buy something in order to maintain my family and my-self, but all the horses look alike to me."

"You mean," she said incredulously, "you couldn't tell the difference between a cause that looked like your new stallion and a cause that looked like a thin, vicious carthorse?"

Colin smiled. "I could tell there was a difference to be seen. But as a novice, I'd look at the stallion and see that he could easily kill a man who mishandled him, even out of ig-norance. Then I'd look at the carthorse, and it would lay back its ears and kick at me. So there I'd stand, between a splendid horse and a vicious one, knowing that because I am what I am, hitching *either* of them to my carriage would kill me, my family, and countless people in the streets. Which horse would you advise me to buy, Nat?"

She smiled back. "I'd advise you to leave the fair and walk home."

He looked over her head at the lantern. "Unfortunately, the way things have been for many years in Mazion, there's no home to walk to; there's only the fair and its choices. I came out here to take leave of the fair in the only way I could."

"Oh, no! There must be some other way—some other place . . ."

67

He shook his head. "Can you think of a single acre in Elyssonne where there is a place for me?"

She looked up and met his eyes—defenseless eyes, incapable of calculation or deception. "No," she said slowly. "But I wish I could."

"So do I," he said. "I have so little desire to die, I can't even take my own life honorably, though I know doing so would save my family from further dishonor and myself from pain." His voice broke and he turned, crossed his arms on Pandosto's stall door, and rested his cheek on them, looking down the aisle.

She'd seen that desolate expression on Eliar's face several times in the past weeks. And before that—she thought back to Castle Mazion and saw Paran, a few minutes after Campion had told him he would have to cease studying with Melibe and join the world of men. He'd been looking out the window, and his face . . . The vision blurred, and there was only Colin before her. She stepped forward hesitantly and placed one shy hand on his shoulder.

His eyes drifted back from the aisle; after a moment, he took her hand with one of his and turned her toward the lantern. She cringed, suddenly remembering that she was supposed to be an apprentice and that it was unwise for attractive lads to show affection. But when she forced herself to look up, she found Colin wasn't looking at her with the kind of tenderness she'd feared. His transparent face reflected only gratitude, then perplexity, then perhaps . . . no, certainly . . . surprise.

He'd seen . . . he suspected . . . She pulled away from him, tensing her muscles for a dash past him, back to the house, to Eliar. Instantly, his hand moved to her shoulder, not holding her, but—strangely—steadying her. Under its gentle pressure, she felt her desire to run fade away. When her eyes finally met his, she saw why: whatever he had seen, whatever he might suspect, he had no desire to know. For perhaps half a minute they looked at each other in silence. Finally, he spoke.

"Do you know," he said, "there's something . . . well, if you were a yearling, I'd say you were unspoiled. Free from the tampering of stupid hands. But not just that—there's some special gift of heart . . ." He smiled apologetically. "I'm sorry for the horseman's terms. But what you are is rarely found . . ." He studied her a moment longer, then sighed. "I hope the world will be good to you."

What could she say? She wanted—wanted very, very much—for the world to be good to him, too. But it seemed absurd even to hope for that. Her eyes filled with tears. "Thank you," she whispered.

He turned her gently toward the main aisle. "Let's go back to the house," he said. "Your master will be wondering where you are."

Tania parted with Colin in the main hall and ran up the stairs as he went to greet the evening's guests. It was more difficult, however, to part with what he'd said. The sense that the world of Campion had been as unjust to him as the world of Ascanet drifted uncomfortably through the back of her mind as she told Eliar about the wine cellar and the horses.

Eliar looked at her keenly. "You've been crying."

"A little. I was talking to Colin, and he said things I found confusing."

"How so?"

"Oh, I don't know," she said evasively. "There's no time to talk about it now, if you want me to get our cloaks down to the wine cellar before you play. The guests are already here."

"Take the cloaks down, then," he said, standing up and looking out the window into the torchlit yard.

She gathered up the cloaks—but paused, for some reason unwilling to leave him. "Are you always so uneasy before you play?" she asked with a lightness she did not feel.

He turned away from the window. "It's you I'm uneasy about, not the playing. I feel your danger all around me." He picked up the lute case. "Well, it will be over soon."

She followed him down the stairs and through the knots of guests, then slipped down to the wine cellar. The company had already assembled in the music room by the time she'd come back up; she crept in and took refuge in a window seat, just as Eliar walked from the shadows to a chair that stood waiting for him. A ripple of horror crossed the room as he stepped into the light, a goblin before gaily dressed, handsome mortals. Ignoring the whispers around him, he sat down, tuned his bottom string, and looked up. Why, he was looking for her! She leaned forward and smiled at him. He smiled back, and for a fleeting moment, she felt they were the only two people in the room. Then he began to play.

Though by now she knew what to expect from her lute when Eliar touched its strings, she leaned back in the window seat, transfixed. He played wonderfully, brilliantly, as if inspired by a thousand musical spirits. The lute's rich tone filled the room with songs, dances, and fugues so complex that they seemed to weave tapestries of sound in the brightly lit air, rising and falling in dynamics that required almost impossible dexterity. The sound lifted the audience out of the world of men; until the lute was finally silent, nobody in the room stirred or whispered.

"Great Theon, Lucot!" said one of the young men after the astonished, rapturous applause had died away. "You told me you'd found a minstrel in the square of Theda, not an enchanter!" He turned to Eliar. "You play too well for a creature of blood and bone. Are you sure you're mortal?"

Eliar nodded stiffly. "Very sure."

"Or perhaps you are his lordship himself, come to us in disguise," suggested a man in the back of the room. "I've heard of such things."

"What?" said one of the ladies. "Is his lordship a lutenist?"

A chorus of assent rose from the guests. "He's said to be beyond compare," said the young man who had spoken first. "Many's the musician who'd sell his soul to study with him. But of course, no musician is worthy of studying with Ascanet." He smiled at Eliar. "Except, I think, this one."

Eliar rose and bowed, but Tania thought she saw a peculiar expression cross his scarred face. As she reflected on its possible meaning, Sir Dolan stood up and smiled. "Perhaps we can present our friend here to his lordship ourselves. That would be a fitting compliment to his talents, don't you think? And"—he rubbed his hands together, anticipating the sensation he was about to cause—"his lordship is coming here, this very evening. I have received word that he will arrive before midnight."

In the excited exclamations that followed, Tania met Eliar's eyes. She could see the worry in them, but she could also see he couldn't leave the group of men who had gathered around him. She bit her lip and shrank into her window seat. When Ascanet came, he—or whoever was with him— would go straight to the stables.

A hand drew back the curtain beside her; looking up, she saw Colin. "Your master plays fully as well as you said, Nat. I'm a fair lutenist myself, but I'd never deign to play in his company—why, is something wrong, lad?" There was no suspicion in his words, only genuine concern.

She forced herself to smile at him. "I just remembered

your groom left a lantern burning for me in the stable when I went to find you," she said. "He said to put it out, but I forgot. I'll go put it out now—but will you tell my master where I've gone? He'll want to know."

The mild blue eyes met hers, and she dropped her gaze. *You lied with a grace and ease that does credit to your upbringing.*

"Of course I'll tell him," said Colin. "Hurry now—I want no lanterns burning in my stable unattended."

She jumped off the window seat. "Oh, thank you!"

As she started to walk past him, he stepped into her path. "Be very careful, Nat," he said gently. He smiled at her the way he'd smiled in the stables, then moved aside.

She fled, running down the stairs, through the wine cellar, into the grain room, to the stalls. She had both horses bridled by the time limping footsteps told her Colin had been as good as his word. The gray mare nickered as Eliar swung on his cloak and took her reins. "Hello, faithless Gwyn," he whispered, stroking her. He turned to Tania. "Are you ready?"

She nodded and led the way down the main aisle. Pandosto pricked up his ears and snorted as they stepped out into the snow; listening, Tania heard the clatter of hoofbeats. Eliar tossed her up lightly onto Pandosto's back, then vaulted onto Gwyn.

"We'll have to circle behind the stables, then ride over the meadows to the road," he whispered. "Follow me."

As they slipped along the shadow of the barn, Tania saw seven silver horses canter into the Lucots' courtyard. A wavering silver figure dismounted and ran to the door. In a moment, torches and cries of welcome filled the courtyard.

"Now!" whispered Eliar. In front of her, Gwyn plunged into the deep snow of the meadows. Pandosto surged after her, and in a few minutes they were flying along the road west.

They rode for an hour at a fast canter, then walked to let the horses breathe. Eliar brought Gwyn up next to Pandosto. "Colin told me he'd look after our lute," he said.

"Did he? He's so kind."

"I daresay," said Eliar, watching their faint gray shadows slip down the road ahead of them. "How much did you tell him?"

She straightened up. "I told him nothing!"

"So you say. But many's the girl who has told a handsome man more than she knows she has. If you told him nothing, how did he know the lute would need caring for?"

"What do you think I am—a little flirt like Flora? Look, Colin knew we were leaving because he has a . . ." She floundered with a concept for which she had no words. ". . . a creature understanding. Something that allows him to understand things instinctively. I suppose that's why he's so splendid with horses."

"I see," said Eliar. "Did he instinctively understand who you were?"

"I . . . don't know."

"Well, if he had any suspicions at all, he'll put two and two together when he finds his new horses are gone," said Eliar. "I suppose it's not your fault, but I'm sorry he knows anything about you at all. Someone will have to lead the Silver Souls after us—and his black mare is the only horse in Elyssonne I'd prefer not to match this pair against." He urged Gwyn into a canter again.

Tania cantered next to him. "I don't think you have to worry."

"You don't? Come, he's not stupid."

"No, he's not. But I don't think he'll follow us."

"Don't be naive. It would be suicide for him not to."

She rode on silently, looking between Pandosto's ears at the starlit road. *I came out here to take leave of the fair in the only way I could.* Eliar looked behind him and cantered faster; Pandosto tugged on his reins. *What you are is rarely found.* They were riding very fast now, but the tears in her eyes had nothing to do with the wind and cold. *I hope the world will be good to you.*

After half an hour, they came to the top of the first foot-hill that led to the mountains before them. Eliar reined in and turned around. Below them, the flat, treeless plain stretched out for miles under the star-crowded sky. It was empty.

"I can't believe it," murmured Eliar. He bowed his head. "I did Colin an injustice. He's a far greater man than I thought."

She nodded, unable to speak.

After a moment, he turned to her. "Was he Campion's man, then?"

"No!" she said fiercely. "Not Campion's man, not Ascanet's man—not anybody's man!" Pandosto pranced as she thumped her fist on his arched neck. "This may come as a surprise to you, Eliar, but there *are* people who do things not out of fear, not out of loyalty, not even out of belief they don't dare express—but just out of . . . of love!"

He looked out at the starlit plain for a long, long time. "Are there indeed?" he said finally, sighing as he picked up his reins. "I never would have guessed it."

CHAPTER
VII

THEY RODE ALL NIGHT. The foothills around them grew steeper; toward morning it began to snow. Eliar pressed on at a relentless trot, though the road dwindled to a mere path. Just before dawn, he drew rein and dismounted. "We'll have to let them rest a few minutes," he said regretfully.

Tania slid to the ground. "Only a few minutes? Nobody is following us."

"Many will be following us soon," he said, pulling his sword out of its scabbard and looking at it. "However heroic Colin may have been in your defense last night, Ascanet will send out hippogriffs at dawn. If one sights us, it will fly to the nearest company of Silver Souls and lead them to us—unless, of course, it disobeys orders and attacks us itself."

Tania shivered. "They do that?"

"They aren't supposed to; they're too delicate to risk. That's why they're not used in battle, though they'd be extremely effective. But they love to hunt, and sometimes when they're on their own, they forget they've been domesticated."

Tania thought of the creature that had flown over the pavilions and terrified Captain Talus's horse. "Hippogriffs are delicate?"

"Well, yes, in their way," said Eliar. "They have a short life span—only ten years or so. And they're very difficult to breed. Ascanet used dozens of them in his invasion, but there are only five left now."

In spite of herself, Tania laughed. "You seem to have made quite a study of the matter," she said. "It never occurred to me one could fancy hippogriffs the way some people fancy hawks or hounds."

"Oh, they're fascinating creatures," said Eliar lightly. "And I have a personal interest in them." He stepped toward her and cupped his hands. "Come—I want to get to the forest as soon as we can." He boosted her onto Pandosto's back, and she looked down at his scarred face to thank him.

Scarred face. Four parallel scars.

Somewhere in her mind, she saw a feathered monster shoot toward the ground, its talons outstretched. It rose, shrieking in triumph, carrying a helpless body high into the air—dropped it, dove beneath it as it fell, tossed it again, caught it with cruel, playful claws . . . She blinked and saw only Eliar before her, studying her with a peculiar expression. In horrified sympathy, she reached out and touched his furrowed cheek. "Oh, Eliar!"

His eyes shut in pain, and she withdrew her hand, afraid she'd hurt him. Before she could stammer an apology, he'd turned and mounted.

They rode for several hours in silence. The trail climbed steeply, first through boulders and shrubs, then through firs of increasing size. Tania hardly noticed. Tired—she was so . . . The branches around her rustled quietly; starting, she gazed into the forest. Next to her—not on the path, but between the thick trunks that lined it—she saw a moving shadow. As she watched it, it skulked from one tree to another, then crouched down, panting, and stared at her. "Eliar!"

Eliar whirled Gwyn around, his hand on his sword. "What is it?"

She pointed—and saw only the great trees. She rubbed her eyes and shook her head. "It's nothing. Or at least I suppose it's nothing. I thought I saw a . . . creature."

"Creature?"

She nodded. "A wolf, perhaps. But I couldn't have, now that I think of it. Pandosto would have seen it. I must be going mad."

"Not necessarily," he said with an irony she found comfortingly sane. "Or rather, perhaps one needs to be a little mad in order to see what's really here." He gazed up into the branches that towered hundreds of feet above them. "It's a peculiar place. I've never seen wolves in it—or any other creature, for that matter—but I've felt . . . escorted."

Tania looked into the forest again; its majestic silence hummed with a life she could somehow feel, but she could see nothing unusual. "You've been here before, then?"

"Many times. I'm taking you to your mother's country—don't you remember? This is the way." He looked at her sympathetically. "You look exhausted," he said. "Unfortunately, I share your fear of madness so acutely that I would never consider stopping here to rest. Take heart, though; there's a way station an hour ahead. We'll sleep there."

She followed him obediently, forcing herself to look nowhere but at his hunched back. Slowly, it slipped in and out of focus, and she drooped forward, wrapping Pandosto's mane around her hands so she wouldn't slide off. She didn't remember arriving at the way station; all she could recall was lying down, so cold that her shivering kept her half awake. After a while, she felt somebody sit down beside her and cover her with something soft. A wonderful warmth enveloped her, and she spun off to sleep.

Gradually, luxuriously, she awoke. Her open eyes fell first on a lighted lantern, then on a dimly lit shed. A few feet from her, Pandosto and Gwyn were eating hay with steady concentration. And she was lying in a deep bed of hay herself, wrapped in Eliar's cloak as well as her own. Eliar was nowhere to be seen.

She got up, shook the hay out of her short hair, and walked stiffly to the door. As she opened it, the smell of horse merged with the smell of fir, snow, and thin air. The stars above her were incredibly bright; there seemed to be nothing between them and the clearing in front of her. Something caught her eye in the forest to her left, and she braced herself for the vision of an observant creature. But the figure that emerged from the trees was two-legged, and it limped. Eliar.

She ran to meet him and saw he was carrying an odd-shaped bundle. "Oh!" she said. "That wouldn't be food, would it?"

"It would indeed," he said, carrying it into the shed. "This is the only place between the forest and your mother's country where one can stop without the risk of running mad with forest visions. Knowing that, your mother's people leave food and fodder hidden near the shed so people who know the way can stay sane during the journey." He unwrapped the last of the canvas, smiling as she bent over him eagerly. "You're hungry?"

"Starved! How long has it been since we ate in Theda?"

"I don't remember," he said, breaking off a piece of cheese, "but I advise you to eat quickly, before I devour everything in sight."

78

She took some cheese herself, and for some time there was no sound in the shed but the munching of horses and people. When all the food was gone, they leaned back in sticky, contented silence against a mound of hay, their shoulders touching.

"This is wonderful," said Tania presently. "I wish we didn't have to ride."

"So do I," he said. "The peace is blissful, isn't it?"

Looking at him, she realized his scarred face looked exhausted. "Didn't you sleep when I did?"

"No," he said. "I rarely sleep. Haven't you noticed?"

She thought of his silent hours in the starlit entrance to the cave. "I noticed you woke at night, but . . . you don't sleep at *all*?"

"As little as I can," he said. "If I sleep, I dream. I prefer not to sleep."

"But how can you live without sleep?"

"Oh, it was difficult at first, but now I'm used to it. I rest, I think."

"I suppose it might be nice," she said. "Like a star, looking down on the mortals who waste a third of their life in their dreams."

He smiled. "Sometimes it's like that."

She looked across the shed, not daring to believe what was happening. Access. She was being granted access to the secret territories of his mind. She almost held her breath, afraid of trespassing further than she was permitted to go.

"We really should get up," said Eliar after a pause. "It's a difficult path, particularly going down; it will take me some time to get back here after I leave you."

She sat bolt upright. "After you leave me!"

"I told you that long ago. I can go no further than the end of the pass; you'll have to ride down by yourself, but the trail

79

is clearly marked and not difficult. When you reach the valley, ask to see Anrican, son of Aldar. He was once my dearest friend . . . almost my second self."

He smiled, and looking at his changed expression, she could almost see the person that lurked behind his scars and his moodiness—the person, she realized suddenly, that had made her curb her tongue after she'd first met him in the Gallery. Sorrow for his loss—sorrow at the thought of losing him—pushed away her fear of entering her mother's country by herself. "What will *you* do, after I've gone on?"

"What I was doing before I gave you the benefit of my sense of direction. I'll find a patron, play the lute . . ."

"Wouldn't you rather come with me?"

He sighed. "I would indeed."

"Was what you did really so terrible that you can't?"

"Yes." He sat so still for so long she began to wonder if he'd ever come back from wherever he'd gone. But finally he said, "Do you remember what the young man in the front row said about Ascanet and the lute?"

She forced her mind back over miles of snowy country to Colin's music room. "He . . . he . . . oh, I've got it now! He said many musicians would sell their souls to study the lute with Ascanet, but none of them were worthy of Ascanet's genius."

"That's right." He seemed to be waiting.

Slowly, she forced herself to grasp the only possible implication of what he had said. "You mean . . . *you* were worthy of . . . ?"

Eliar nodded. "I studied with him for over a year. His playing was—is—incomparable. Complete understanding, mediated by impeccable technique. Music like his is worth any man's . . ."

Please, please, Eliar—don't say it . . .

He stared unseeingly across the shed. "Ascanet told me he wanted no lease on my soul. His gift to me, he said, would be permanent: life on the Mainland, surrounded by instruments I'd never seen—wonderful instruments, with a range of sound and texture I'd never heard. All those instruments, all the music they played would be mine, provided . . . provided that I delivered your mother's people into his hands."

"My mother's people? Aren't they already in his hands?"

"They're the last people in Elyssonne who aren't." He sat forward. "For five hundred years, Ascanet has been unable to complete the subjugation of Elyssonne because he can't contaminate them. That's why everybody who had been to your mother's country is under oath never to reveal where it is."

She stared at him. "And Father knew where it was?"

Eliar nodded. "A hermit led him to it when he was exploring the island."

"But surely, if Father could enter it, Ascanet could!"

"No," said Eliar. "Theon has protected it—and will continue to, so long as its purity is uncorrupted. But if it ever becomes corrupted, Ascanet will be able to conquer it as he has conquered the rest of the Elyssonne. Once that has happened, the island will sink into the sea, and there will be nothing between Ascanet and his desire to rule the world. And that's what Ascanet asked that I do in return for all musical knowledge: return to my people and corrupt them. It was a relatively simple task. All I had to do was incite one act of violence or injustice."

"And you . . . you agreed to do it?"

"No," he said softly. "I refused."

She looked up slowly from his hunched shoulder to his scarred face. There was no need to ask what his punishment had been. Finally, she brought herself to speak. "But since you refused to betray your people, why can't you go back to them? If I were they, I'd welcome you as a hero."

He shook his head. "Ascanet's offers cannot be refused so simply. Do you think I would be alive if he hadn't decreed it? Don't underestimate him; he let me live, but his offer is still open. Any time I wish to betray my people, I will be preserved from Elyssonne's destruction and become the master of all music." He crumpled a few stalks of hay in his hand. "And the knowledge taints me."

"How . . . how can you be sure of that?"

"By what I dream," he said. "When I sleep, I hear music so beautiful it would make Orcus weep: music played on instruments I've never seen, music of quality I've never heard —the essence of music, as it sounds in the souls of men who compose it, not just the pale imitation of that essence which emerges when they play. And when I wake, I know that I can never trust myself to go to my people again. It would be too easy to slip, knowing all that music would be mine if I did."

"But, Eliar," she said, half pleading, "how could you slip, if you knew that you'd destroy Elyssonne?"

"How could I slip?" he echoed. "I spent all last night realizing how easily I could slip." He got up and began to pace up and down the shed. "For the past four years, children have run from me in terror, men have looked at me with horror, women with revulsion—not knowing that for all those years, I've stayed awake night after night lest my dreams tempt me to destroy the island on which they live. Sometimes, I long to repay the people who have made me an outcast by sinking their island into the sea—as, of course, Ascanet knew I would. I've learned to resist such longings, as I resist my dreams. Or at least, I thought I had."

He stopped pacing and stood with his back to her. "But

last night," he said, "I watched you sleep, and I realized that when we reached the valley and said farewell, I would lose to my own people the one person who has looked upon me with sympathy and affection since Ascanet took vengeance on me. And the agony I felt then was so great that I wished —more bitterly, more poignantly than I have ever wished before—that I could flatten Elyssonne with my fist." He smashed his hand against his palm, then shook his head and looked down. "And having felt such pain," he said, very softly now, "I wondered how I could bear to let you go."

Outside, wind stirred the giant firs, accentuating the stillness of the shed. Tania got up slowly and walked to the door. It opened at her touch, and she leaned against its frame, staring out into the snow. What he had asked her was all too clear: to save Elyssonne by . . . not leaving him. Marrying him, presumably. He'd presented the necessity very clearly —just as Paran had presented the necessity of marrying Radnor. She looked out at the stars in despair. Had nothing changed at all? Had she lost a father and brother, seen a castle fall, eluded the Silver Souls, and arrived at the edge of her mother's country—only to find that there was no point in her existence but the role she thought she'd escaped?

She heard footsteps behind her, then a pause. "Tania . . ."

She turned, and she saw something in his face she'd never seen in any face before—hesitant, gentle, the product of some kind of longing, not frightening in any way she recognized. But . . . she *was* frightened. Steadying herself against the door frame, she fought a panicked urge to run from him into whatever madness the forest might bring. She couldn't, she wouldn't . . . There must be some other way of serving Elyssonne than marrying somebody who looked at her so!

He took another step toward her and touched her arm. "Tania . . . I . . ."

"Please! Don't!" she cried, shrinking back.

He stopped. "Don't what?"

"Don't . . . don't come near me! *Don't touch me!*"

He looked at her as though she'd slapped him; for a moment, they stood in frozen silence. Then he turned, limped across the shed, and picked up the bridles. She leaned against the doorway, her face in her hands.

When he spoke again, his voice was little more than a whisper, and cold as ice. "My lady, your horse is ready."

Where was he going to take her? She crossed the shed, but as she gathered her reins, her question died in her throat. His scarred face was totally expressionless. All Access Denied. They were strangers.

Outside, clouds had covered the stars. After they had ridden into the forest, Tania could see nothing, had no sense at all of their direction. For all she knew, he could be taking her back to . . . to Ascanet.

"My lady?" Eliar's voice was so close that she jumped.

"Yes?"

"We've reached the passage that separates your mother's people from the rest of Elyssonne. It's a tunnel of sorts. You'll have to lie flat."

"We're . . . going to my mother's country, then?" she whispered.

"Of course." His voice sounded faintly surprised as he disappeared into the darkness before her.

Tania slipped her arms around Pandosto's muscular neck, feeling his warmth and strength. The stallion snorted, then stepped cautiously into what felt like a vault. A few cramped minutes later, he stepped out into starlight and sniffed the air around them. Tania sniffed, too. It didn't smell like the air on the other side of the passage. She turned to Eliar in surprise, but he had already started up the path ahead of them.

She trotted Pandosto after him. He was taking her where he had said he would; apparently, he'd never considered taking her anywhere else. Her refusal to marry him—if that's what it had been—had had no effect. That was certainly not what she'd expected; political refusals usually had harsh consequences.

She pushed Pandosto up the nearly vertical path and found Eliar waiting for her at the top. "Are you all right, my lady?" he asked coldly.

"Yes," she said, suddenly hurt by his voice.

He turned without a word, and she followed him, sick with the sense that her refusal *had* had a harsh consequence: it had made them strangers. Who would have thought the void between them would be so painful? After all, as he'd said weeks ago, she'd needed neither beauty nor virtue, merely a guide.

"Steady him, my lady."

Ahead of her, Tania saw Gwyn step carefully across a narrow, railless bridge. Tania stroked Pandosto soothingly as he put one wary foot on it, then looked down and saw . . . nothing. When they finally arrived on solid ground again, she found she'd stopped breathing. What would have happened if Eliar hadn't warned her to take care?

Care. All at once, she realized he'd been far more than a guide: he'd cared for her, as he'd cared for her lute, in circumstances that would have led most men to relinquish care and save themselves. He'd had no reason to care for her lute, except that she had asked him to, and that he valued it. For that matter, he had no reason to care for her, except that she'd asked him to, and that he . . . he valued *her*.

She stared at the idea as it rose before her. Everyone she knew would have been shocked by its peculiarity—the Ladies of the Tower who had no part in the progress of history, the kings who had left her standing alone in the Hall, the people in Colin's box who had assumed that Campion would save only his son, not his daughter, from a doomed castle. Yet, so it seemed: Eliar had risked his life, not once, but several times, to keep her safe. And he could have done it only because he valued her; a princess without a realm was politically useless.

That must have been what he'd told her: not that he wanted her to save him, not even that he wanted her to save Elyssonne, but that he . . . cared for her. And instead of being grateful for his care, she'd . . . She looked up the trail at Eliar's silent, rigid . . . hurt . . . shoulders. *Oh, Eliar, Eliar . . . please forgive me!*

Pandosto's hoofbeats echoed her anguish for the rest of the night: I'm so sor-ry, please for-give me. But there was no place to say it; the trail was too steep and dangerous. They'd part strangers, and there was nothing she could do but ride helplessly behind him, weeping for the damage she had done.

The stars had faded by the time they reached the top of the trail, and the sky was beginning to turn gray. Tania looked out over the wide, flat pass ahead of them, trying to determine what was unusual about it. "Oh!" she said suddenly. "There's no snow!"

"There's been no snow since we came through the passage, my lady."

She looked at him, hoping for an ironic smile, but his face was blank, deliberately averted from her. "Eliar . . ."

He moved Gwyn forward, scanning the sky. "It's lighter than I'd like it to be," he said. "We'll have to hurry."

He set out at a trot, and she rode miserably after him. The pass was bleak, silent—she heard nothing but the far-off cry of some bird of prey. After a few minutes, she heard it again, closer this time. The sound made her think of the vultures that had hovered over Castle Mazion.

Eliar looked at the sky over his hunched shoulder, then dropped his gaze to her. "Run," he said quietly.

The order was unnecessary. Pandosto shot forward as Gwyn did, pulling the reins from Tania's surprised hands. As they hurtled across the wide valley, a shriek split the air around them, then ricocheted off the mountain peaks. Above them, a huge, winged shadow kited, then drifted toward them through the gray light. Pandosto laid his ears flat back and spurted forward, moving up beside Gwyn. Eliar leaned toward them.

"When you get to a place ahead where two cliffs come close together, vault off and send him on by himself!"

She nodded and dug her heels frantically into Pandosto's sides. She felt him lengthen his stride, and they shot past Gwyn. Three hundred yards in front of them, two cliffs loomed high into the air, forming a V as they came close together at the ground. That must be the place . . . She looked at the rocky path that spun past her, wondering what would happen if she slid off at this speed.

"Tania! Look out!"

She looked up and saw the huge kiting shadow above her extend its talons and dive. Pandosto swerved to the side, and the great body swept by them, screeching in fury. In two gigantic, haunch-sliding strides they'd stopped; the stallion whirled around, facing their attacker as it hovered above them. "No, Pandosto!" Tania pulled at her reins, but he stood his ground, rearing and striking out as the hippogriff shot toward them.

"Tania!" Eliar shouted through the turmoil of wings. "Slide off and run!"

She let go of the stallion's mane and slid to the ground,

rolling to the side of the path. Pandosto dodged, and as the hippogriff swept by him, he struck it in the ribs with his iron hind legs. The hippogriff screamed in pain and paused in the air, shocked at meeting opposition.

Tania saw Gwyn shoot by her, then Eliar flew through the air, landing almost where she had fallen. "Up!" he shouted, pulling at her hand. Hardly seeing where he was going, she felt him drag her near a cliff and shove her roughly against its wall.

"Don't move!" his voice whispered in her ear. He looked out between the cliffs. "And don't watch," he added, putting his hand over her eyes.

But she did watch. Pushing his hand away, she saw the hippogriff dive again, saw Pandosto rear to meet it. He struck out with forefeet that had been the terror of enemy soldiers, but the hippogriff ignored the blows and closed with him, pushing him over backward. He fell heavily, and Tania heard a hideous snap amidst the roar of wings. The hippogriff leapt into the air, circling for another dive. Below it, Pandosto writhed from his back to his side. Looking up at his enemy, he lurched onto his forefeet—but his hindquarters collapsed uselessly under him as he struggled to rise.

Eliar put one hand on Tania's shaking shoulder. "Turn away," he said grimly. "There's nothing we can do for him."

As he spoke, the hippogriff dove, its beak and talons outstretched. Pandosto bared his teeth as the creature bore in under his jaw, then went down silently under the rush of feathers. The hippogriff dug its talons into his still quivering flesh as it worried his throat, lashing its tail in the blood that gushed out onto the ground.

Tania buried her head in Eliar's cloak. "No! No! No!" she sobbed. "It can't be so! He was good, and beautiful, and brave! What could Ascanet possibly want from him?"

"Hush, hush," he said soothingly. And then, not soothingly at all: "Stand back against the wall."

She brushed the tears out of her eyes and looked: the hippogriff had whirled around at the sound of her voice and was crouching at the end of the two cliffs, growling. "It's too big to get in, isn't it?" she whispered, backing away.

It decided it was. Shifting to one side, it reached in with one of its front legs, then tore at the sides of the cliff with its beak. After a few minutes, it backed away and disappeared, ignoring Pandosto's bleeding body as it passed him.

"Has it gone?" whispered Tania.

"I doubt it." Eliar drew his sword and handed her his dagger. "Don't use this unless you have to."

His words were covered by the shriek of the hippogriff as it dove, feet first and wings aloft, between the two cliffs. Tania watched its descent in mesmerized horror—then suddenly realized it couldn't brake. Fluttering frantically, it crashed to the ground, its body trapped between the granite walls. As it howled and spat and struggled, she saw that the narrow passage kept it from furling—even from moving—its huge wings. Eliar nodded and took a step forward.

So fast that Tania could hardly see what happened, the hippogriff's forefoot shot out, tearing Eliar's cloak and sending him spinning against the wall. It pounced, but its wings caught on the cliff walls and it dangled several feet above the floor, howling in fury. As it squirmed its way down to the floor, Eliar crawled under it and struggled to his feet; Tania saw his sword flash just in front of the helpless left wing. The creature shrieked, kicking at Eliar with its hind leg and turning to slash him with its wide-open beak. Eliar's sword flashed again; the hind leg dropped to the ground. In the fury of feathered struggling that followed, Tania heard Eliar groan and saw him fall.

"Eliar!"

The hippogriff's head snaked around at her cry. Holding her dagger in front of her, Tania edged toward it. Its front leg shot out; jumping back, she slashed at the talons as they swept by. Growling furiously, the hippogriff lurched forward on three legs, still impeded by its trapped wings. Tania backed away as it forced its body between the walls. After she had taken five steps, she looked behind her and realized that if she took five more, she'd be out in the open. The hippogriff knew it; taking another step toward her, it purred in anticipation.

Above them, something moved, and a hail of pebbles bounded into the chasm. The hippogriff looked up and tried to rear, but its hamstrung hind leg couldn't support it. As it slumped to one side, a boulder hurtled down between the cliffs and crashed onto its back. With a spitting screech, the creature fell forward, writhing and fluttering its broken wings. Its head flopped down, but it gasped and struggled violently for several minutes before it finally collapsed in a moaning mass of blood and feathers. And then it looked at Tania.

She had seen that expression before, once in a kitten that had been stepped on by a horse in the stables, again when a colt had slipped on the ice and broken its back . . . the terrible, helpless expression of an animal in pain, full of the trusting plea that some wiser creature make the agony stop. How long would it lie there, gasping out its life, if she did nothing? An hour? Two hours? It closed its eyes and moaned in unspeakable misery, then opened them and looked at her again. She could bear it no longer. Drawing a deep breath, she stepped forward and slit its throat with Eliar's dagger.

Pain shot through her left arm so quickly that for a moment she thought she'd misjudged the length of the stroke and cut herself, but as she looked down, she saw the hippo-griff's beak was still imbedded in the slash. Its eagle eye gazed at her in pain and anguished terror, then froze open as the creature shuddered and died.

Tania stepped out of the pool of blood that was collecting around her ankles and looked at her slashed arm. Blood spurted out of it in even gushes that matched her pulse beat. Clenching her teeth, she dropped the dagger and grasped her upper arm with her right hand, forcing herself to breathe as evenly as she could. She couldn't faint; she had to help Eliar.

She heard running footsteps and turned to face the entrance of the cliffs. A silhouette stood against the morning light, listening; then it entered cautiously and leaned over the dead hippogriff with a murmur of surprise. Tania leaned against the wall. "Please . . ."

What happened next, she really couldn't say, but presently she found herself lying outside the cliffs; something was tied securely around her upper arm, and there was a sweetish taste in her mouth. Slowly, her vision began to clear, and she saw somebody was kneeling next to her, rolling a bandage.

"Eliar . . ." she murmured.

Her companion bent over her. "What was it you said, child?"

Peering at the form above her, Tania focused first on gray hair, almost white, then on a face lined with deep wrinkles, finally on patient eyes the color of Eliar's. An old man? No —a woman, dressed in a tunic, breeches, and a sheepskin cloak.

"What was it you said, child?" the gentle voice prompted again.

Tania concentrated. "My friend," she said, fighting the slowness of her tongue. "He's hurt . . ." She tried to raise her arm, but it throbbed so terribly she shut her eyes. When she opened them again, the old woman's face had disappeared. Making a tremendous effort, Tania lifted her head and saw her emerge from between the two cliffs, push back her cloak, and unsling something from her shoulder. A moment later, the sound of a horn echoed off the mountains and drifted with the wind.

The woman reslung the horn on her shoulder and walked back to Tania's side, only a little stiffness revealing her age. "I can't help your companion alone," she said. "He's pinned under the hippogriff. But he's breathing, and help will soon come." She knelt next to Tania and finished rolling the bandage. "I'm going to bind your arm now," she said, "and I'm afraid it will hurt. It needs stitches, but I can't clean it properly here."

Tania looked down for the first time at her throbbing arm. It was laid open almost to the bone.

"Yes," said the old woman, binding it gently. "It's more than a scratch. Is this your reward for putting the creature out of its misery?"

Tania nodded.

Her companion frowned. "They're vicious creatures."

"When it slashed me," said Tania weakly, "it was only frightened and in pain. I should have anticipated that, but I didn't. Poor maimed thing."

The woman looked at her in surprise. "You pity the monster? It would have killed you."

"I pity its suffering, yes."

The old woman finished tying the bandage. "I've known only one other person who would say such a thing," she said, "and she died years ago, many miles from here. It's peculiar —when I first saw you in the light, I thought of her . . ." The quiet, searching eyes met Tania's. "My name is Bellanca, daughter of Allison," she said. "Tell me who you are, child. And have no fear; if you've fled injustice, I won't betray you."

No. That patient, compassionate face was not one that knew betrayal. "I am Tania, Princess of Mazion."

"Then you're the daughter of King Campion and his wife, Marinda?"

Tania nodded. "My mother died when I was born, but I learned a few weeks ago that she was one of your people."

"She was indeed. And by adoption, your father, too, for a time." Bellanca looked off across the mountains, then down at Tania. "Your father and brother died when Castle Mazion was betrayed, were they not? We heard that all the royalty of Elyssonne fell to Ascanet."

"You heard truly," said Tania. "Except that I escaped. My brother saw the attack was coming; he told me to take Father's horse and ride."

"If he told you to ride here, your father broke a sacred oath," said Bellanca, frowning. "Neither you nor your brother should have known . . ."

"Father broke no oath," said Tania. "I was brought here by the man who's wounded in there." She pointed. "He's a master lutenist, and his name is Eliar."

Bellanca's sea-green eyes opened wide. "Eliar! Yes, I thought I heard you say the name, but I didn't realize . . ."

She broke off and looked behind her. Tania peered past her and saw six men climbing down the steep path on one side of the chasm. They were led by a stocky, open-faced man and a black sheepdog that trotted at his heels. The man ran to Bellanca and took both her hands.

"Have you taken to dragon slaying in your old age?" he said, half laughing, half worried. "Surely you could have called us before it was dead!"

"The dragon was nearly slain when I appeared," said Bel-

93

lanca. "This child was injured as she slit its throat, and I had only to bind her wound. It's her companion who needs your help; he's pinned underneath it." She looked up at the young man. "The child says his name is Eliar."

The man dropped Bellanca's hands and looked at Tania, who nodded in confirmation. "Eliar," he said, almost in a whisper. "Eliar . . . truly?"

"He led me here," said Tania. "But he said he couldn't return himself because of something he had done."

The young man threw off his cloak. "There is nothing Eliar could do and not be welcome among us," he said. He turned to his companions. "But I'm afraid our welcome won't be a pretty task."

The other men nodded as they threw off their cloaks and followed him into the space between the cliffs. Bellanca looked after them. "Stay here, Tania. You've lost too much blood to help. But I should go, if you think . . ."

"Please go," said Tania. "I'll be fine, so long as I lie still."

That wasn't true, she reflected as she shut her eyes; the world was spinning around her. Occasionally, it stopped and she saw Eliar playing the lute, Eliar sitting in the mouth of the cave, Eliar telling her about his dreams of music, Eliar riding stiffly up the mountain ahead of her. Then the world spun again, driven on by sorrow and regret.

"Tania?"

She opened her eyes and saw the young man who had led the others. His tunic was covered with blood and feathers.

"I am Anrican, son of Aldar," he said, wiping his sweating forehead with his sleeve and sitting down next to her. "When Eliar and I were boys, we were inseparable; now that we are men, we are still—I trust—friends." He looked at her. "I say this because I want you not to fear for him."

"Is he . . . alive?" she whispered.

"He's alive, but he hit his head when he fell. Bellanca would like to take him to the hermit whose cave is near here. It's a shorter journey than the one to the valley, and the hermit is skilled in healing. But we thought you should be consulted."

"Is the hermit one of your people?" asked Tania.

Anrican smiled. "The hermit is of no people, I think. He's wise, and he's so good that nobody I know can look him in the face and feel virtuous himself. He lives in his cave only now and then; sometimes none of us sees him for months, even years. But he's there now."

"Then take Eliar to him," said Tania, "if you think it's best."

Anrican nodded and began to get up, but she touched his sleeve. "When . . . if . . . Eliar recovers, will I be able to see him, if he's with the hermit?"

"Of course," said Anrican. "As soon as you're well enough to do so." He smiled at her. "Let me take these cloaks to my companions and help Bellanca lay Eliar on the stretcher we've contrived for him. Then I'll fetch my horse and lead you down to the valley. It will take me some time, but I'll leave Sacra here to keep you company." He gestured to the black dog, who reluctantly lay down near Tania's side as his master hurried away. Tania lay back and felt the sun shine on her face, aware only of its unaccustomed warmth and its gradual movement. It was, in fact, high in the sky by the time Sacra jumped up joyfully, welcoming Anrican and a brown horse that was as stocky and gentle-eyed as he was. The horse snorted when it saw Pandosto's body, but stood still as Anrican helped Tania mount it.

"I'm afraid this is no substitute for the horse you've lost," said Anrican sorrowfully. "He's just a horse I ride to tend our sheep. But he's one of the few horses we have that we can trust when the air and the ground—and we—smell of blood."

Once settled on the horse, Tania looked down at Pandosto's gray body, then at the kites that were beginning to circle overhead. Anrican glanced up. "My friends will be back to take care of what needs to be done," he said.

"Thank you," she said. "He was . . ."

"A king among horses," said Anrican. "I was very young when he left, but Sena, our herdsman, says he was the best colt he ever bred."

She stared at him. "Pandosto was bred here?"

Anrican nodded. "He was our people's wedding gift to your mother and father."

A wedding gift. Tania thought suddenly of the two portraits in the Gallery, now ruined, crumbled into the earth. As they started off, she looked behind her and saw the great horse's mane blow in the wind.

Anrican put one hand on her knee. "Dry your eyes," he said gently. "He died full of years and full of spirit, having brought you safely to us. He did well."

She nodded, looked back once more, then fixed her gaze on the trail ahead of them. It was steep and twisting; after a mile, her grief dwindled into a numb consciousness of pain. Anrican stopped the horse. "I'm going as slowly as I can. Are you all right?"

"Yes," she said weakly.

"We'll stand here a minute or two," he said. "Try putting your arm on your leg."

She did, and it helped. As she looked up to thank him, she saw he was studying her. "Have you always known Eliar as he is now?"

"As . . . ?"

"Not wounded, I mean, but . . . maimed, I suppose I

must say, though I dislike the word. When I first saw him, I scarcely recognized him."

Scarcely recognized him? Of course. When Eliar had left his country, he must have been . . . whole. It was strange to think of that. "I've known Eliar only for the past few weeks," she said. "So, yes. Always as he is now."

"He has suffered terribly," said Anrican, looking down the mountain. "I . . . felt it, I suppose one could say, in a sort of waking dream while I was watching my sheep. That was four years ago, and he'd been gone for two years before that. I came to myself thinking he had died, but seeing him now, I realize that whatever I sensed happened to him was far more painful to him than death." He glanced at her. "Do you know what it was?"

Tania looked at Anrican's wide, reflective face. He had asked out of love, not curiosity. And yet . . .

Anrican started the brown horse down the slope again. "You're quite right," he said. "And I apologize. I shouldn't ask to know more than Eliar himself chooses to tell me."

The mist thinned around them as they continued, and Anrican took off his cloak, throwing it over the saddle in front of Tania. She slipped off her own cloak after a few more minutes, wondering at the heat of the gray, filtered sunlight that warmed her stiff shoulders. All at once, they rounded a corner and stepped out into full sunlight that fell upon a wide ledge. Anrican stopped the horse and pointed. "Look," he said softly.

Below them, white and golden cliffs plunged through wisps of fog into a valley newly touched by the sun. The valley was green—so green the long light seemed to spring out of the earth instead of falling from the sky. A river wound across it, bordered by trees that stretched into the translucent meadows in gray-green groves. Here and there she could see

97

the roofs of scattered cottages; far from them, in foothills that led to forests of great firs and from there to protective cliffs, she saw hundreds of small, grazing animals whose white backs caught the still-slanting rays of the sun. She looked at Anrican in speechless wonder.

"This is Dacaria, your mother's country," said Anrican. "Most of our people are shepherds, like myself. At this hour, they should have finished herding the sheep to the feeding places; if you listen, you'll hear their pipes."

Tania strained her ears, listening to the silence—not the dead quiet of the snow-imprisoned world she was used to, but silence filled with the rustle of leaves that brushed against each other in the light breeze, and with the far-off roar of water rushing down the mountainside. Through the active quiet there suddenly rose the plaintive notes of a flute, rising and falling in a lonely, distant melody. Tania sat still, her tears blurring the valley into a watercolor wash of green and white.

Anrican stood next to her, his hair blowing in the warm wind. As the flute reached the end of its song, he looked to the left, and as if his anticipation had drawn the sound out of the air, another tune rose through the trees below them. As its wistful notes floated up to the ledge, it was joined by a new tune from the first flute, and the two melodies wound around each other in harmonious discord.

Anrican smiled. "The shepherds can't hear each other's flutes because of the way the hills lie," he said. "This is the one spot where you can hear them both. When Eliar and I were young, we used to take our flocks to these hills and try to play duets with each other so the sound that reached this ledge would harmonize."

"And did it?" she asked.

"We liked to think so," he said, "though of course we

98

could never tell. We were very young then; we hadn't learned we had no control over our melodies once we'd played them."

The second flute stopped; the first continued its wandering melody. Anrican laid his hand on his dog's head for a moment, then turned from the ledge. "We must go," he said. "You must get to Elissa as soon as possible."

"To Elissa?"

He smiled. "Elissa is my wife. She's also the wise woman of herbs for the valley, and she'll take care of your arm."

Tania's wound throbbed as they started off; in her wonder at the beauty below her, she had almost forgotten it. But now, the pain seemed the only thing about her that was real; everything below her was a vision of peace and perfect order. Looking out over the approaching valley as often as the trail would allow, she thought again of the portraits in the Gallery—of her quiet, serene mother and the restless, golden-haired young man who had loved her. Of the young man himself, who had come upon this beauty and sworn that all Elyssonne would share it. This was what had sustained him, then, after his wife died and his country sank into endless warfare: the memory of wondrous, living green, of sweet-smelling air filled with drifting melodies. She saw it now and understood. Dacaria. Her mother's country. The uncorrupted core of vanquished Elyssonne. *Let it remain so,* she prayed. *Preserve it. Cherish it.*

The path turned away from the valley, but as the brown horse plodded around another curve, she looked out again and saw it drawing closer to her. As she felt its peace envelop her, she realized why Eliar felt he could never return. The beauty below her was so perfect, so innocent, that it was almost frightening in its fragility.

CHAPTER
VIII

AT THE BOTTOM OF THE TRAIL, Anrican led the brown horse through a grove of oaks, then out into a field filled with flowers and grazing sheep. On the far side of the field stood a cottage surrounded by berry bushes and pungent-smelling plants. A woman stood in the midst of the plants, holding a baby on her hip. Next to her, a little girl in a tunic and breeches sang as she weeded yellow and red flowers. The horse plodded faster as he saw them, and the little girl looked up as she heard his hoofbeats.

"Papa!" she cried, breaking off in the middle of her song. She stepped carefully on the earth between the flowers until she reached the path, then ran toward Anrican. "Papa, we heard the horn—were you in the high pastures? Did you . . . ?" She caught sight of Tania and stopped, her eyes growing rounder and rounder.

"That's no way to greet a guest, Corinna," said Anrican gently. "This is Tania, daughter of Marinda. Can you greet her properly?"

Corinna dropped her eyes and made a little bow. "Welcome, Tania, daughter of Marinda," she said shyly. "May Theon grace your days." She glanced at Anrican and beamed as he nodded in approval.

"May he grace them indeed," said the dark-haired woman, smiling as she reached them. But her face grew serious as she looked at Tania's bound arm. "You're hurt?"

Tania tried to answer, but she found she could hardly whisper.

"Bellanca did what she could," said Anrican. "But it's the work of a hippogriff, so it's not just a matter of stitching."

The woman frowned. "There's no time to be wasted, then," she said. She gave the cooing baby to Anrican and led the horse up to the cottage door. "I am Elissa, daughter of Celia," she said, helping Tania dismount. "No—don't try to speak; just lean against me and let me help you inside."

Before she could comprehend all that happened, Tania found herself lying on a bed of sweet-smelling herbs, listening absently to hushed voices—Anrican's, explaining something, then Corinna's: "Eliar, Papa? The friend you thought was dead?" Shortly after that, she felt someone bathe her aching arm, then stitch it with a jab that sent flames through her whole body. She was about to scream, but darkness closed about her. Gradually, the pain—and everything else —drifted away.

She woke, sweating, in suffocatingly hot air. Opening her eyes, she saw three-legged demons feeding a fire whose flames leapt up toward an invisible ceiling. Standing apart from them, a transparent figure shimmered in the red and yellow light; through it, she could see a wavering black demon that bent over a workbench cluttered with ingots of silver, scraps of jewelry, and a clutter of precious stones. The black demon finished its work with a flourish, and the figure through which she saw it quivered, rings of anticipation spreading out across its transparent surface. Slowly, slowly, it moved toward the workbench and picked up the completed object, then carried it across the cave. Through its rippling body, she saw a young man in a blue cloak extend his hand, take something . . . then leap into her sight in his own shape as the watery figure suddenly disappeared.

". . . fever . . . infection . . ." A quiet voice put out the suffocating flames, and a fragrant cloth touched her forehead, letting her sleep.

It grew cold, and she was in a forest, surrounded by staring eyes and gray shadows. Listening, she heard a clatter of hoofbeats, and she crawled into a thicket, trembling. Twenty silver riders galloped silently past her in perfect formation, their swords drawn. A lone rider followed them, bent to one side of his horse, studying the imprints in the snow. He reached the place where her footsteps led to the thicket and wrenched at his horse's mouth. It reared in pain, and his hood fell back. Where his face should have been, there was a blank shell, cut by two staring eyes that met hers as they searched the thicket. He studied her silently; then the lower portion of his faceless visage slit open, and he laughed a high-pitched, shrieking laugh as he rode toward her.

"No, no!" she cried. "You can't have it! Eliar! Help me!"

Somebody lifted her gently and gave her something sweet and warm to drink. ". . . fever has broken . . . very ill . . . exhausted . . . poor child, so many losses . . ."

She sank back, feeling sleep drift slowly around her—peacefully, this time, without dreams. When she at last opened her eyes and looked around her, she found she was lying in a small, dimly lit room. There was little to see in it: the sweet bed of herbs on which she was lying seemed to be the only piece of furniture, except for the table next to it that supported a candle . . . candle? The light in the room didn't look like candlelight. Carefully, she turned her head. No, there was no candle, only a small object that shone with a silvery light.

The ring.

For some time, she lay there, grasping in her mind for half-remembered dreams, but she couldn't call them back. All that remained was a sense that the ring was linked with whatever she had dreamed about—and the knowledge that it should not lie in the open. She sat up quickly, then steadied herself as the room tipped and spun. As the spinning diminished, she stretched out her good arm. She couldn't reach it. She'd have to get up.

The door opposite her bed swung open, and Elissa stepped in, carrying a candle that looked warm and bright in the twilight of the room. "You shouldn't try to sit up," she said gently. "You've been ill for two weeks; it will take you some time to recover."

Two weeks! "How long . . ." Tania's voice cracked, and she swallowed. She concentrated, trying to frame the words she needed. *How long had the ring been lying next to her, unattended?*

Elissa sat on the bed beside her. "Not very long," she said. "I found it in your pocket when I was washing your tunic a few days ago, and I asked Corinna to put it on your table so it wouldn't get lost."

Corinna. The little girl. *She* had brought the ring inside?

The door opened once more, and Corinna tiptoed in. "I put it right where you told me to, didn't I, Mama?"

Elissa smiled as she placed a cool hand on Tania's forehead. "You did indeed."

Corinna trotted across the room and sat on the rustling mattress, looking at the ring. "It's the strangest-looking seed I've ever seen," she said. "What's it grow, Tania?"

Some of Tania's uneasiness slipped away. "Nothing," she said, smiling weakly at the eager little face. "It's a decoration. Where I come from, people wear such things to make themselves look beautiful or important."

Corinna's eyes grew huge in the candlelight. "Wear it! But

how? It's much too small to keep anybody warm."

Tania was about to explain that people wore rings on their fingers, but a warning flashed in her mind. "People do many strange things in my country," she said. "After I've rested, I'll tell you about them."

"You will? Really?" Corinna bounced up and down. "Oh, get better really fast, Tania, so you can start right away!"

"Tania can hardly get better with you bouncing on her," said Elissa, raising her eyebrows. "Maybe you should get her some soup."

Corinna scampered out of the room, and Tania heard her bustling around outside the door. Elissa smiled at her. "Your arm has healed well," she said. "Can you move your fingers?"

Could she possibly *not* move her fingers? Tania wiggled them furiously.

"You must do something with those fingers to be so worried," said Elissa.

"Yes. I play the lute."

"Do you?" Elissa looked pleased. "We have one—Anrican used to play, though he hasn't touched it for years. I've kept it strung and in tune, but I'm no lutenist. When you can sit up, I'll bring it to you; it will give you something to do."

"Oh, wonderful!" said Tania. Then, hearing Corinna's footsteps outside the door, she glanced at the ring.

"Is that what you were trying to pick up?" said Elissa, handing it to her. "You needn't worry about its safety. I have medicines in the house; Corinna has learned not to play with things that are fragile or might hurt her."

Things that might hurt her. Did Elissa know the ring's powers?

Elissa looked at her curiously. "Do rings like this have powers, like herbs? Sena, our herdsman, takes horses to

104

Theda once a year for the Great Fair, and he says that people trade horses for a little thing the size of that. But I thought he was joking."

"No, he's right," said Tania, inwardly resolving to control her thoughts more carefully. "Though not because rings have powers. In Theda, rings have value because of their stones and the craftsmanship of their bands."

Elissa bent over the ring. "Its stone? If you wished, you could pick hundreds of stones like this off the paths that lead through the oak groves. They don't shine like that, but perhaps they would if you washed them." She shook her head.

Corinna walked carefully into the room, holding a steaming bowl in both hands. She gave it to Tania and sat down on her bed, looking at the ring. "It's pretty," she said. "If it's something to wear, why don't you wear it, Tania?"

"Because it doesn't belong to me," said Tania, sipping the pungent soup. "I found it and put it in my pocket until I decided what to do with it."

"I still think we should plant it," said the little girl. "Maybe it would grow a silver bush with blue flowers. Wouldn't that be pretty?"

Tania looked at the ring. Plant it. Yes, if she buried it here, where Ascanet couldn't come, it would be forever out of his grasp, its powers ineffective. "Maybe we should do that," she said.

As the days passed, the idea of burying the ring became increasingly attractive, and Tania had plenty of time in which to do it, for Anrican and Elissa spent most of their days tending their sheep and their garden. But while she told herself every morning that she would do the deed that day, every evening found the ring still in her pocket. Her reluctance surprised her, and one evening, she examined her fears and decided they were cowardly. What harm could the ring possibly do if it lay beneath two feet of Dacarian soil? Yes, she would bury it. After all, she would know where it was; she could always dig it up again.

The next morning Tania took Elissa's trowel and slipped off to the brook that ran near the cottage. She dug through the damp soil until the trowel struck rock, then reached into her pocket and pulled out the ring. It sparkled in the mist, and when she dropped it into the hole, blue light radiated out of the earth with such intensity that all her earlier fears returned. Shaking, she dropped an experimental handful of dirt on it; the light dimmed, then went out altogether. She quickly filled the hole and stamped down the loose soil, half expecting something unusual to happen. But the thrushes sang on in the shrouded forest, the oak leaves dripped distilled mist onto the grass, the brook flowed on over its slippery stones, just as if nothing of importance had occurred.

And perhaps nothing of importance *had* occurred. Perhaps, like Elissa's healing roots, the buried ring had no power unless someone knew how to use it. Tania marked the spot with a white rock, then walked back to the cottage, feeling that she had relieved herself—and Elyssonne as well—of an immense burden.

Corinna remarked on the ring's absence, then forgot about it as Tania distracted her by talking about castles and pageants, ladies who wore dresses, and men who wore chains of state. When the little girl tired of stories, Tania took up Anrican's lute and began to sing songs of the court. Corinna found the structured melodies and verses fascinating, and in the long twilight evenings, Anrican and Elissa joined her, listening as avidly as she did.

"Would you object," asked Anrican one evening, "if someone besides us listened to your songs? I told Kylian about them yesterday, and he was interested. He's a good friend of Eliar's."

Tania started, as she always seemed to do when Eliar's name was mentioned. "Of course I wouldn't object," she said. "But you should warn him I'm no Eliar. Judging from the flute playing I've heard drifting through the valley, Dacarian musicianship is a little intimidating."

"Kylian's not difficult to please," said Elissa. Then she laughed and exchanged glances with Anrican. "But he's more than a little intimidating."

Anrican nodded. "He always was, and he has become more so since he left the valley."

"Left the valley?" said Tania in surprise.

"It's not all that unusual. Most of us stay in Dacaria all our lives; a few others, like Sena, make yearly trips to the horse fair in Theda. But now and again, there are men and women whose minds range more widely than these hills permit. And they leave—perhaps for years. But they also return, unless they come to grief." He looked out into the twilight for a moment. "Kylian has an extraordinary . . . curiosity, I suppose I'd call it—not just about things of the mind, but about things the mind alone can't comprehend. I'm sure I wouldn't know him as well as I do if it hadn't been for Eliar, for he's several years older than we are—and I was then, as I am now, a simpler man than either of them. But Eliar could match wits with him, and I enjoyed watching them together, so in the year before Kylian left, we formed a peculiar threesome."

"Did Eliar leave when Kylian did?"

"Oh no. Eliar left two or three years later, when he was just shy of twenty. And Kylian returned about a year after I'd dreamed of Eliar's misfortune, not greatly changed in essence, but . . . well, you'll see."

She did see—the very next evening, in fact. When Sacra's

bark of welcome told her Anrican had come home, she emerged from the cottage to see a stranger kiss Elissa affectionately, then swing Corinna up on his shoulder with a lithe grace she had never seen any man display. She crossed the garden to greet him, and he stepped forward.

"Greetings, daughter of Marinda," he said, extending the hand that wasn't steadying Corinna on his shoulder. "I am Kylian, son of Thyrsis."

She took the hand. "May Theon grace your days," she began, then met his eyes and fell silent. They were a peculiar light green, almost yellow, and she felt they looked at her from some place she had once seen in her dreams. The feeling fled as he talked wittily at dinner, but when she looked across the table, she was struck by how different his alert, wary face was from Anrican's wide and open one. There *was* something intimidating about him, something not quite . . . tame.

He proved, however, as receptive an audience as Elissa had promised; he listened to her songs with an attention that drove her to her best efforts, and the evening sped by in a decorous whirlwind of courtly music. At last, it grew dark, and he stood up.

"I must leave," he said. "The sheep will be reproachful if I let them starve because I sleep far into the morning."

"My heart aches for the poor things," said Elissa sardonically.

Tania giggled; Elissa didn't like sheep. Lambs, she admitted, were sweet, but they quickly grew up into animals that were, even in the best of circumstances, rude, demanding, and dirty. Tania had initially been shocked by Elissa's heresy, but when she'd become strong enough to help tend the ewes and newborn lambs, she'd decided the opinion was, if anything, charitable.

Kylian looked at her for a moment, and she sensed she and Elissa had an ally. But he kept his face straight as he turned to Anrican, smiling only with his peculiar eyes. "I will see you in the pastures tomorrow," he said.

"And here in the evening, I trust," said Elissa. "Unless Tania has run out of songs."

"Oh, no!" said Tania. "Please come."

Kylian bowed. "Thank you," he said, smiling. "I'll be happy to." He walked into the night, his feet soundless on the gravel path.

Elissa slipped her hand into Anrican's. "I hadn't realized until tonight that he was lonely," she said.

"He is lonely," said Anrican, "but not in the usual sense. He keeps to himself in the pastures, though we welcome him when he joins us. Whatever he's lonely for is not to be found in Dacaria."

Tania plucked at the lute strings, thinking that Anrican was right, but wondering how she knew. She'd been aware of strange things lately; that very afternoon, she'd stopped weeding the garden, convinced that Eliar was thinking of her . . . She called her straying thoughts back and frowned at herself. She had no right to think Eliar missed her; she had made them strangers.

Kylian came not only the next evening but all those that followed, and Tania sang song after song, calling long-forgotten melodies and ballads to her mind during the day. Soon, however, she found herself hesitating to sing all the ballads she remembered, and she began to repeat songs she'd sung before. Anrican and Elissa seemed not to mind; in fact, they sometimes asked for songs they had particularly liked. But Kylian's odd smile told her he knew she was keeping something back. That smile and her own reticence disturbed her.

One evening, after Corinna had asked her to sing a new song and she'd protested that she didn't know any more, she got up with Kylian as he prepared to leave. "Could I walk part of the way back with you?" she asked.

She had expected him to answer with his usual aloofness, but he accepted her offer with obvious pleasure. In fact, after Anrican and Elissa said good night and carried the sleeping children inside, he offered her his arm. She took it, noticing with surprise the coiled power beneath her hand.

"So," he said, walking softly by her side, "you wish to talk to me about the songs you're *not* singing."

"I . . . well . . . yes," she stammered.

He stopped beneath the oaks by the brook, and she could feel him smile. "They're ballads of great heroes and battles, are they not?"

"Yes," she said. "I haven't sung them because—well, you saw how much trouble Corinna (and even Anrican and Elissa) had when I tried to explain the songs that depended on knowledge of precedence, degree, and the separation of sexes at court. How could I make them understand songs that assume killing people is heroic?"

"You probably couldn't," he said. "And I pray that may always be so." He looked up into the trees; when he spoke again, it was in quite a different voice. "But you see, in singing only songs of love, you've forced yourself to ignore the reason for the court's being, which is to draw men together to make war against their rivals. There are many people who could do that without being disturbed by the distortion, but you seem not to be one of them."

"I don't know," she said hesitantly. "At first, I didn't realize how much of a distortion it was, and when I did—well, I didn't know what to do."

"You could draw songs from the world of imagination

rather than from the world you used to know," he suggested. "Have you had no dreams, visions that you could set to music?"

"I? All the time. But they're only fantasies, not the truth that others see."

He shrugged. "There's truth and truth," he said. "Are your fantasies less trustworthy than your distorted versions of history, in which people of perfect beauty love each other without causing each other pain and in which battlefields are settings for bloodless heroism?"

"I hadn't thought of that." She stared across the brook. "I'll try the world of imagination, then—if only for Anrican and Elissa's sake. They seem to enjoy the singing, and there's very little else I can do to thank them for all they've done for me."

"You've done more than you can possibly know," he said. "Anrican is a changed man since you've come here."

"Anrican? I've seen no change."

"That," he explained patiently, "is because you've only seen him since you've come."

She smiled, understanding why he and Eliar had enjoyed each other's company. "Tell me what he was like before."

"As he is now: wise, kind, modest, affectionate—but without song. When I left Dacaria, Anrican sang all the time: in the pastures, at home, with his lute, with friends. When I returned, he'd shut song out of his life as completely as any Dacarian can."

"That's terrible! Why?"

"Because his singing had been an essential part of his friendship with Eliar, and when he thought Eliar had died, he couldn't bear even to hear songs, let alone sing them himself. When I first saw him after I returned to Dacaria, I could hardly bear the loss."

"And Elissa said nothing?"

"What could she say? She understands the forms grief takes. But she is as delighted as I am that Anrican likes to listen to you play his lute and sing. That may be his first step toward singing again himself, and until he can do that, he and Eliar will never be to each other now what they once were."

"How can that be?" she asked.

She felt his peculiar eyes look at her in the darkness. "Can you truly have as little experience with friendship as your question implies?"

She thought for a minute. "Very little, I suppose. I was close to my brother when we were young, but though I dressed like a boy, I was a girl and a princess and so shut off from my brother's comrades. My tunic shut me off from women, too, until my father sent me to live in the Ladies' Tower. And I found no friendship among them."

"Had I been you," he said, "I would have left the Ladies' Tower and run off into the forest before I tolerated such a life."

"I thought of it," she said. "Asphodel had been the constant companion of my fantasies when I was a child. But when I thought of living as she did, I couldn't bring myself to leave the castle."

"Why not, in the name of Theon?"

Why not? Standing in the warm breeze of a Dacarian night, it seemed incredible that she would have spent two years alone with her lute, gazing at the forest but staying where she was. "I suppose I didn't because I assumed that freedom and friendship, like politics and war, belonged to the world of men," she said. "And besides, I assumed my father would defeat Ascanet and bring back Elyssonne's Golden Age, thus enabling me to live as I chose."

"Can you truly have believed in your father so deeply?"

"It never occurred to me not to. He spent all of his waking hours planning Ascanet's defeat; it was as impossible not to believe in him as it was impossible not to love him."

"I see," he said, with a gentleness that surprised her.

She gave herself a little shake. "But we were talking about song and friendship. Why must Anrican sing again before he and Eliar can be what they were?"

"Because a friendship like theirs is a harmony between two people that requires each of them to carry a whole part," said Kylian. "In his grief for Eliar, Anrican destroyed the element in himself that expressed itself in song, just to enable him to bear the pain in which he lived. But until he finds that element, he won't be able to take part in their harmony again. He and Eliar would, of course, still have memories in common. But they wouldn't be the friends they had once been, and both of them would know it. Eventually, that knowledge would drive them apart."

What would happen to Eliar, she thought, if he saw Anrican again and realized that they could no longer be to each other what they had been—Eliar, who had borne so much pain already? She shivered. "Do you think Anrican will ever be able to sing again?"

"I don't know," he said. "When I heard that Eliar had returned, I hoped he would start then, but he hasn't." He sighed. "Elissa is upset; Bellanca told her two days ago that Eliar is well enough to be visited, and she knows Anrican will go see him soon."

Tania pursed her lips. "Perhaps if you sang with me, he'd join us."

"No, he would get up and leave us," said Kylian. "He has done it many times in the pastures. He seems to be able to listen only to you, perhaps because you . . . you and Eliar . . ."

She drew an uneven breath, and he stopped. "It's late,

daughter of Marinda," he said, "and the trees are whispering oddly. We should go. But I'm glad you walked this far with me."

"So am I," she said. "I'll spend all my free time tomorrow trying to think of songs. If Anrican and Eliar found they could no longer be friends, I don't know how he . . . I mean, how I . . . could bear it."

He bent down and kissed her forehead. "May Theon grace your days," he said softly.

When Tania awoke the next morning, she felt the cottage was empty. She got up and slipped through the main room; bowls and cups stood half full on the table, and the dirt floor wasn't swept. She hurried outside into the mist, listening.

To her right, she heard voices and muffled hoofbeats. Turning in that direction, she ran until she saw a tall shape and a short one standing at the edge of the sheep pasture. The short shape looked around and trotted toward her, emerging from the mist as Corinna. "Sena's here!" she announced, smiling all over. "You know—the master herdsman. He hasn't come for ages—that's because Mama couldn't ride when Baby Talin was on the way. But he's here now, with a new colt. Come meet him!"

She pulled Tania eagerly forward, and the tall figure turned to see what the commotion was. Corinna stopped in front of him and let go of Tania's hand. "Sena," she said, bowing a little, "this is Tania, daughter of Marinda."

Tania looked up at a white-haired man who bowed with a grace that would have done credit to a young knight, even though he held Baby Talin in his arms. "May Theon grace your days, daughter of Marinda," he said, smiling at Corinna's formality. "I am the husband of Bellanca, who found you and Eliar on the pass."

Tania returned the bow, reflecting that Sena, like Bellanca, looked far younger than he was. But his face had none of his wife's serenity; the eyes that gazed at her were distant, almost resentful. "Eliar and I are much in Bellanca's debt," she said, wondering at the peculiar expression. "If she hadn't helped us, we'd both have become hippogriff fodder."

"Bellanca didn't put it quite so baldly," he said, "but I daresay you're right. As it was, you lost only your horse."

Her horse. Pandosto. Tania dropped her eyes, remembering that Sena had bred him. "Yes . . ." she murmured. "I grieved for him."

"I grieved for him, too," said Sena. "But from what Anrican told me, I gather his bravery gave you and Eliar time to reach the cliffs. And it was perhaps just as well that he died as he did. We could not have kept him in the valley."

Tania opened her eyes wide, but Corinna asked her question. "Why couldn't he have stayed here, Sena? Papa took Eliar's horse straight to you."

Sena glanced at her. "Eliar's horse is a mare, and she was fully trained when she left the valley," he said. "Now, little one, will you tell your mother to ride the new colt over here, so Tania can see him?"

Corinna darted off; Sena turned back to Tania. "Pandosto was a war-horse," he said. "He couldn't have come back to the valley to become one of ours again."

"But . . . but it's unfair to condemn him for doing what he was taught to do!" Tania protested.

"I don't condemn him. A horse is never to blame for his training."

"And Father needed a war-horse! Why else did your people give him . . . ?"

Sena sighed and stroked Baby Talin's dark hair. "When

115

your father returned to his own country with your mother, he vowed that he would lead Elyssonne back to the Golden Age by peaceful means. While your mother lived, he kept that vow. But then . . ." Sena looked off into the mist. "I don't know what happened. All I know is that when your mother died, Pandosto was a four-year-old, ready to be trained. And he was trained to attack, to defend, and to kill. He would have brought that training with him to Dacaria, where it cannot exist."

Everything in Tania's soul wanted to leap to Campion's defense, but she could think of no apt reply. In her moment of confused silence, she heard Corinna's voice; then a chestnut colt pranced through the lifting mist, shying as he caught sight of them. Elissa moved easily with him and brought him gently to a halt.

"He's more skittish than most of your youngsters," she said to Sena. "But he has beautiful gaits."

Sena sighed. "They're all skittish this year. That's because I have to rely on my skittish lad to help me. Sometimes I think they'd be better off untrained."

Elissa pursed her lips. "Perhaps you could leave me this one," she said. "I have very little time, but . . ."

"Oh, Mama!" cried Corinna, jumping up and down. "Could we really keep him? It's so sad to see Papa's horse grazing all alone, and Papa's horse is nowhere near as pretty as this one."

"Perhaps," said Sena. "But Papa's horse has six times the sense. I'd been meaning to teach you to ride that horse this year, but with Damon so difficult and Sylvio off to the fair, I don't know where I'll find the time."

Tania stroked the young horse's sweating neck. "Perhaps I could teach Corinna," she said. "I taught the younger children to ride at the castle." She looked hesitantly at Sena. "And the chief groom let me start all the colts."

"Oh!" said Corinna—then remembered herself and stood still, holding her breath.

Elissa and Sena exchanged glances, and Sena rubbed the dirt with his heel. "Swing down, Elissa, and let her try the colt."

It was the first order Tania had heard since she'd come to Dacaria, and it took her completely by surprise. Elissa looked surprised herself, but she dismounted and handed Tania the reins. As Tania vaulted on, the colt snorted and pranced, but she patted him gently, then urged him forward. Gradually, his stride lengthened into a vigorous walk, and he asked to go faster, shaking his head when she refused to let him. She'd ridden horses like this one before, the ones young knights "fired up" so the Ladies of the Tower would admire their horsemanship. Carefully, she asked the colt to trot. He bucked and tried to run, but she settled him into a steady gait and guided him in a circle, laughing as he snorted at the ewes and lambs that scattered before him. She could hardly bring herself to pull him up, but she knew it would be unwise to ask him for more. Walking him back to Sena, Elissa, and Corinna, she dismounted and patted him.

Sena looked at her; again she saw pain in his face, this time mixed with something else. "You handle him well," he said, rubbing the colt behind the ears without looking at her. More softly, he added, "If only I could bring him and three others to you . . ."

"Oh!" she said, flattered. "I'd love to work—" She stopped, frozen by his look of surprise. Then she realized that he hadn't voiced the request; she had heard the question as it formed in his mind.

Very slowly, he smiled. "Thank you," he said. "I'll bring them Thursday morning, and it will take a heavy load off my shoulders. I think there's no harm done that you and Elissa can't cure." He handed Baby Talin to Elissa, bent down to kiss Corinna, then took the reins from Tania and mounted stiffly. The colt stood like a statue while he adjusted his reins and stirrups; then, at his quiet command, it moved off in perfect harmony with itself and with him.

Tania watched in awe as the pair trotted off rhythmically into the oak grove. "He's truly a master."

"He is indeed," said Elissa. She took Corinna's hand, and they started back to the cottage. "Did you know that your mother trained colts with him? She was an incomparable rider, and it was out of love for her that Sena gave her and your father Pandosto when they left, as a present from us all. I was only Corinna's age, but I can remember how he wept as we all watched the two of them ride out of the valley. At the time, I thought he wept only for his colt, but I'm wiser now." She glanced at Tania. "I saw your face when I rode up —I gather he had told you how deeply it hurt him when he found that the colt had been trained for . . ."

"Yes," said Tania. "And he blamed my father for that."

"Sena isn't a man who blames, merely one who grieves for what is lost," said Elissa gently. "There are men on whom the cares of the world rest heavily because they see more clearly than the rest of us. He is one of them." She smiled at Tania. "But seeing you ride has reminded him that you are not just Campion's daughter, but Marinda's. Perhaps that will ease him of the anguish he has felt watching his son spoil his colts."

"His son? A lad? Surely . . ."

Elissa laughed as they entered the cottage. "Nothing so prodigious as that," she said. "About seventeen years ago, Sena was returning from the market at Theda, and he found a newborn baby hidden in the hay at the way station that's near the bottom of the trail. I suppose some poor girl must have been driven out of her home and had found the place.

At any rate, the baby was almost dead when Sena came upon him; only Bellanca's care saved his life. They named him Damon, and they raised him as their own.'' She frowned and laid the bowls down. ''He has grown up to be a handsome lad, blond, like most of your people, with eyes like none I've ever seen. But though he rides well, he's too impatient to school colts.''

''Perhaps he'd be happier doing something else,'' suggested Tania.

''Perhaps. But . . . well, when you meet him, you can decide for yourself. I suppose he'll help Sena bring the colts here on Thursday. And that night there'll be dancing.''

''Dancing?'' Tania looked up from the dishes she was washing.

''Yes!'' said Corinna. ''And it's so much *fun,* Tania! I've learned lots of steps now, and I can dance in all the sets!''

Elissa smiled over the little girl's head. ''Every fortnight, all Dacaria joins in music and dancing; last time, you were too weak to go, and the time before that you were very ill indeed, but this time, you'll enjoy it.'' She picked up Talin and gave him a kiss. ''You'll find yourself popular, I should think. Short hair or no, you're one of the comeliest girls in the valley.''

Tania blushed deeply, and Elissa and Corinna laughed at her.

For the rest of the day, Tania thought a little about horses, a little about dancing, but mostly about songs. Now that she thought about it, she found she knew many songs from the realm of fantasy—Melibe had taught them to her. She had put all of them out of her mind when he left the castle, for she had found it impossible to disassociate them from his face and voice; but as she began to sing them now, they no

119

longer filled her with pangs of loss. Delighted with her discovery, she spent the afternoon recalling the once familiar tunes, reconstructing the rhymed verses, and finally recalling them word for word. As she walked back to the cottage, she was humming with a tranquility she hadn't felt for years.

Kylian joined them for supper, as he had for many days now. Nothing in his face or manner indicated tension, and yet Tania could feel that he was waiting for her to sing. It made her feel self-conscious, but Corinna gave her courage by bouncing into her lap, asking for a new court song.

"I thought I'd sing you another kind of song," she said. "Would that be all right?"

"Of course!" Corinna fetched Anrican's lute and settled herself expectantly.

So Tania began to sing Melibe's songs of maidens who had wept for their lost loves and turned to willows, of faithful lovers who merged into great, single oaks in their old age, of lakes whose waters caused men to forget their past miseries. As she sang, she suddenly realized she was singing about Dacaria—or a country very like it—in which the impossible lived in easy conjunction with the ordinary and in which the only permanence was change. The knowledge filled her with a joy that surged through her voice; as he listened, Anrican slipped his arm around Elissa and leaned against her shoulder. Tania went on, not daring to look at him but reaching out to him with each new melody, begging him, in song, to sing.

When she finally laid down the lute, it was nearly dark, and Corinna was curled up beside her, sound asleep. Around them, fireflies began to flash and the valley hummed with a music of its own. Tania looked at Anrican; his face was still hidden in Elissa's tunic. Afraid to intrude upon him, she began to get up. "I'll take Corinna to bed," she said softly.

Anrican raised his head and smiled, blinking as if her words had awakened him from a dream. "There's no need to hurry," he said. "She's comfortable. Would you mind if I sang a song that answers the last one you played?"

Tania picked up the lute and gave it to him silently. He looked at the instrument affectionately, fingered a few chords . . . then something changed, almost imperceptibly, in the way he sat. Smiling absently, he played an introduction and began to sing, huskily at first, but with increasing confidence and tone, until at last his warm tenor voice filled the night, caressing each note that rose to the early stars.

Later, Tania could never remember what Anrican's song had been about; she could remember only the beauty of his voice, the tears that slid silently down Elissa's cheeks as she listened, and the expression on Kylian's face as his eyes met hers.

CHAPTER

IX

ANRICAN AND SACRA were late coming home the next evening, and when they finally appeared, Anrican needed to explain neither his lateness nor Kylian's absence—his face lit up the room as he walked in the door. Elissa jumped up and put her free arm around him. "You've seen Eliar!"

"I have indeed," he said, laying his cheek on the top of her head. "And we talked as if we'd never parted." He bent down and kissed Corinna, took Talin from Elissa's arms, then turned to Tania. "Eliar told me far more about you in an afternoon than you've told us in over a month," he said. "He wants very much to see you."

Tania stared at him. "Did he say so?"

Anrican laughed. "He did, but he had no need to. I could see as I first greeted him that he'd hoped I would bring you with me."

Tania looked down, almost afraid to believe Anrican's words. If Eliar had talked of her, if he wanted to see her . . .

A hand touched her shoulder; raising her head, she saw Elissa looking at her with an expression she couldn't quite fathom. Puzzled, she glanced at Anrican and saw much the same look on his face. Then she realized that she had said nothing—not even asked Anrican when she could go with him to visit Eliar. Of course she should speak. But when she did, she found herself saying, "I think I'll go sit by the brook awhile."

They said nothing to stop her, so she wandered out into the gathering darkness and down the still-warm path to the brook. She sat for a long time, trailing her bare feet in the water and listening to the ripple of the current. Eliar. She hadn't lost Eliar, after all. Perhaps he'd felt her remorse as she rode up the mountain behind him—or perhaps he had understood that her first terror had been followed by second thoughts. Possibly, when she saw him, she could undo some of what she'd done, now that she'd talked with Kylian and seen that friendship in Dacaria, unlike its shallow counterpart at court, was something to be wished for.

The trees whispered above her, breaking into her reverie. Looking up, she suddenly felt as she had in the forests where she'd seen Asphodel and the shadow-gray wolves—not enchanted, exactly, but part of something larger than herself. What was that feeling? A vision? A . . . warning? She looked uneasily over her shoulder and saw a figure leaning against one of the old oaks. Suddenly afraid, she scrambled to her feet.

"It's only I," said Anrican's voice. "I wanted to talk to you, but I didn't want to intrude."

Her fear faded. "Your company is never an intrusion," she said, extending her healed arm toward him. "Come sit down."

He crossed the wet grass and sat down next to her, watching the moonlit reflections of the trees ripple in the brook. "Today, Eliar told me he couldn't come back to Dacaria," he said. "And he told me why."

Disappointment flooded through her, though until that moment, she hadn't realized she had hoped he would come.

123

"Do . . . do you think he is right to doubt himself?"

Anrican nodded. "The burden he bears is too heavy for one man to bear without stumbling." His voice drifted into the noises of the night; she could feel his pain drift with it.

"Do you suppose that if we—you, Elissa, Kylian, and I—told him we would watch over him, he would think of coming?"

"He has thought of that," said Anrican. "And with what longing perhaps only one who has lived behind his face for four years can understand. But we must not ask."

Tania pulled her feet out of the water and rubbed them with her tunic. "It would seem to me that the decision to stay or to go is Eliar's alone," she said. "He's a free man."

"A free man is exactly what he isn't," said Anrican. "And that means that those of us who love him aren't free either. Tania, if I asked Eliar to come to Dacaria, to be my friend as he once was, to share, as a friend can, my happiness with Elissa and the children—if I asked him to do that, I would imply that I was strong enough to stand between him and the forces he's chained to." His voice dropped. "And I'm not, though I wish with all my heart I were."

He spoke so sorrowfully that Tania bowed her head, accepting his superior wisdom and wishing she shared it. "Does that mean when he's well enough to leave the hermit, I . . . we . . . will never see him again?"

"I don't know," he said. "I think his decision depends on other people than myself." He paused, and she felt his thoughts surround her, but she couldn't interpret them. "You will come up the mountain with me day after tomorrow and see him, won't you?" he asked.

"Yes," she said. "Yes, I will."

They sat still, listening to the whispers of the trees above them. It flashed through Tania's grieving thoughts that the whisper was louder than it had been.

124

Anrican rose. "Will you walk back with me now? The trees are peculiar tonight."

Tania got up. "They are, aren't they?"

"They've been so for the past two weeks. Their whispering has woken me at night, but when I come out to see what the matter is, they're still, as if I were not the person for whom they bear a message. It's strange; I can't remember when it has happened before." He shook his head as they started up the path.

Back in the quiet cottage, Tania lay on her sweet-smelling mattress, wishing she could beg Eliar to come to the valley, wishing she had not thrown away what he had once offered her, wishing he did not have to leave, wishing . . . She leaned on one elbow and listened, aware of some change in the noises of the night. No whispering met her ears, only a deep silence that reminded her of the mornings she'd woken up in the castle and known it was snowing. The trees had stopped, then. Perhaps they'd delivered their message. She lay back, wondering for whom the message had been meant, if not for Anrican, whose depth of understanding mystified her even while she envied it. She drifted off to sleep, listening to the strange silence—then woke, sitting bolt upright.

The ring. She'd buried the ring by the brook, near the trees that had started to whisper at night. And as she'd sat by the brook, she'd felt the trees about her . . . Was it possible? Had the warning, the plea she had sensed been for her? She opened the cottage door and slipped outside.

For a moment, she was puzzled by her discomfort, but then she realized the breeze that blew by her was cold and the grass next to the path to the brook was covered with snow. Could the ring have . . . could she have . . . ? She ran to the back of the cottage to fetch Elissa's trowel. The garden stretched out peacefully before her under the stars, and the ground under her feet still held the warmth of the sun.

Whatever had frozen the earth hadn't reached this point, it seemed. She could still . . . maybe, possibly . . . prevent it from spreading.

She dashed back to the front of the cottage, feeling the grass grow colder at every step. By the time she'd reached the bottom of the path to the brook, snow came up to her ankles, and her feet ached with the cold. Above her head, the trees moaned; looking up, she saw the snow was falling from their gently swaying branches, drifting to the ground like leaves. She tripped over something and fell. As she scrambled up, she saw what it was. A rock . . . a white rock.

She plunged the trowel into the snow, but it stopped as if it had hit stone. She shoved the snow aside with her hands, then looked down in dismay. The ground was frozen; the trowel had made no mark on it. She chipped furiously, then started to stab the ground in frantic, widening circles. Three feet from the spot the ring was buried, the trowel sank into soft soil and she began to dig toward it, first using the trowel, then, when it would go no further, her hands, tearing at the frozen dirt, warming it with water she scooped from the brook, working so desperately for so long that she didn't see the sky lighten above her. But as she stood up to get more water, she suddenly realized that she could see—and that in the furthest corner of the trench she'd dug, something glistened. She leapt forward and pulled at it, scrabbling madly with her broken fingernails. It clung to the soil that surrounded it, refusing to come loose. Finally, chipping madly with the trowel, she pulled and tugged the whole block of frozen soil out of the trench.

A sigh drifted from the thick branches above her as a warm breeze blew through them. Under the trees, the snow melted into green grass and flowers and the ground grew warm. Across the brook, a thrush's ascending song greeted the mist-touched day and the sounds of morning began to stir in the valley. Tania sat down on the grass, sobbing in guilt and relief, and chipped at the block until the ring came loose and fell into her lap. The remaining soil crumbled in her hands and sifted through her fingers onto the ground.

Wearily, she walked to the brook, dipped the ring in the water, then dried it on her tunic. Free of dirt, it lay shining in her hand, its silver band and blue-gray stone unscathed. She looked up to the now peaceful trees, listening to the song of the brook mingle with the thrush's voice. *Fragile.* Eliar had told her; Sena had told her; Anrican had told her; she had even sensed it herself. But she had not fully understood. Sena, Anrican, Eliar, Kylian, Elissa—all of them knew that the only thing standing between Dacaria and Ascanet was their ability to prevent corruption from entering the valley. That knowledge caused them deep pain; yet they never questioned it. Nor must she. Much as she hated the ring, much as she feared it, she would have to carry it. She squared her shoulders and began to slide it into her pocket.

Unless . . . she stopped. *Was* it harmless in her pocket? What if it did to her what it had done to the earth, what Pandosto would have done to Sena's herd, what Eliar knew he could do to the valley? If there were even the slightest possibility that it would, and if she could not rid herself of it, then she was as much a threat to Dacaria as Pandosto and Eliar. She stared out into the trees, shaking in defenseless terror. If she had to leave, where would she go? Outside of Dacaria, she was a fugitive, sought by Ascanet, the Silver Souls, hippogriffs. In the face of their combined forces, she would be captured in a matter of days . . .

"Tania! Ta-a-ania!" Corinna's voice piped through the mist.

Tania stuffed the ring into her pocket and hastily filled in the trench. What could Corinna want from her at this hour? Then she remembered. Sena had said he would bring down the colts this morning; he must have come. Hurriedly, she stepped into the stream, washing the mud off her face and arms. As she ran back to the cottage, she heard the jingle of bridles in the fog; she arrived at the bottom of the path just as Anrican and Elissa opened the door.

"Here she is, Corinna!" called Elissa.

Corinna ran around the corner of the cottage and gave Tania a hug. "I've been looking all over for you, Tania . . ." She stepped back, wrinkling up her freckled nose. "Why, what have you been doing? You're all dirty!"

"Um . . . I've been digging," she said, brushing the dried mud off her tunic and pushing her hair behind her ears. "But look—here they come!"

Six horses emerged from the mist, two with riders and four on lead-ropes. Tania could tell that one of the riders was Sena; his horse moved in perfect rhythm with itself, and the two followers trotted alongside it obediently. The other rider, she guessed, looking at his prancing horse and two snorting, shying colts, must be Damon.

"Hold up, lad," said Sena as they reached the cottage. "Give Anrican your colts."

Anrican stepped forward and reached for the lead-ropes. "Here, take this one, Tania!" he called as the colts cavorted around him.

Tania took a lead-rope and led the colt a few steps away from the others. As she patted it, she recognized it as the chestnut she'd ridden two days before. "Easy, my beauty," she whispered.

"He's a handful as well as a beauty," said a voice behind her.

Turning, she found herself suddenly speechless; the young

128

man who had spoken was the most beautiful creature she had ever seen. Tall, broad-shouldered, gracefully muscular, with a perfect, tanned face framed by hair so blond it was almost silver, he looked like the gods who assumed mortal shape in Melibe's tales. But it was his eyes that struck her most; they were blue-gray, almost smoky, and as they met hers, they opened in an undisguised interest she found most flattering.

She swallowed several times before her throat was wet enough to speak. "I don't know," she said, patting the chestnut. "When Sena rode him the day before yesterday, he behaved as beautifully as he looked."

"Sena's a master horseman," he said, nodding.

That was hardly what she'd been expecting, after the fired-up colts and Elissa's description. She looked past him in perplexity and caught a smile on Anrican's face that had a great deal of Eliar's irony in it. Sena was looking at her, too, with much the same smile. "Come," he said to Damon, "let's get these colts in the pasture."

He led the way, and Damon fell into step beside Tania. "I'm grateful to you for taking these colts off my hands," he said. "There are so many to work, I never get to do what I'd like with any of them. They go beautifully for Sena, of course, but with anybody else, they're skittish—and there's never time to exercise them properly. If you and Elissa can take these four, Sena and I will have the others quieted down in no time."

Could he possibly be sincere? She'd seen him ride, and she knew the chestnut colt was no firebrand in Sena's hands. And yet, as she looked up into his absorbing face, she found it difficult to doubt him.

They reached the pasture and turned the colts out, watching as they sniffed at Anrican's brown horse, then galloped around their new surroundings. Sena turned to Tania. "Sometimes I think I became a herdsman because I love to watch horses run," he said, smiling. She nodded, smiling too. But Damon looked bored and flipped the lead-rope over one of his broad shoulders. "Are you coming to the dance tonight, Tania?"

She turned away from the colts reluctantly. "I am indeed," she said. "Though I may be tired from working these youngsters."

"Oh, give them a day to settle in," he said. "They'll go better tomorrow, and you'll have the energy to dance the night through."

Tania laughed. "They might go better, but I'll hardly be able to work them after a sleepless night." After *two* sleepless nights, she added wearily to herself.

Damon danced a few steps, moving as beautifully as the running colts. "We'll see about that when the time comes."

Sena turned to him. "If you're going to be useless tomorrow, you'd do well to make up for it today," he said. "There are four horses waiting for you in the pastures; ride back now and begin on them. I'll follow you soon."

Damon threw back his head, and the air between him and the old man snapped. The tension was one Tania had felt before, when stableboys resented the orders of the chief groom or when young guards disagreed with their captain's plans. But she'd never felt it in Dacaria.

Damon glanced at her, and his rebellious look transformed itself into a smile. "You're right, Father—there is much to do," he said. "But you'll see soon that I can dance all night after a full day's work—particularly in the company of the beautiful."

Tania curtsied in mock solemnity. "Thank you, kind sir," she said. "I'll look forward to seeing if you can live up to your words."

Damon bowed, his smoky eyes laughing at her; then he turned away with a nod to Anrican, Elissa, and Corinna and strode gracefully down the path toward the cottage.

Sena watched him go. "He's obedience and charm itself when he wants to be," he muttered.

"He is indeed," said Anrican, smiling. "I must go," he added, stepping forward to sort the brown horse out from the snorting youngsters. "Damon isn't the only man who must work before he dances."

"I'll come back to the cottage with you and help you tack up," said Elissa as Anrican boosted Corinna up on the horse's broad back. "And then I have work of my own. Selinda is very near her time, and I said I would stop by her cottage early this morning." She smiled at Sena. "We'll see you at the dance tonight."

Sena watched Anrican and Elissa stroll down the path, talking to Corinna. When they'd disappeared around the corner, he turned to Tania, and his expression changed from one of tenderness to one of keen appraisal. "Something is troubling you," he said.

She knew it would be useless to deny it, so she nodded.

"I am troubled, too," he said, "though the cause of my distress is merely a heritage to you, not even a memory." He studied her a moment, his eyes straying from her snarled hair to her tunic. "But what troubles you, I think, is something more immediate. You have not spent the past night dancing."

"That's true," she said, wondering how many of her thoughts she had let him see.

"Last night," he said slowly, "I dreamed that Dacaria was freezing before my eyes, that snow fell from the trees, that ice gripped the earth. When I awoke, I couldn't convince myself that my dream was only a product of my troubled memories of your father."

131

"Whatever you dreamed," she said, stung out of her fear by his injustice to Campion, "you shouldn't blame it on my father! He had nothing to do with how I spent the past night!"

Sena rested one hand against the oak that stood near them. "That is, I think, not true—though your loyalty is commendable."

Tania stared at him in frustration. He had decided—without evidence—that Campion wished to hurt Dacaria. And he had decided, equally without evidence, that she was the heir to that wish. In the face of his aged stubbornness, what could she say?

Sena looked at her gravely. "You're listening to your thoughts instead of mine. There's little to be learned that way."

Under his steady gaze, she found herself thinking of the doubts she'd ignored as she buried the ring, of the whispering trees whose warning she'd ignored because she was thinking of Eliar. Suddenly, she felt no older than the colts and far less intelligent. "Tell me your thoughts," she said humbly. "And I'll try to listen."

"Thoughts become clumsy and accusing when they're reduced to words," he said. "That's why I've hoped to make you understand them without speech. But I see I can't do that." He paused a moment, as if phrasing something carefully in his mind. "I have long felt that your father, while deeply loving Dacaria, nearly betrayed it—possibly would have, if he'd lived," he said slowly. "That is a feeling for which, as you've just observed, I have no evidence, and it is one I can't—and don't—ask you to share. But for the moment, open yourself to the possibility that I might be correct."

Tania looked down at the grass. "I will . . . try."

He nodded. "Last night," he said, "I dreamed your father's work had been completed. I was wrong; as I rode here, I saw that the valley was untouched by what I'd feared. And yet, I arrived to find Campion's daughter weary, dirty, and frightened." He raised his sea-green eyes to hers. "I don't know what you've done, child. But I know you have somehow encountered forces you don't understand. If you ignore them, even out of fear, your peace will be destroyed, as your father's was—and perhaps Dacaria's peace as well."

As Tania looked up, she saw that Sena's face reflected no condemnation, no resentful equation of her with her father, only deep concern for her. "What should I do?" she whispered.

"You should seek help from a man older and wiser than I."

She raised her eyebrows. "Is there one?"

"I choose to take that as a compliment on my wisdom, not a comment on my age," he said, smiling. "Yes, there is one; the hermit who is caring for Eliar. Sometimes, I think he is as old as Elyssonne itself, though he has a face which does not age. And he is wise beyond mortal comprehension. If there is any man in Elyssonne who can help you, it is he."

Tania looked at Sena gratefully. "I'll go this instant, if you'll excuse me from my work with the colts."

He shook his head. "It's a long ride, and none of these young fools will carry you there safely. You're going with Anrican to see Eliar tomorrow, are you not? See the hermit then, and at the dance tonight, I'll bring you a horse that knows the mountains."

"Thank you," she said. "You're very kind. And I . . ."

He picked up a lead-rope. "And you, daughter of Marinda, are causing me to spend a morning in talk that should be spent in schooling colts. Use this to catch the gray. He's further along than the others, and I want to make sure you know what needs to be done for him."

133

CHAPTER

X

"I'M AFRAID you'll have to meet people during the dancing," said Elissa as they hurried away from the cottage. "I'd hoped we could get there for the shared feast, but this was Selinda's first baby, and it took a long time to come. I really should have sent you and Anrican on earlier."

"And me!" said Corinna, pulling Tania's hand. "I've been waiting for hours!"

"Perhaps, perhaps," said Anrican, shifting Talin from one hip to the other. "But Selinda is well, and her new daughter is healthy and strong—that's worth waiting to know. Besides, I think Tania made good use of her time." He threw her a teasing look; he'd had to pour water on her to wake her.

Elissa laughed. "I forgot to tell you what a taskmaster Sena is, Tania. I hope you're not too stiff to dance."

"Oh, no!" said Tania. In truth, all her muscles ached, but she felt more like dancing than she had for weeks. The thought that the hermit would be able to solve the problem of the ring for her had sent her spirits floating. And then, of course, there was the prospect of seeing Eliar again . . . She looked down at Corinna, who was skipping by her side, and wished she were a few years younger so she could skip, too.

The sound of dance music floated through the twilight; peering ahead, Tania saw a bonfire through the trees. "There they are!" cried Corinna, dropping Tania's hand and running down the path.

Tania hurried after her, drawn by the rhythm of the drums and the haunting melodies of the flutes and rebecs. But the sight that met her eyes as she slipped into the circle made her stare in dismay. She had known, of course, that dances in Dacaria would not be like those at court. But she had not expected what she saw: people of all ages whose vigorous, intricate steps moved them in squares, circles, ellipses, stars, all so quickly that she couldn't follow what they did. As she watched, Corinna took her place in one set and fitted herself into the pattern, never missing a turn or step. The other dancers called out to Anrican and Elissa, who had just arrived. They looked at each other, then at Baby Talin.

Tania stepped to Anrican's side. "I'll take him."

Anrican's eyes shone, but Elissa shook her head. "You should be dancing yourself, Tania!"

"I've never seen dancing like this before, and I could never keep up," said Tania, laughing. "If you let me hold Talin, at least I'll feel useful."

They hesitated a moment, but the music changed and the dancers whooped as they heard the new tune. Anrican handed Talin to Tania, then spun Elissa into the set.

"Tania?"

She turned and saw Bellanca and Sena standing arm in arm. "Good evening," she said, smiling. "You see, I can still walk."

"And ride, too, I hope," said Sena. "We brought you a mountain horse. Come let us show you where we've put him." They led her into the oak grove behind the dancers and stopped beside a shaggy bay pony. "This one," said

Sena, chuckling. "He's no beauty, but he'll take you anywhere."

"He's a beauty in his own way," said Tania affectionately, shifting Talin so she could stroke the pony's whiskery nose.

Hoofbeats echoed through the grove as a horse rounded the corner of the path and pulled up. Its rider dismounted gracefully and walked toward them with a lithe step she suddenly recognized. "Kylian!"

"Ah, you've met, then," said Bellanca.

"We have indeed," said Kylian, smiling at Tania. He turned to the tree that sheltered the pony. "May I leave my horse here?"

Sena nodded, and Kylian tied his horse, looking around him at the other horses who stood tethered to trees. "I see nothing that your firebrand would dream of riding," he said. "Is he not here?"

Sena shook his head. "No—he's sulking because I wouldn't let him ride the stallion he likes. But he'll recover when he recalls that Tania will be here."

"I'm sure he will," said Kylian. "And perhaps I'd do well to take advantage of his absence." He turned to Tania and bowed. "Would you consent to dance with a man old enough to be your brother before the lads your own age sweep you away?"

"I told Elissa I'd hold the baby," said Tania, reluctant to admit to any ignorance before him.

Bellanca looked fondly at Talin. "I'll happily hold him."

"What?" said Sena, "You've decided your husband is too old to dance with?"

"Oh, I expect Elissa will reclaim him eventually," she said, smiling.

They walked back through the shadows of the oak grove, then stopped as a sad, clear bird song drifted through the gay music of the dance. It was still a moment, then sounded again, nearer this time.

Sena slipped his arm around Bellanca. "A white-throated sparrow," he said softly. "They still sing here, just as they did when I walked you home after we first danced together."

"Yes," she said. "I can never hear one sing without remembering that evening and how I wept, wondering if it was for joy or sorrow."

Tania listened to the four clear notes as they sounded again. When she looked back at Sena and Bellanca, the old couple leaned upon each other—and the lines that distinguished them softened, weakened, and disappeared. Before her, she saw not two people, but one. The song stopped, and a small brown bird flitted by them in the twilight. Tania rubbed her eyes with her free hand and saw Sena and Bellanca moving slowly down the path ahead of her.

"Kylian . . ." she began.

"Ah," he said softly. "You saw it, then."

"It was . . . real?"

"To those who can see it, yes."

"And who are they?"

"Those who long to be to somebody what Sena and Bellanca are to each other."

She looked up at him with interest. "I wouldn't have thought you wanted that for yourself," she said. "You seem so complete as you are."

He paused, and she suddenly felt the tension she'd felt before Eliar had opened the secret territories of his mind to her. But the moment passed, and he led her out of the grove into the crowd. "Perhaps someday I'll tell you," he said. "But it's a long tale, and this is not the time. Shall we dance?"

"I . . . I don't know any of the steps," she said, flushing.

137

"Really?" His moodiness vanished in an instant. "Well, you'll learn quickly, I'm sure. Surrender that child you carry so sweetly to Bellanca, then meet me behind the fire—unless you want to learn to dance in front of everybody."

"No, indeed!" she laughed.

Bellanca was waiting for her at the edge of the circle. "I'll look forward to seeing you dance with Kylian," she said. "Since he's returned to the valley, he has come to the dances only rarely and danced more rarely still. It's a pity, for his dancing is extraordinary."

Tania slipped off, feeling that she should tell Kylian to find a partner more worthy of him. When she met him, however, he looked so eager that she couldn't find the words, so she set herself earnestly to her task. He was an excellent instructor, and within half an hour, she was dancing the intricate steps with only a few pauses of confusion.

Kylian watched her with satisfaction. "That's very good!" he said. "Let's go back to the circle now and we can . . ." He looked past her, and his voice faded. Turning around, she saw Damon standing with his back to the fire.

"I've just gotten here," he said. "But I hope you're free to dance with me."

"I will be soon," she said. "But Kylian has just finished teaching me the steps, and we were going to try them together. May I look forward to dancing the next dance with you?"

"I'll count on it," he said, turning away.

She turned to Kylian and held out her hand. "Shall we go?"

Kylian looked at her curiously. "There was no need to send him away, Tania. I would have waited."

"Nonsense! It's you who has taught me to dance, not he."

"That's true," he said. "But Damon's not used to waiting for girls to fall into his arms."

"In that case," she said tartly, "it's time he learned. Nobody's good looks entitle him to be arrogant."

Kylian grinned. "Not even yours?" He laughed as she blushed, but when she looked up, she saw his eyes were serious. "Have you talked with Damon?" he asked.

"Very little. I met him only this morning."

"Well, after you have, tell me if you can hear what he thinks, as well as what he says. I've never been able to, but there are some men who let their thoughts be seen only by women, not by other men."

"That's an interesting idea," she said thoughtfully. "I hope I'm enough of a Dacarian to be able to tell. I still tend to listen only to spoken words."

"That's a habit you'd do well to break," he said, frowning a little. "But come—I'm getting to be a schoolmaster."

They joined a set, and the instant the music began, she saw all the lithe, unnerving strength she'd felt in Kylian's movements suddenly freed. His power and control astonished her—and those about her as well. In a few minutes, the people about her fell away one after another, watching. She felt self-conscious at first, but she gradually found she could follow him instinctively, swirling and leaping as he did, spinning when he spun her, letting him lead her through complicated sequences as if his power had enchanted her. The drums beat faster and faster; the rebecs joined the flutes in a wild crescendo—and Kylian caught her up, lifted her in one last, impossible leap, and caught her as she descended. The music stopped, and he bowed deeply, kissing her hand.

"That was wonderful!" she said breathlessly through the shouting and clapping that filled the air around them.

"It was indeed," he panted, his strange eyes shining. "You dance like Asphodel herself."

The other dancers surrounded them, clapping Kylian on

the back and hugging Tania, whooping and shouting their approval. Anrican hurried toward them, bearing two mugs of cider.

"That was magnificent!" he said. "Have you the strength to go on?"

"Yes—go on! go on!" Shouts rose from all sides, and Kylian looked at Tania, smiling. "Perhaps . . . if you'd like to . . ."

"Wait!" said a deep voice.

Silence fell all around as Damon shouldered his way through the crowd and stood next to Tania. "The next dance has been promised to me," he said.

Kylian bowed gracefully. "Forgive me," he said. "I should have remembered. I was present when the promise was made." He looked around the circle. "Shall we form sets?"

A sigh of disappointment floated around Tania, but the dancers began to form into circles and squares. She let Damon lead her to the center set, but as she began to talk to him, Corinna came running toward her.

"Tania! Tania!" she called. "Your ring fell out of your pocket when Kylian lifted you on that last leap, and I picked it up so it wouldn't get stepped on." She bounced to Tania's side, gave her a hug, and opened her hand. "But you'd better take it now—here."

Tania felt herself go cold as she took the ring, but looking about her, she saw that the people about her were commenting only on Corinna's sweetness, not on what she'd given back. Relieved, she slipped the ring into her pocket and smiled up at Damon.

"What did she give you?" he asked casually.

"Just a trinket I dropped."

"It shines very brightly for a trinket. May I see it?"

"It's hardly worth seeing," she said. "And besides, the music is starting."

They began, and though Damon danced well, she couldn't follow him with the ease she had followed Kylian. Several times, she became confused in the complex patterns of the set and had to ask him to set her straight. He didn't seem to object, however; at the end of the first dance, he asked her for the next—and though several young shepherds stepped toward her at the end of the second dance, he waved them away. In surprise, Tania watched them retreat to the edge of the circle. Who was Damon that they should obey his wishes? And for that matter, what right had he to assume she wanted to dance with nobody but him? The people about them switched partners every time the music changed.

As she turned to him to excuse herself, however, she sensed the answer to both her questions—for the words she'd been about to speak died on her lips as she met his blue-gray eyes. They were courteous, but they were commanding and completely without warmth. She remembered with trepidation that even Kylian had declined to cross him. Still, everything in her rebelled at being forced to dance with him. Surely there must be a way of escaping him without bringing whatever lay behind those eyes to the surface . . . With relief, she realized there was. "I think Sena would dance with Bellanca if I took the baby from her," she said. "So if you'll excuse me . . ."

"That's a kind thought," he said, ushering her out to the edge of the circle. As they neared Bellanca, he smiled. "Mother, Tania and I think you should dance with Father while we hold the baby."

Bellanca stared at him, her face lit up in wonder. "Why —you're not going to dance?"

"Oh, we'll dance later," he said airily, "but no harm will come to us if we sit a few out."

Sena smiled at Tania as he and Bellanca started into the circle. "You have a good effect on all my skittish colts," he said.

Well, at least Damon's attentions made *somebody* happy. She tapped her foot as she stroked Talin's curls and looked at the youths who turned away in disappointment as they saw her arms were full and her guard had no intention of leaving her. Not that she really wanted to dance with them; their timid admiration was only slightly less irritating than Damon's possessiveness. No, she just wanted to be free to choose her own partners. Or perhaps she didn't even want to do that. Sighing, she realized that Eliar's easy, restrained companionship had spoiled her for the shallow admiration that lurked behind dances, both in Dacaria and at court. If only he were here, she could enjoy herself, the way Sena and Bellanca so obviously were.

"They're very good," she said, watching the two old people move in and out between the other dancers in their set.

Damon nodded. "They're good at all things," he said. "And they're very kind. I suppose you've been told how they brought me up, even though their own children were all grown. I won't forget that soon, I can tell you—even after I leave the valley."

She looked at him in surprise. "You want to leave Dacaria? You wouldn't if you knew how cold and bleak the world outside it is."

He pushed back his silver-blond hair. "I do," he said. "At least I've been told so too many times to ignore it. But go I will. I don't belong here. You must realize that; everybody else does."

She nodded, suddenly sympathetic. "It must be difficult to live here, knowing that," she said.

142

He stretched one hand gently across her and pushed back a lock of hair that Talin had started to pull. "Do you think some lord would train me as a knight?"

"Six weeks ago, I would have been able to tell you the names of countless lords who would have been eager for your service," she said sadly. "But now, I can tell you nothing."

"Nothing?" he said. "The trinket Corinna gave back to you isn't a tie to someone outside the valley?"

"Oh, no," she said. "It's nothing of the sort."

"I see," he said. "Well, then—I'll have to wait for my brother to return from the fair at Theda. He's due back soon, and I asked him to inquire for men who needed knights to serve them."

She looked at him. "Does Sylvio know—do you know—that most of the men who are looking for knights in Mazion now serve Ascanet?"

Damon shrugged. "To serve a servant of Ascanet is not to serve Ascanet himself," he said. "I can take care of myself."

She was about to protest, but Anrican appeared out of the crowd and held out his hands for the baby. "We're going home now, Tania. But there's no reason for you to do so." He looked at Damon and smiled. "I'm sure you'll have no trouble finding someone to ride back with you."

Tania jumped up, seeing her way to freedom at last. "No, I'll come with you," she said. "Just let me get Sena's pony."

Damon frowned. "May I come see you tomorrow?"

"I'm afraid I'll be gone all day," she said, noting with a wave of irritation that he looked quickly at Anrican for confirmation. "Perhaps some other time—though I'm seldom free."

Damon's eyes narrowed and glinted, but as Elissa and Corinna drew near them, he bowed and kissed Tania's hand. "I'll be sure to ask Father to give you some free time," he said. "And I'll tell him it's for a worthy cause." Smiling, he stepped into the crowd and disappeared.

Relieved to be alone, Tania hurried into the oak grove to fetch the pony. After she'd gone a little way, she wished she'd brought a torch; it was very dark, and she sensed, with a fear she hadn't felt since she'd ridden through the forest with Eliar, that something was watching her. Reaching the tree where the pony was tethered, she stopped, listening; she heard nothing, but Kylian's horse snorted and sidled against her, and the pony threw his head up, sniffed the air, and began to jerk on the rope.

"Easy, easy, love," she said, releasing the knot. "There's nothing to be afraid of." But the pony backed so fast she had to follow in order to hold it. Left alone under the oak, Kylian's horse pawed the ground. All around her, the other tethered horses began to neigh and pull at their ropes. Ashamed of herself, but truly frightened, Tania vaulted onto the pony's back and galloped him toward the music.

As she reached the edge of the grove, she saw Sena, Anrican, Elissa, and Kylian running toward her, followed by other men and women with torches. Kylian reached her first. "Are you all right?"

"Yes, but the horses are terrified of something in the grove, and I felt . . . I don't know. I think there's something there."

Kylian and Sena looked at each other; then each took a torch and hurried past her. Anrican and Elissa stayed by her side, but Anrican looked into the grove thoughtfully . . . "I should go join them."

"Please don't," said Elissa, touching his arm. "Sena and Kylian have all the help they need, and we left Corinna dancing."

Anrican hesitated, then turned back to the fire. "Very

well," he said. But he walked with a tension that made Tania wonder if he'd thought of something she had not.

Back inside the circle, Corinna was in tears because she couldn't find them. Anrican comforted her quickly, and Tania, seeing that the pony had recovered from its fright, slipped off and let her ride it home. It wasn't until she'd put the pony into the pasture and walked sleepily back to the cottage that she wondered why Damon hadn't joined the people who had hurried into the oak grove to see why the horses were frightened.

CHAPTER
XI

WHEN TANIA AND ANRICAN reached the high pastures the next day, Kylian strolled through the flowers to meet them, pushing a few stray sheep out of his way.

"Dancing seems to agree with you," he said, looking at Tania. "Or is it the prospect of seeing Eliar that makes you look so happy?"

She blushed deep red, and he laughed and turned to Anrican. "I thought I might take her up to the hermit's cave right now, since she's radiant with longing . . . ouch! Tania —watch where you back that pony!"

"Oh, did he step on your foot?" she said innocently. "I'm *so* sorry."

Anrican shook his head in quiet amusement. "And I thought I'd left the children at home," he said. "By all means, go ahead; I could use the peace and quiet. Leave the pony here, Tania—the trail to the cave is too steep for horses." He whistled to Sacra and cantered off.

Tania followed Kylian across the meadow, looking at the huge pines that grew up the steep pasture sides and the granite crags that rose above them.

"It's very beautiful here," she said, wishing to make peace.

"Yes, it is. But the view from the hermit's cave is more than beautiful. It took my breath away the first time I saw it."

"Do you go there often?"

"I've gone there several times since Eliar has come," he said. "And before that, several more. The hermit's cave is wonderful and strange; and the hermit's wisdom is a marvelous antidote to pain."

She glanced at him, wondering if what caused him pain was what he'd decided not to tell her at the dance, but his face discouraged all questions. Well-schooled by Eliar's moodiness, she waited until they'd walked a little way, then changed the subject. "Did you find what had upset the horses last night?"

"No," he said. "We saw as little as you did, but Sena and I agreed that the horses were right to be frightened. Something was very strange."

"Yes, it was," she said, for some reason thinking again of the forest. "But there are no wild creatures in Dacaria, are there? Wolves or other animals that would threaten sheep or horses?"

"Not usually."

His voice sounded odd, and when she caught up with him at the top of a steep incline, she saw his greenish-yellow eyes were shining strangely. "Not usually—then there are sometimes?"

He looked out over the mountains below them. "According to the tales the shepherds tell, the last time wolves came to Dacaria was shortly after Ascanet came to Elyssonne."

"You mean, they were his forerunners?"

"No, no—they came to warn Dacaria of its danger, and because they came, the people of Dacaria blocked off all the entrances to the valley except one, saving themselves from

Ascanet's corruption. And the wolves disappeared. Legend has it that they became the protectors of Asphodel." He ran his fingers through his hair, then turned to her. "Let's go on," he said abruptly.

She followed him, reflecting first on the strange tale, then on the fear she'd felt the night before. But as they climbed higher and the trail grew steeper, she gradually found herself thinking of little but her screaming muscles and laboring lungs. "Kylian," she panted. "Can . . . we . . . rest?"

He waited for her, leaning against a sun-warmed cliff. As she collapsed next to him, she noticed with irritation that he wasn't even winded.

"You talked to Damon a long time last night," he said after she'd caught her breath. "Tell me, now—could you hear his thoughts?"

It struck her suddenly that she hadn't been able to. Perhaps that was why she'd felt uneasy about refusing to do his will. "No," she said. "I couldn't—not even when he talked of leaving the valley and I could assume his heart was in what he said."

"He talked of leaving the valley?" Kylian's eyebrows shot up.

She nodded. "He said he doesn't belong there. And I agree—he's too much a courtier to live in Dacaria."

"A courtier! Well, I suppose that's true; and yet I'll be most concerned if he asks to leave. I don't like the side of myself that suspects him without cause, but I've always felt he'd sell his knowledge of the valley in a second if he could gain preferment by doing so."

Tania nodded. *To serve a servant of Ascanet is not to serve Ascanet himself. I can take care of myself.* Whatever Damon might have been thinking when he'd spoken so last night, he'd certainly put his own safety and interest before Dacaria's. But . . . "But, Kylian, if Damon wants to leave the valley and the Dacarians refuse to let him go—wouldn't that be a way of imprisoning him? And wouldn't imprisoning him constitute the act of force and injustice that would destroy Dacaria?"

"I'm afraid it would."

"Then what can be done?"

"Well, the best thing would be to find him something in Dacaria that would make him content to be where he is. Sena and Bellanca certainly aren't alone in hoping that he'll fall in love with a pretty girl and stay in the valley for her sake."

Tania thought of the old couple's delight when they'd seen that Damon had chosen to talk to her instead of dancing. She looked at Kylian, fighting back a familiar surge of resentment. Was he—were Bellanca and Sena—silently asking her . . . ?

"Nobody's asking you to do anything of the sort," said Kylian, a little sharply. "Think for a minute: would forcing you to marry for the sake of preserving Dacaria be any improvement over forcing Damon to stay in the valley?"

"No, I suppose it wouldn't," she said, sifting some gravel through her fingers and watching it fall onto the path.

He reached out and caught the last few pebbles. "You cling to your ideas very stubbornly," he said, but without his former sharpness. "The point is *not* that you're free of an obligation to marry Damon only because forcing you to marry him would do Dacaria no good."

She looked up at him, puzzling over both the double negative and the strangeness of the idea. "What is the point, then?"

"That you have an essential personal worth that transcends even the importance of preserving Dacaria," he said.

"If you're robbed of that—for any reason—Dacaria might as well not exist."

"Then . . . then being forced to marry, even to bring back the Golden . . . I mean, even to preserve Dacaria . . . would rob me of the essence of myself and so defeat the very purpose it was supposed to serve?"

He smiled the way Paran had smiled in the schoolroom when she'd finally struggled through a logical problem he'd solved in five minutes. "That's right."

She did not return the smile; her conclusion threatened to set off an avalanche of corollaries that would bring down all the carefully structured ideas of her upbringing. Picking up a little rock, she tossed it over the side of the path and watched it bounce from cliff to cliff as it fell.

Kylian looked at her for a minute, then stood up. "Let's go on."

The trail became a series of steps cut out of the cliffs, and the air grew cold and thin. At last, Kylian reached what seemed to be the top of the stairs and turned, holding out his hand. Tania took it, and was glad she had, for as she stood erect, she found herself on a thin bridge of rock between two immense pinnacles. To her right, hundreds of feet below her, stretched the golden cliffs and green valley she had left. To her left, treeless mountains dropped into snow-covered forests, foothills, and, finally, a great, gray plain.

"Mazion," she breathed, looking at its bleakness in awe.

"Yes. In fact, if you climb that pinnacle," he said, pointing, "you can see the whole of Elyssonne." He shielded his eyes against the sun. "As the hermit seems to be doing now."

Tania shaded her eyes and looked: a man stood at the very top of the crag, his cloak billowing in the cold wind. Looking back at Kylian, she saw he'd walked across the bridge and was standing by a fissure between two rocks. From out of the fissure emerged the muffled tones of a lute.

Kylian smiled. "Tell Eliar that Anrican and I will come this afternoon," he said. "We won't be able to stay long, but . . ."

Suddenly, the idea of meeting Eliar alone filled her with shyness that was close to fear. "You're not coming in now?"

He looked at her anguished face, and his own softened. "Don't worry," he said. "When you see him, you'll find whatever words you need." He turned and walked back across the stone bridge; soon he had disappeared. Tania drew a shaking breath and slipped into the fissure.

Inside, she found herself standing in a torchlit space that faced three stone arches which appeared to have been shaped by natural forces, not human hands; yet as she looked at them, her eyes rested on stone reliefs: animals that seemed to be struggling out of the ground, trees that emerged from the soil fully grown, and a strange figure she couldn't quite identify, holding something in its cupped hands. She stared at them in wonder, then started through the center arch, drawn by Eliar's lute.

The arch led to a high-vaulted room lit with rays of sunlight that filtered in through openings she couldn't see, and warmed by a fire that burned brightly in a natural recess. The circular walls were lined with books—great leather-bound tomes with brass clasps, tiny volumes smaller than her palm, and books of ordinary size, leaning toward each other across friendly spaces where other books had been taken down to read. The room itself was furnished mainly with tables, piled high with unbound sheets of music. But there was a settle in front of the fire, and next to that, a chair with its carved back turned to her. On the chair sat Eliar, absorbed in his lute.

Tania hesitated a moment before she spoke. "Eliar . . ."

He turned his head, then laid the lute carefully in its case. "Tania," he said wonderingly. "I hadn't expected you so soon." He rose to his feet, his eyes searching the arch behind her.

So he, too, had wished to meet in the company of others. Did they have so little to say to each other, then? "Anrican and Kylian can't come until this afternoon . . ." she began. But as she looked at him, words left her entirely. He was terribly thin: his scars practically covered his sunken cheeks, and the bones of his hunched shoulder made uneven lumps in his tunic. But it was his eyes that she found most disturbing; they were set in a masklike attitude of pain.

"You must be cold," he said into the silence. "Come sit by the fire."

"Thank you." She crossed the room and sat on the edge of the settle. He sat down in his chair without looking at her.

"How long have you been well enough to play the lute?" she asked after another silence.

"A week, I think. I tend to lose track of the time."

"There seems to be a wonderful selection of music here."

"Yes, there is."

"It belongs to the hermit, doesn't it? I wonder how he got it here."

"I've often wondered, myself."

The stillness of the room seemed to envelop them both. Tania looked desperately into the fire and tried another subject. "Anrican told me you didn't feel you could come to the valley . . ."

"You know as well as he does why I can't," he said, preoccupied with a spider that was crawling across the space between them.

"Yes, I do," she said. "But I was sorry to hear it."

"You were?"

The surprise in his voice stung her. "Of course I was! Did you expect me to rejoice because you can't live in Dacaria, where you have friends who love you? Or to be happy because you'll have to go back to a place where people turn away from you in fear, and you lie awake all night, afraid to shut your eyes?"

"No. But I know that such thoughts are soon forgotten when one is busy."

"I see," she said. "Then I'm not a monster—merely an ungrateful wretch."

Eliar shifted in his chair. "I've always thought gratitude was merely an unselfish form of forgetfulness. Somebody does you a kindness; you thank him, and the two of you never have to think of each other again."

Tania looked across the eight feet that separated them, wondering how to bridge the void it so poignantly represented. In his present mood, he was certainly not going to reach across even half of it. Eight feet! It might as well be eight miles . . .

Suddenly, the memory of her own panicked voice cut through the long silence that stretched between them. *Don't . . . don't come near me! Don't touch me!* She'd forgotten those words; she'd remembered only the terror she'd felt in the face of his expression of longing. *That* she hadn't forgotten; every time she remembered it, her fear had welled up again. Looking at him now, though, she found herself thinking not of her fear, but of the harsh words that had spoken the thoughts he'd seen in every woman's face—except hers. What she had said to him, then, had hurt him as deeply as his look had frightened her. And if she wished to bridge the void between them, she'd have to put aside her fear and assure him she'd never hurt him so again. Drawing a deep

breath, she forced herself to speak. "Would you come sit . . .
next to me?"

She saw his feet move back and heard the chair creak as he
stood; then the settle moved gently as he lowered himself
onto it. She looked up and saw a shadow of the face she remembered struggling through the mask he'd turned to her
before. For a moment, she was tempted to throw her arms
around him in relief; but the memory of the look she'd
feared made that gesture seem peculiarly inappropriate—as
childish as Corinna's hugs. In renewed awkwardness, she
groped for some alternative. The coquettish smile of a Lady
of the Tower? The impassioned verses of the heroines of
courtly songs? Affected . . . absurd! What did *real* people say
when they felt as she did?

Eliar's mouth suddenly twisted into his familiar, sardonic
smile. "They say, 'I'm glad to see you again.' "

"But that's just as silly as everything else!" she objected
before she thought. "It's so . . . obvious!"

"Not always," he said, no longer smiling.

Not always! Then he hadn't known . . . ? In a wave of
self-reproach, she reached out and took the thin hand that
rested on his knee. "I *am* glad to see you! I missed you
dreadfully—not just because you were up here, but because I
thought after what I'd said . . ." She tightened her hand
around his and bumped them both against his knee in frustration. "Oh, Eliar . . . I'm so *stupid*!"

He turned his hand over and closed his fingers around
hers. "Not consistently," he said. "And—who knows?—
perhaps not even incurably."

She smiled into his wonderful, hideous, ironic face.
"You're terrible!"

"You'd thought a month of pain would improve my
disposition?"

154

"No—only that it would teach you not to wallow in your misfortunes."

He shook his head, smiling wryly, then raised her hand to his lips and kissed it. For a moment, both of them looked into the fire in a silence far different from their earlier ones. Then Eliar stood up. "I made you something," he said. "Let me go get it."

He limped across the room and out the arch. When he came back, a hand-sized object hung from the belt of his tunic. He sat beside her again and detached it. It was a little instrument, fashioned in a graduated series of reeds.

"Oh!" she said, delighted. "A panpipe! I've never seen one before, except in pictures." She picked it up and gave an experimental puff, producing two squawks.

"Tighten your lips a little more," he said, "so you'll play only one note at a time. That's right. Now, pull it from right to left as you blow, and see if you can play its whole range."

She slid the pipe slowly across her mouth; something rather like a scale resulted. Encouraged, she tried a few more times.

Eliar smiled. "You'll find it's a rewarding instrument. An hour's practice will make you a master."

"Have you had an hour's practice with it?" she asked.

He nodded.

"Would you show me how it sounds in the hands of a master?"

He took the pipe from her and blew; a Lydian melody wafted sadly about them. He smiled as he handed it back to her. "I'm afraid the scale it plays is something of a limitation if you want to play cheerful songs," he said. "But the old shepherd who taught me to make panpipes told me his grandfather said pipes in the Lydian mode had magical properties."

"And do they?"

He laughed. "I have no idea. I'm even cynical enough to suspect that shepherds know only one way of making pan-pipes and have invented the story to excuse their ignorance. But I followed their example, nevertheless. One never knows."

Tania looked at the little instrument. "I think you were wise. It looks vaguely . . . well, not magical, but Dacarian." She held her lips the way he'd told her to and began to blow.

He watched her. "Then you've noticed things you see and hear in Dacaria are . . . shall we say . . . flexible in their reality?"

She nodded, frowning with concentration as she played the panpipe's strange-sounding scale.

"I thought you would," he said. "Look, start in the middle of its range, then play three descending notes . . . that's right . . . now skip a fifth . . ."

They worked with the panpipe for some time, passing it back and forth as Eliar showed Tania different tunes. By the end of the morning, she had a whole repertory of sad melodies at her command.

"It's really a delight," she said. "It's so simple."

"Yes," said Eliar. "But eventually you'll find that's its weakness as well as its strength. You play it well; in a month's time, you'll play it no better. The lute, now . . ."

He bent down and picked it up. She slipped the panpipe onto the belt of her tunic and leaned back against the settle, listening to the music he drew from the instrument and thinking that he somehow became complete only when he was absorbed in it. He played on and on, and as her thoughts drifted with the sound, she, too, became absorbed —not just in his playing, but in the memories of other times she'd heard him: in the Hall at Castle Mazion, in the firelit cave above the ruined valley, and in Colin's music room . . . His music drew her far into that oddly foreign world, then through it, into a world she'd seen only in visions.

She started as she felt his hand cover hers; turning to him, she realized with a jolt that he had stopped playing and was looking at her. "Where did you go?" he asked softly.

She stumbled back into the world before her. "I was . . . re-seeing . . . I guess you'd say, something I saw last night. Sena and Bellanca were standing arm in arm, listening to a white-throated sparrow, and as I watched them, I was jealous."

He looked puzzled. "Of Bellanca?"

"No, no—of both of them, of what they were to each other. They became . . . one person."

"Ah." His voice became absolutely still.

"And I was thinking that I'd once longed for that myself, but I'd made myself forget such things. Marriage at court was a woman's duty and a man's route to preferment; wishing for anything else made the reality only more painful."

"You certainly make it sound distasteful," he said lightly. "Is that what you expected when you said you'd marry Prince Radnor?"

"I didn't have very much time to think about it; I was still in the middle of realizing I had to marry him to save the alliance. I suppose I'd hoped for a little more than politics, in spite of myself; I was upset when I saw how hard Radnor was. But I didn't know, really, what to hope *for*. I'd seen lords kiss their wives in formal greeting, and I didn't particularly want that. I'd seen guards kiss servant girls in corners and heard my attendants giggle about what they'd done, and I didn't want that, either—especially since what the young brides said about their wedding nights made it seem just brutal . . ."

Eliar tapped his fingers gently on the back of her hand, but he said nothing.

"And yet," she went on, "when I think of Sena and Bellanca together—or, for that matter, when I see Anrican and Elissa sitting together on the doorstep with the children—in spite of everything I know, I wish . . ." She shook her head. She couldn't say it—not even to Eliar.

He nodded. "If it's any consolation to you," he said, "sometimes, when I think of Sena and Bellanca or Anrican and Elissa, I wish . . . too. What they are to each other is very rare, even in Dacaria."

As she looked up, she found he was looking at her with an expression very like the one that had so frightened her in the way station, but it seemed gentler and less threatening. "And . . . and you envy them? But what you and Anrican are to each other is also very rare."

"It is rare," he said. "As rare as a perfectly made instrument—and as inexplicable."

"And even so, you wish . . . ?" .

"Even so."

They sat quietly, listening to the small noises of the fire. In the silence, Tania felt a surge of longing so intense she could hardly bear it. There was nobody to turn to in her pain and confusion but him, and she did, sobbing as she dropped her face on his hunched shoulder.

He slipped his arms around her and stroked her lengthening hair. "What is it?" he asked.

"I don't know," she said, her voice muffled by his tunic. "I . . . Eliar . . . I longed for you so . . ."

The hand that was stroking her hair stopped at her chin. Gently tilting her head back, he kissed her forehead, her cheeks—then stopped, his hand shaking.

She looked at him, ducked away, and hid her eyes in the safety of his tunic. "I'm afraid . . ." She felt him stiffen, and she quickly put her hand on his. "No, that's not the kind of fear I mean." She groped for words. "If . . . I must have known, but I never thought about it before . . . it's different when it's only a fantasy. If two people become one, there's no place they can hide from each other, and that's so . . . vulnerable. Do you see?"

"Oh, yes."

"But you aren't afraid?"

He sat very still. "Look at me."

She raised her head obediently, then reached up hesitantly to stroke his scarred cheek. The instant her hand touched his face, she saw the same pain and panic she'd seen in the forest when she'd expressed her horror at his torture by the hippogriff. "Oh!" she said softly, taking her hand away. "Then you are afraid."

He nodded. "It's not a visage I would wish on the other half of myself."

"Even if the other half of yourself were sensible enough to realize that it's an inseparable part of what you are?" she asked, caressing it again.

He winced as she touched him. "That's just the point: it *is* inseparable from what I am, not just because it's deformed, but because it's a living reminder of the powers I'm attached to. You know what I've done. You know what I can do. I'm not free, Tania."

She turned her head away. "Neither am I," she said softly.

"You will be if you don't attach yourself to me," he said. "That's why . . ."

Tania sat up, though she still leaned against him. "It's more than my attachment to you," she said. "It's . . . it's a . . . problem of my own. Sena said that when I came up here, I should talk to the hermit about it."

Eliar said nothing for a moment; then he looked at her.

"You may find the hermit is already aware of it," he said. "I meant to tell you earlier, but I was . . . distracted." His face grew serious. "He's concerned about you."

"But how could he be? He doesn't know who I am!"

"Sometimes," said Eliar, "I think the hermit knows who everyone is. And it worries me that both he and Sena fear for you. Can you tell me what has brought you to see him?"

"Of course," she said. "I meant to tell you after we left Colin's manor, but then we rode so hard, and so much happened . . ." She slid her hand into her pocket and drew out the ring. "It's this."

He bent over it, then drew back and stared at her, his face ashen under his scars. "Great, merciful gods . . ." he whispered.

"Do you know what it is?"

He didn't answer; instead, his twisted eyes searched hers with a sick fear that had been totally absent when he'd drawn Paran's sword against the hippogriff. "Who . . . who gave this to you?"

"Nobody. The Captain of the Silver Souls gave it to Radnor as a bribe, and when he stabbed him, it rolled in my direction. I put it in my pocket so he wouldn't find me—" She told the rest of her story, watching his fingers clench and unclench as they lay on his lap. "And I wish I'd told you about it at Colin's manor," she concluded. "I don't know what I would have done, but . . ." She looked up at him. "What do you know about it that I don't?"

"Little more than you've found out for yourself, except that Ascanet never took it off, even when he played the lute —which struck me as strange, since the stone is so large it interfered with his fingering. I came to suspect that he was somehow dependent upon it." He tapped his fingers on the settle. "So *that's* what the Silver Souls were looking for in the ruins of Castle Mazion, and why they had a new, young captain at the demonstration. And, I suppose, why Ascanet rode to Colin's so quickly, then risked a hippogriff . . ."

"And . . . and do you think he knows it's in Dacaria now?"

"If he does," he said grimly, "the knowledge must give him tremendous pleasure. He couldn't have wished for better fortune."

"That's what I was afraid of," she said. "And it's why I came to see the hermit—to ask him where I should take it."

"Where *you* should take it? Why you?"

"How could I give it to anyone else, knowing what it is?"

"Don't be ridiculous!" he said, taking her hand. "Tania —do you think anyone who loves you could stand by and watch you leave Dacaria with Ascanet's ring?"

"Perhaps not happily," she said. "But think: wouldn't my giving the ring to somebody else, knowing what it was and what it could do, be the kind of selfish action that would allow Ascanet to gain a foothold in the valley?"

He gazed into the fire. "Yes," he said finally. "Yes, it would."

She slipped the ring back into her pocket. "You say you know where the hermit is?"

"He's usually through the arch on the left as you come in. Do you want me to come with you?"

"I do—but I think I'd better go alone," she said.

He nodded, and she started slowly toward the door. As she reached it, she heard his uneven footsteps stride across the room.

"Tania . . ."

Turning around, she saw his outstretched hand and, above it, eyes filled with all the fear and sorrow and longing she felt herself. She took the hand and let it draw them into each other's arms; and for a moment all the loneliness that stretched out before her disappeared. Sighing peacefully, she lifted up her face and smiled at him.

His kiss was so much a part of all he was that she found the courage to return it.

CHAPTER
XII

WHEN SHE FINALLY BROUGHT herself to leave Eliar, Tania walked through the arch he had described, then stopped in dismay as three more arches opened in front of her. Suppose each of these opened into three more arches, and each of those . . . She peered through the arch furthest to the left and found to her relief it opened into a room. It seemed to be empty, but she could see very little of it from where she was. She entered and found it was indeed empty . . . but the stone walls about her muffled the echo of her footsteps, and the floors under her feet felt softly carpeted. She circled it curiously, instinctively avoiding the places where tables and chairs should be, but seeing nothing. Very odd.

She stepped back into the hall and turned to the arch on the right, which led to a warm, comfortably furnished room. Just as she was about to enter it, something made her extend her hand; it met solid rock. Bewildered, she traced the images of tables, chairs, and books with her fingers, unable to believe they were two-dimensional, even as she touched them. Was this what Kylian had meant when he said the cave was strange and wonderful? No doubt.

Shaking her head in bewilderment, she moved slowly toward the remaining arch, both hands in front of her, and emerged in a low-vaulted room that held a few books, a bed, a high, slant-topped desk, and a white-haired man who stood at it, writing. She waited nervously for him to look up, wondering if he had heard her come in. Just as she raised her hand to knock on the side of the arch, he put down his pen and turned.

"Greetings, dear child," he said. "It has been a long time since I saw you last; I see I can no longer think of you as a child. But I'm very glad that you've made your way here."

Tania stared at the familiar, finely sculpted face, the white beard that flowed over his simple tunic, the tapered, ringless fingers that rested on the desk—and was suddenly overwhelmed by memories of the schoolroom in Castle Mazion. "Melibe," she whispered. "How is it possible?"

"All things are possible," said Melibe, smiling. "Though not at all times or in all places. Have you forgotten your lessons so quickly?"

His voice, his words were so familiar that Dacaria, the mountain, the strangeness of the cave all faded away, and she ran to him as she'd done when she'd been much younger. He held her tight for a moment, then stepped back and looked at her carefully.

"You've cut your hair."

She nodded, flipping it behind her shoulders. "Eliar cut it so I could travel as his apprentice, after . . ." She looked at him, wondering how much he knew of the world beyond his mountain. Everything, most likely. "I suppose Eliar told you Castle Mazion fell to Ascanet, and Father and Paran were . . ."

"He told me the details; the facts I'd learned already." Melibe sighed. "I grieved for your brother—and for your father, too, though I lost him so long ago, his death was hardly a parting."

She puzzled over the remark, looking around the room. "Is there somewhere we could sit and talk? One of the other rooms . . . ?"

He laughed. "They're unavailable, I'm afraid."

"Well, yes—I noticed. But I thought perhaps you could make them . . . more cooperative."

"I doubt it," he said. "The one on the right is furnished with memories; the one on the left is furnished with plans. I could play with them a little, I suppose, but it's unwise to make the progress of history fit one's immediate desires. I'm afraid the sparsely furnished room we're in at present is the only one left to us, unless you'd like to join Eliar in the library."

He spoke so naturally that she accepted his explanation without a second thought. "I'd rather talk to you here—for a little while at least," she said. "Eliar said you were worried about me."

"I am indeed."

She pulled the ring out of her pocket. "Because of this?"

He looked at her without surprise. "Yes, because of this. Do you know what it is?"

"I know that it's something Ascanet values beyond all things. I know that it has great power. I know that it's extremely dangerous to anybody that wears it—but that's all."

"You've learned enough about it to treat it with the respect it deserves, at least."

"But what is it, that it should be treated with such respect?"

He looked at her with the face she'd often seen in the schoolroom. "Do you recall the conditions under which Theon imprisoned Orcus before the flood?"

165

"Of course," she said, wondering why the lesson was necessary. "He decreed that Orcus could emerge again only if he took some visible, ordered form."

"That's right," said Melibe. "And though Orcus found the idea of form repugnant, after many centuries he bowed to the inevitable and took one." He pointed at the stone that lay glistening in her hand. "This form."

Tania looked at him incredulously. "The form of the ring?"

"Not at first. He couldn't truly become free—in any form —until he had corrupted some mortal. He took the preliminary form of a star sapphire; but when Ascanet, Prince of Adesh, found the stone by the sea and felt its call, the stone was only the spirit's minion, not his essence. The sapphire led Ascanet to the mountains, and from thence deep into Orcus's cavern, and there the spirit drove a bargain with him —an unequal bargain, since Ascanet could not possibly understand the terms until he had executed his part of it."

For a fraction of a second, Tania glimpsed the dream she'd had in her fever: the transparent figure that rippled in anticipation as it carried something to a young man in a blue cloak. Dacaria had tried to warn her of her danger, then, just as the trees had warned her of theirs. "And the bargain?" she whispered.

"The bargain was that Orcus would have the stone set in a silver band, and that if Ascanet willingly put it on, he would be able to conquer first Elyssonne, then the world. For this, the ring would be his means: its power would enable him to offer—and give—men what they most desired for a period of five years; after that, their souls would be his and their bodies would obey his every command. There was one proviso: if there ever lived a man who refused to sell his soul to preserve or advance his own interest against those of his fellow mortals, that man would destroy the ring, and Ascanet would lose both his power and his life. But as Orcus pointed out, the proviso was minor—for if such a man could be persuaded to wear the ring, even for a few minutes, he would become Ascanet's vassal.''

"And Ascanet accepted the offer?''

"He accepted by putting on the ring; and he thus became the first person Orcus had corrupted for a thousand years. Orcus was freed; he became the ring, and the ring gave its wearer all his power to destroy.''

Tania stared at the glittering sapphire. "Then . . . I'm holding the corporeal form of Orcus in my hand?'' she asked in horror.

"Yes, you are,'' said Melibe. "And that's one of the reasons I've been concerned. I can see by your face that you haven't worn it, but even so, carrying it for eight weeks would have corrupted you beyond recall if you were other than what you are.''

"I . . . I hadn't realized what a blessing lack of importance was until now,'' she said, slipping the ring back into her pocket.

"That's not what I meant,'' he said, smiling. "But no matter. The point is, even when it cannot corrupt, the ring can destroy. You saw yourself what it did to the soil of Dacaria.''

"You know it did that? How could you possibly . . . ?''

"I felt it,'' he said, "and I nearly despaired, until I found that you, too, felt it, and did what needed to be done. But the ring could do to you what it would have done to the trees.''

"It could kill me?''

"Not directly. But it could attract somebody to you who would kill you to get it.''

"In *Dacaria?*"

"Yes, even in Dacaria," said Melibe. "The power of Orcus lies in his ability to make strengths into weaknesses; if the innocence of the Dacarians has allowed some latent evil to lurk in the valley unidentified, the ring would find it—and you would suffer because of it."

"Even in Dacaria . . ." Tania murmured. "Is there *nothing* that's safe from the perversion of the ring?"

"No," he said simply. "In fact, though you do not know it, that perversion has affected every day of your life."

"Before I found the ring? That's impossible!"

"Not at all," said Melibe. He settled back against the wall, as he'd once settled in his chair before he told her stories. "Ascanet has used the ring only twice in his long reign," he said. "He used it first to corrupt one who, in all the years he ruled, was the only man whose desire to defeat him was truly selfless." He looked at her. "That man was Campion of Mazion."

She stared at him. "Oh, no! Father never would have yielded!"

"You're thinking of yielding as complete, immediate surrender; with your father, it was a lengthy, steady process—impeded, I might add, by as much unwelcome advice as I could thrust upon him, until at last he could bear it no longer and ordered me to go."

"He . . . banished you? You said nothing about it at the time! If you had, I'd have gone with you—and Paran, too, I'm sure!"

"What would that have achieved, beyond taking from your father his last link to Dacaria? No, I could only go, hoping that his children would somehow escape his coming destruction."

"You make it sound as if Father's care for the Golden Age

was merely a front for service to Ascanet," she said. "The people of Mazion certainly didn't think so! They thought he was the only man strong enough to liberate Elyssonne!"

"And so he was," said Melibe. "That's why Ascanet had to use the ring; only thus could he turn Campion's strengths into weaknesses. It was a difficult task, for Campion's strengths were deep, unqualified love for his friends, devotion to the innocence of Dacaria, and determination to liberate Elyssonne, no matter what the cost to himself."

"Exactly! Father was incorruptible!"

Melibe nodded. "Very nearly so. He clung stubbornly to his vow to liberate Elyssonne by peaceful means, and he wouldn't be shaken. For years, Ascanet had tried to corrupt him in the usual way, by encouraging the kings of Fami and Dolc to invade Mazion and take pieces of it for themselves, and by urging Campion's knights and lords to beg him to defend his realm. But when he saw all this urging was of no avail, Ascanet bided his time, waiting for the most auspicious moment to offer him the ring. That moment came when your mother's death filled Campion with grief."

"And Father took it? From Ascanet himself?"

Melibe shook his head. "Even in the deepest grief, Campion would never have done that. No, first Ascanet arranged an alliance between himself, Fami, and Dolc that threatened to destroy Mazion. Once all Elyssonne knew of that alliance, Ascanet sent the ring to Sir Colin Lucot, with the message that if Campion wore it into battle it would enable him to defeat all the enemies of Elyssonne's Golden Age—perhaps not immediately, but eventually. Sir Colin knew nothing of the ring or its dangers, but he loved your father, and when he arrived at Castle Mazion, he begged Campion to put on the ring and call up troops of his own. And Campion yielded to the danger, to the messenger's promise and to his friend's pleas. He put on the ring, called up his troops—and won a decisive victory. Then, as the message had instructed him, he sent the ring back to Theda the next morning with Sir Colin."

"But the battle he thought he'd won made him Ascanet's slave?"

"No, calling up troops made him Ascanet's slave. For in taking up arms, Campion took the first step away from his vow to liberate Elyssonne without using force. After that, it was only a question of time. Slowly, under the influence of the ring he'd worn only for a day, Campion increased the size of his army, trained his troops to kill without mercy, and found brilliant generals to serve him . . ." Melibe sighed. "In short, he made himself a living contradiction in terms: in the name of bringing back Elyssonne its Golden Age, he followed the one course sure to loose the powers of Orcus upon the island."

Tania stared at him. "Then all the hours Father spent planning campaigns, training troops, forging alliances—all those days, weeks, years—he was defeating his own deepest desires?"

"Yes," said Melibe. "But—perhaps mercifully—he didn't know that. The ring's power lies in its ability to make its victims shut out what they see in order to preserve their illusions. If it didn't have that power, it couldn't be effective." He looked at her. "So when you think of your father, remember that in his own mind, he was never untrue to himself. He died as he lived—believing in the beauty and goodness of Dacaria and hoping to bring the virtues of the valley to the island he loved."

Tania looked at Melibe's sorrowing face, then let her gaze drift around the room. On every wall she saw visions of her father, walking along the battlements early in the morning, sitting by the fire with Sir Colin Lucot and talking far into the night, leading troops on the horse Sena had given to him and Marinda. And finally, she saw his fingers close around hers in the State Chamber. *I had hoped to spare you the clumsy hands of politics . . . but time has mocked me . . .*

Melibe touched her wet cheeks. "Ah," he said gently. "If you can weep for your father's undoing, you are indeed no longer a child."

"How could I condemn him?" she said, choking on the last of her sobs. "I might have done the same thing in his place; after all, I brought the very ring that destroyed him into Dacaria." She looked at Melibe in despair. "It seems that all of us are helpless in front of its power."

"Nobody is helpless who allows himself to think," said Melibe. "Tell me, who was the second man to whom Ascanet offered the ring?"

Tania forced her grieving mind into action. "Prince Radnor of Dolc, I suppose," she said. "Though I can't see why he should have, if he was supposed to give it only to unselfish men. The term hardly describes Radnor."

"That's true," said Melibe. "In fact, Radnor was one of those rare men who is naturally corrupt, without any urging from exterior forces. Because of that, Ascanet feared him, and his fear led him to give the ring to the last man on earth who should have been given it."

"So offering the ring to Radnor to keep him from defecting was a mistake?"

Melibe nodded. "A serious mistake. It cost Ascanet control of the ring."

"I see," she said. "But it didn't cost him the castle; and, in fact, it would have made no difference if the ring hadn't rolled to me, or if I hadn't picked it up so the Captain wouldn't find me."

"So that's how it came to you," said Melibe. "I feared it was so."

"Feared? If I'd gotten it any other way, I'd be lost!"

"True," he said. "But I feared because . . . well, you set the prophecy to music yourself: *When the ring is found alone, Winter shall be all undone.* You found the ring when it was alone; you haven't succumbed to its powers by wearing it; and you know what those powers are. In short, your possession of the ring enables you to drive Ascanet from Elyssonne."

"Enables . . . *me?*"

"Indeed it does. And yet, I don't find myself able to rejoice. What you'd have to do is very dangerous."

Tania leaned against the wall. She, whose position in the world was merely that of an interested observer . . . *she* had obtained the ring in a way that obliged her to do a deed even Campion had been unable to do? It was beyond belief. "What . . . what . . . would I have to do?"

"Go to Ascanet's castle and spend a day and a night without wearing the ring."

Tania stared at him. "Go to his castle! What's to prevent him from killing me the minute I ride into his courtyard?"

"The fact that you sought him willingly, though you had nothing to gain for yourself by finding him. It follows, of course, that you must not be captured and taken to him."

"But that's impossible! He knows I have the ring; the moment I leave Dacaria, I'll be beset by Silver Souls, hippogriffs . . ."

"Not if you travel through the forest," he said. "Ascanet has left the forests of Elyssonne ungoverned since the days of Asphodel. That is the other mistake he was led to by fear, and you should take advantage of it."

"But Ascanet has every reason to be afraid of the forests! They're terrifying!"

"You might find them less terrifying now that you've lived in Dacaria," he said. "What's frightening about the forests is their creation of visions that can't be distinguished from reality."

"Precisely!" she said. "And that's madness!"

"Not necessarily," he said. "What makes people go mad in the forest is their assumption that the real and the visionary belong to different realms. If you allowed the border between them to blur, you'd be in no danger of madness." He smiled at her. "And if you became truly terrified, you could play the panpipe that's hanging on your belt."

She looked down at it. "Does it really have magical properties, then?"

"Play it," he said.

She unhitched it and played; its sad scale filled the room.

"The Lydian mode," said Melibe, nodding. "Yes, you may think of its being magical if you want to. It would protect you, in any case."

"From Ascanet?"

He shook his head. "No, I'm afraid it doesn't have the power to do that. But it would protect you from your fears in the forest, and that would help you."

She hung the panpipe back on her belt, then looked at him. "And this journey . . . if I had the courage to make it . . . would defeat Ascanet?"

"I cannot promise you that," said Melibe. "I have no control over what's in the room to our right. You've thought only of your physical danger; but it's the least of the dangers you'd face. There is nothing Ascanet won't do to get his ring back, but he has learned—learned since he saw you in Theda, learned since he sent a hippogriff in pursuit of you— that what he willingly took from Orcus he can only get back if you willingly wear it. In order to defeat him, you would have to refuse to wear the ring, no matter what he said and

173

no matter what he offered you. That would be difficult; he is extraordinarily intelligent."

"I've discovered that," she said. She tapped her fingers on the panpipe. "And if I managed not to put on the ring, no matter what he offered me—what then?"

Melibe shook his head. "Then your danger would be physical, and it would be great indeed. Ascanet and Orcus will not accept defeat quietly."

"And so," she said, trying to keep her voice steady, "If I go, I have little chance of coming back, whether I defeat Ascanet or not?"

Melibe's eyes fixed upon the wall opposite him. "Very little," he said softly.

She looked at the floor, then at the bed, then at the tall desk, not seeing any of them. "Well," she said at last, "since the ring threatens my life even when it's lying in my pocket in Dacaria, and since its very presence in Dacaria threatens to corrupt the valley, and since I have very little chance of living if I leave the valley, I will be in only a little more danger if I attempt the journey than if I don't. So I'll make it. As Eliar says, one never knows."

Melibe's face looked far older than she had thought of its being. "Are you sure, child?"

"Yes," she said, surprised to find that she was.

Melibe sighed. "I should be pleased," he said, "to find that one of my students has embraced an active role in the progress of history. But I find, instead, that I regret the thoroughness of my instruction." He glanced at her. "And I think I'm not the only person who is concerned about you. Eliar has been pacing up and down the library for the past half hour."

She stared at him, wondering how he knew. "May . . . may I go to him?"

174

Melibe hesitated. "Do you love him?"

The question was so plainly put, and the idea of her loving anybody was so new and strange, that for a moment she didn't know what to say. But, finally, she nodded.

He tapped his fingers together. "I would say that you had chosen well, if he were a free man."

"He has asked me for nothing!" she cried.

"I'm sure he has not," said Melibe. "He's too intelligent and honorable, and he loves you too well. But your love—by the mere fact of its existence—will make your task even more dangerous than it otherwise would be. If Ascanet were to discover that you loved the man who refused to betray Dacaria to him, he would take Eliar hostage and use him to weaken your resolve. And he would have no mercy." He looked at her. "It follows, of course, that you must not let Eliar accompany you to the Waste, as he will certainly ask you to do. He shouldn't, in any case—he has been very ill, and any strain or shock would bring on dizziness and faintness, neither of which are desirable companions on a journey. So you must tell him to stay here."

Tania swallowed. "That will go hard with him."

"Yes, it will." He looked at her sympathetically. "Would you like me to come with you and explain to him—and to Kylian and Anrican also, since they've just arrived—what it is that you must do and why they must let you go alone?"

"Oh!" she said. "Would you? I know they'll try to stop me, and I know Eliar will want to come with me . . and I'm afraid I'll listen to them." She looked down. "I'm afraid I'm not very brave."

Melibe laid his hand on her shoulder. "It's not necessary to feel brave in order to be so," he said. "Come, let's find your friends."

CHAPTER
XIII

THEY SAID VERY LITTLE as they rode down the mountain. In front of Tania, Anrican's back was unyielding; behind her, the one time she dared to look, Kylian's eyes were gleaming so intensely that she turned around quickly. When they reached the fork at the bottom of the trail, she stopped.

"I'll take the pony back to Sena," she said. "And I'll come home through the groves." They nodded, and she rode off at a choppy trot, almost glad to quit their company.

They'd been even more difficult than she'd anticipated. Oh, they'd understood the prophecy, and they'd agreed that somebody should take the ring to the Waste and spend a day and a night without wearing it. But with an obstinacy she would have found comic if she hadn't known it came from deep affection, each of them had asked to bear the ring himself, thus sparing her and his friends. It had taken all Melibe's skill and tact to make them see that they could not; she was very glad he'd been there. Even as it was, in the few moments the others had left them tactfully to themselves, Eliar had persuaded her to let him meet her at the ledge from which she'd first overlooked Dacaria and walk with her to the place they'd fought the hippogriff—just to say goodbye. She knew that if Melibe had left her alone to tell him he could not come, she wouldn't have been able to manage it.

The pony pricked up its ears and trotted a little faster; as they rounded a corner, she saw Sena's cottage ahead of her. Damon was sitting on the doorstep, polishing his boots.

"Well, hello, Tania!" he called, getting up and smiling. "It's good of you to come and visit me! Would you like a mug of cider?"

"Thank you," she said, dismounting, "but I came to return your father's pony, and I don't have time to talk. Where shall I put him?"

"The pony? Oh, out there, I suppose," said Damon, waving his hand at the pastures. "I don't think Father has any need for him right now."

"Is he here?"

"Father? He's in the grove over there, trimming the colts' feet."

"Doesn't he need your help?"

"Oh, I helped him awhile, but he didn't like the way I was doing it. You know how he is. So I left him to do it alone. Come—surely you can spare me a few minutes. You could show me that trinket Corinna handed you last night. I'd really like to see it; Father has talked about Mazion jewelry, but I've never seen any."

"I . . . don't have it with me right now," she said. "And I really do have to go. I'm sorry."

His blue-gray eyes appraised her carefully, and for a fraction of a second, she was reminded of another pair of eyes she'd seen that color, set in a face older and more sensitive than his, but very like it. She shook the idea away before it had time to form fully, and led the pony to the pasture.

Damon followed her. "Will you tell me nothing about the trinket?"

Tania let the pony loose and slammed the gate a little too

hard. "I *told* you, Damon—I have to hurry back to Anrican and Elissa's, and I'm just going to stop for a moment to talk to Sena. We'll have to talk some other time."

He shrugged. "As you will." As she turned to go, he went back to the doorstep and his boots.

Pleased to have escaped him so easily, she ran across the field. As she entered the grove, she heard the sound of struggling; soon she came upon a wide-eyed yearling, dragging a half-prone old man across the clearing. She ran to the colt's head and grasped the lead-rope. He reared and plunged, but she talked to him gently, and finally he stood still, though he held his ears back. As she began to walk him, she saw Sena collapse against a tree and rub his thigh.

"Did he kick you?"

Sena nodded. "The colts were watching me trim, but one of them got stung by a bee and started to run. The others went with him—this was the only one that was tied, and I was trimming his hind foot." He struggled to stand up, grimacing in pain. "He's almost done," he said. "If you'll just hold him . . ."

"Don't be absurd!" she said. "You can hardly walk! If you'll hold him, I can finish him."

Sena looked at her in surprise. "Who taught you to trim colts?"

She smiled as she picked up his tools. "Father. He made Paran and me trim and shoe our own horses as soon as we were old enough. He said no horseman should be at the mercy of his farrier."

She heard Sena chuckle as she picked up the colt's foot. "He didn't forget all my lessons, then," he said. "By the way, did you talk to the hermit?"

"Yes," she said. "Wait a moment, and I'll tell you." She shaped the colt's hoof carefully, keeping one eye on his pinned-back ears. When she'd finished, she let him loose and sat down next to the old man. "You were right," she said humbly, "both about my having come upon a power I didn't understand, and about . . . about Father." She told him her story, and he listened intently, his head bowed. When she reached the end, he sighed.

"It's a sad tale," he said. "And it makes me see I've been unjust. But you see, I'd had great hopes for him and for your mother. After she died, I grieved for her, and it was perhaps too easy to think he'd willfully forgotten all he learned in the valley. When I brought the colts down the other morning and saw you, I . . . I feared he had even tainted the consciousness of Marinda's only daughter. But I see I was wrong." He looked off into the grove. "And perhaps I shouldn't have judged him as harshly as I did in any case," he added. "I, too, have threatened the valley, though that was not my intent, by thrusting an unruly boy upon my people."

Tania touched his sleeve gently. "Damon's no more unruly than your chestnut colt," she said, wishing she believed what she said. "And we've agreed that when the colt settles down, he'll become a fine horse."

"So I've tried to tell myself for years," said Sena. "But I'm afraid he reminds me more of the colt that has laid me low here. When I pay attention to him, he will stand well, as he stood for you. But none of the others would have kicked me, no matter what the provocation. There are some temperaments that training can contain, but not reform." He looked at her. "But that is my burden, not yours. Do you plan to ride on your journey? I can supply you with any kind of horse you think you'll need."

"Thank you," she said, "but I'm going through the forest, and I think I'd better go on foot."

"The forest? Alone?"

"Yes," she said. "And immediately. I'll leave tomorrow, an hour before dawn." She tried to smile at him. "I must hurry back to Anrican and Elissa's; I have preparations to make. Do you want me to help you walk back to your cottage?"

As she spoke, something rustled behind them in the underbrush. Sena looked around, but there was nothing to be seen. "Thank you, but if you can travel to the Waste by yourself, I think I can manage to hobble two hundred yards. Your path lies there." He pointed into the grove. "Follow it for half a mile, then when it forks, turn left. You'll see where you are when you get to the ford."

"Thank you," she said. "And say goodbye to Bellanca and Damon."

He nodded, and they looked at each other. "You are indeed your mother's image," he said. "I hope that will give you strength." He leaned over and kissed her forehead, then limped off toward the cottage.

The grove was dark; the sun had slipped over the mountains, leaving the valley in their shadows, though there would be daylight for at least another hour. Tania walked quickly, thinking partly of Sena and partly of her coming journey—then some instinct made her stop and listen. Everything seemed peaceful enough, but the silence was unnatural; the ferns were still, and the birds had stopped singing. She looked around her, straining her ears, but she saw and heard nothing.

Nothing. And here she was, afraid. That boded ill; if she let her fantasies frighten her here, what would happen to her in the forests Outside? She squared her shoulders and walked on. As she turned left at the fork, she was sure she heard something rustle, but she refused to allow herself to run. This was Dacaria; there was nothing that could harm her—unless, of course, what Melibe had said about the ring's ability to draw evil to her was right . . .

Through the silence, she heard the noise of running water. The ford. Yes, she'd soon be there, and she'd probably meet the shepherds who came home at this hour. Company would be welcome . . . A branch snapped behind her; she looked over her shoulder and broke into a half trot. Her fear was absurd, of course—but if something *were* following her, the river's noise would cover approaching footsteps . . . Her eye caught a flash in the trees ten feet to her left, then a movement in the bushes. Abandoning all her resolutions to be calm, she flew down the path and splashed across the ford.

Ahead of her, two shepherds and a dog turned as they heard her noisy crossing—then froze, staring. The dog crept behind the younger man, its tail between its legs; the older man shakily pointed his crook at something behind her. Choking back sobs of terror Tania stopped, turned, and looked. In the middle of the ford stood a great silver wolf, panting as if it had been running long and hard. As she started to inch slowly away, it lowered its head and drank, then looked back into the grove and snarled. Slightly to the right of the path she had just left, Tania saw something flicker as it changed direction. The wolf looked the way she had and sniffed the air; a moment later, it stepped quietly through the water and disappeared into the trees, following whatever it had seen.

Tania heard footsteps behind her; turning, she saw the two shepherds hurrying toward her. In answer to their breathless questions, she assured them she was all right, only frightened.

"I should say so!" said the younger one. "It leapt out of the grove only a few feet from where you were! Was that what you were running from?"

Tania recognized him as one of the youths who had been hoping to dance with her the night before—eons ago, it seemed now. "I didn't know what I was running from," she said. "I only heard noises; I saw nothing."

"Well," said the older shepherd, "if you're not hurt, all's well, but I'm glad you're fleet-footed." He frowned pensively as they began to walk on. "You live with Anrican and Elissa, don't you? I'll walk back that way with you and speak with them. They're good people to know when things go amiss; likely some of us will meet at their cottage tonight and talk things over."

They came to a fork, and the younger shepherd turned to the right. "If you decide to meet tonight, tell me," he said. "I'm going to go tell my mother to bring her sheep in."

When the young man was out of sight, the old shepherd stopped and looked at Tania. "My eyes aren't what they used to be," he said, rumpling his dog's ears, "but I thought that wolf was snarling when it stood in the ford."

"Yes, it was," she said.

"At you?"

She shook her head. "It was looking the other way. And I thought I saw something move."

He started walking again. "That's what I was afraid of," he said. "Things have come to a sorry pass in Dacaria if our people need wolves' protection."

It was still dark when Tania woke, and when she crept out of the cottage, carrying her pack and her cloak, it was so foggy she could scarcely see. As she started off into the mist, she heard the door open behind her.

"I'll walk with you to the bottom of the trail," whispered Elissa. "I'm afraid you'll lose your way."

"Oh, please," whispered Tania. "You were up so late with the shepherds! I know you must need sleep. Every time I woke up, I could still hear them."

"They left only an hour ago, but don't worry. I'll go back to sleep when I get home," said Elissa. "Even Talin won't be awake for two hours. And besides, I've hardly had a chance to talk to you since Anrican told me where you were going." They started down the path together.

"I feel badly about slipping off like this," said Tania, "but . . ."

"But you're wise," said Elissa. "I think Anrican would have tried to stop you from going entirely if he hadn't collapsed out of sheer exhaustion. He was upset about your journey yesterday, and last night's meeting has only made him more so."

Tania glanced at her. "But you're not upset?"

"Oh, I am," said Elissa. "I'm as frightened as anyone else about the state of the valley, and I shudder at the thought of your danger. But I also think you have a reasonable chance of doing what you've set out to do; and if you're successful, you will do more for the valley than any of us can. So while I grieve to see you go, I wouldn't dream of stopping you."

"You *really* think I have a reasonable chance of success?"

"Would you be less shocked," said Elissa, smiling, "if I said 'unreasonable chance'?"

"I don't know," said Tania. "I've not let myself think about it, because I'm afraid of losing whatever courage I have, but . . . well, the lords and kings who have tried to defeat Ascanet have all failed."

"Yes, but you have an advantage that none of them had," said Elissa. "You're the same age Asphodel was when she defied Ascanet, the same age Marinda was when she left the valley. Of course, I never knew Asphodel, and I knew Marinda only as Corinna knows you—with the worship of a little girl. But I suspect you have whatever quality it was that gave them extraordinary power over people's imaginations."

"What quality is that?"

"I don't know," said Elissa. "I saw it, just for a second, when you were riding Sena's chestnut colt—longer, when you were dancing with Kylian. It's . . . at least, I think it is . . . whatever made Anrican sing again. And, long ago, it's whatever made Sena think it would be Marinda, not Campion, who would drive Ascanet from Elyssonne." She sighed. "Perhaps she would have—who knows? When I heard that Marinda had died, I was only ten years old, but that's when I decided to become a midwife. I couldn't—I still can't—accept her death as a quirk of fate. Perhaps knowledge and skill could have prevented it and let her live to do what she was meant to do."

They had reached the bottom of the trail, and both of them stopped.

"I'll leave you here," said Elissa. "I trust you know we'll all be praying for your safety."

"Thank you," said Tania—and embraced her as tightly as her cloak and pack would allow, unable to say more.

As she started up the trail, she wished she had said more. And as she looked behind her at Elissa's figure disappearing into the mist, she also found herself wishing she'd had a sister, though she'd never felt the lack of one before.

It took her longer than she'd expected to reach the ledge; the mist was thick, and the rocks on the path were so slippery that she fell every time she tried to go faster. Consequently, she wasn't surprised to see a dark figure leaning against the cliff when she finally got to the ledge. Sick or well, Eliar

184

knew the mountains far better than she did; undoubtedly, he'd made the long trip down from the hermit's cave in less time than it had taken her to come from the valley. She hurried toward him.

"I'm sorry I've kept you waiting! Have you been here long?"

"What—were you expecting me? I'd hoped to surprise you."

Tania stopped, staring. The voice wasn't Eliar's—nor, now that she could see it more clearly, was the shape. "D-Damon?"

"Yes, Damon. I heard you were undertaking a journey outside the valley, and since I'd been planning to leave myself, I thought I might join you."

"How . . . how did you know I was leaving?"

"Oh, I strolled over to the grove yesterday afternoon to ask if I could walk you home, and I heard you tell Father you were leaving before dawn."

She bit her lip, wondering what else he'd heard. "And did you tell him you were leaving?"

"No. If he knew, he'd worry. I'm not as inconsiderate a son as everybody thinks." He smiled at her. "But you aren't as pleased at the prospect of my company as I thought you'd be."

She looked at him curiously, wondering what thoughts were hiding behind his words. "Well, you see," she said, "I'm going on a journey which I must make by myself. The hermit has said so, and he has prevented several of my friends from accompanying me."

"Does he mean that if somebody accompanies you, you'll fail in whatever you have to do?"

"It's a little more complicated than that," she said. "But, yes." An idea suddenly struck her. "And besides," she added, "you've never left the valley before, have you? You can't leave until you take the oath never to reveal its whereabouts."

"Have you taken it?" he challenged.

"I have indeed; the hermit made me swear."

"Well, if you insist that I take it, I will. Do you know the oath?"

"I'm not the person to administer it," she said. "And besides, there have to be witnesses."

"Oh, come, Tania! Where will we find witnesses?"

"In the valley," she said with private triumph. "And I'll not stir a foot further with you unless you take it. I don't want all Dacaria to think I've spirited you away."

"Dear me," he said. "I certainly wouldn't want you to lose the valley's esteem. Perhaps it would be better if I went down and took the oath. But that wouldn't be worth my while unless I was *sure* you were going to be here when I came back to join you."

"You mean you want my word?"

He laughed. "Words mean very little; I'd rather have some kind of pledge. Not an important one. The trinket Corinna gave you the other night will do."

His smile had no malice behind it, nor had his words any threatening overtones, but as she stared at him, she saw he had no cloak and no pack. He didn't mean to leave the valley, then . . . With sick certainty, she suddenly knew why he'd come to meet her. He'd been fascinated by the ring from the moment he saw it; he'd mentioned it twice at the dance and again yesterday. And of course, if he'd heard her talking to Sena about it, he'd gained some knowledge of its power. She looked at the empty path, the fog-shrouded cliff, the tremendous drop from its edge into Dacaria, and she thought of Melibe's warning.

If she could just convince him she didn't have it! "Oh, the trinket," she said casually. "Corinna's fond of it, so I left it

186

with her. I'll have to pledge you something else."

Damon raised his silvery eyebrows. "Come, Tania, I know as well as you do that trinket is not a child's toy." He took a step toward her. "In fact, I'm worried about your carrying it in your pocket; it's far too valuable to be kept so casually. Why don't you let me take care of it while you're gone?"

He took another step, then another. As he came closer, she realized how much taller and stronger he was than she. But she mustn't, *mustn't* let him force it from her! That would be the end of her journey, the end of Dacaria. As he reached out to grasp her wrist, she ducked under his arm and darted up the path.

Before she'd taken two steps, she heard him sprint after her; in a second, he'd grasped her wrist and dragged her back to the ledge. Frantic with pain and fear, she dropped her head and bit him as hard as she could. He jerked his arm away, leaving a sizable chunk of flesh between her teeth. "You little vixen!"

His eyes blazed as he stepped toward her; before she could run again, he'd caught her by the shoulder and whirled her around so her back was to him. His arm closed around her, crushing her ribs. She tried to stamp on his feet, but he lifted her off the ground and ran his free hand down her side, searching for her pocket. "Don't struggle so," he said between his teeth as she kicked at him. "I might have to move nearer to the edge, and there's a crack all the way along it."

All of a sudden, he jerked backward and spun around, releasing his hold on her with a grunt of surprise. She rolled toward the cliff, then sat up, gasping and dizzy. In the first foggy morning light, she saw Damon and . . . and . . .

Eliar, with his sword drawn. Consciousness came back to her in a sick rush, and she scrambled to her feet. "Eliar!" she gasped, her ribs aching. "You can't!"

He glanced at her—and Damon sprang at him. Eliar side-

187

stepped quickly, but as Damon shot by him, there was no silver flash. Damon landed in the dust, unharmed.

"Coward," he snarled. "Are you really going to fight an unarmed man with a sword?"

"No," said Eliar. "In fact, if you leave her alone, there's no reason to fight at all."

"There will be no reason indeed," said Damon, getting to his feet and resuming his usual air of indifference, "if Tania will simply deliver the little trinket she has in her pocket to me."

"Tania shouldn't be forced into giving you anything she has in her possession," said Eliar. "If you have asked her for it and she has refused to give it to you, that should be the end of the matter."

"It would be," said Damon, "if the trinket were merely a trinket. But since it is what it is, she shouldn't be carrying it. I was only trying to preserve her from its dangers."

Eliar's crooked eyebrow shot up. "Your method of preservation left something to be desired."

Damon shrugged. "She misunderstood me, and in her scuffling, she bit me. For a moment, I lost my temper, but I wouldn't have harmed her." He took a step to the side.

Eyeing him warily, Eliar took a similar step. "That's good to know," he said. "Well, if the matter is settled, she should go on up the mountain, and you should go back down the trail. I suggest that you do so at once."

Damon moved sideways once more; Tania saw he had maneuvered Eliar into a position between himself and the cracked rim of the ledge. "It's easy for an armed man to 'suggest.' "

Eliar glanced over his shoulder and sheathed his sword. "That's true," he said. "But when I've taken off my sword, I'll make the suggestion again." He unbuckled the belt that held his scabbard at his side and leaned over deliberately to put the weapon down.

With the speed of a striking snake, Damon sprang at him, his arms stretched out. But Eliar seemed not to be taken by surprise; he dove forward under Damon's flying body, rolled over several times, and came up on his feet, whirling to meet a new attack. There was no attack to meet. The momentum that was to have knocked Eliar into the valley carried Damon halfway over the edge; he teetered helplessly on his hips over the three-hundred-foot drop, managing to keep his balance only by grasping the cracking lip with his hands. Eliar's eyes narrowed as he stepped toward him.

Tania seized his arm. "No!" she screamed. "How can you even *think* of it?"

He shook her off impatiently, watching Damon struggle with the same expression she'd seen on Damon's face as he'd sprung.

"Eliar!" she pleaded. "Eliar . . . please look at me!"

He turned his head obediently, and as his eyes met hers, she saw the strange light in them flicker, then turn into a look of dazed horror. Slowly, she felt the arm under her hand begin to tremble.

He would be all right now, she knew. Leaving him where he stood, she edged carefully toward Damon. He was breathing hard, and his face was dead white. As she came nearer, she could see the crack along the ledge was widening.

"Damon," she called, in the voice she used to soothe young horses, "I'm going to take hold of your feet and pull you back. Don't kick at me. Do you understand?"

He started to nod, but the motion threatened to unbalance him altogether. She took one more step and reached out toward his legs. The ground seemed to shake a little under her; perhaps it was just her nervousness.

"Tania!'

Looking behind her, she saw Eliar leap forward. "Don't pull from there! Look—the whole edge is about to give way. Come over on this side, where it's firmer. No—here. Let me help you . . ."

He moved quickly to Damon's right side, but as he started to pull on him, Damon lashed out viciously, and Eliar let go. For one terrible second, everything stood still except the rising mist. Then Damon screamed, and Eliar grabbed Tania's hand, pulling her back against the cliff. In front of them, the lip of the ledge broke off with an ear-splitting crack and leaned slowly out over the drop below it. Damon looked desperately over his shoulder and pushed himself backward—but his struggling broke the fragile bond between the edge and the cliff. With a great roar, half the ledge gave away and spun down the mountainside into the valley.

CHAPTER
XIV

THE MIST THINNED, and the sun shone weakly through it. As the warm rays fell on Tania's stunned face, she looked blankly at the broken lip of the ledge. Eliar was slumped against the wall next to her; she touched his knee, hoping for some assurance that what she'd seen and heard had been only the work of her imagination—or that Damon had survived the impossible fall as one survived the falls in dreams. But Eliar didn't move.

"Eliar! Did he hurt you?"

"No." His eyes were fixed on some point beyond her.

"What is it, then?"

"Look."

She looked out beyond the ledge. Two hippogriffs circled high above the valley, their voices silent, their wings unmoving. She stared at them in disbelief. "I didn't know they were allowed to fly over Dacaria," she whispered.

"They weren't," he said. "But they are now. Remember? All I had to do to yield Dacaria to Ascanet was provoke one act of violence."

A chill swept up her back. "But . . . but, Eliar! You didn't provoke it—you had a sword, and you didn't use it! You could have pushed him over . . ."

"And I would have, if you hadn't stopped me."

"But you didn't! Don't you see? And later you tried to save him! Anyway, you didn't *cause* the violence; Damon did. You stopped him from hurting me!"

"Yes," he said patiently. "But the violence occurred. That is all that matters."

"Are you sure? You stopped him before he hurt me; you never touched him; he fell by accident as you were trying to *help* him. And besides, this is the trail *out* of Dacaria, not the valley itself."

"Logic chopping won't change what happened," he said.

"Call it logic chopping if you wish," she retorted, "but the point remains: everything you did—except for the one moment when I stopped you—was done to *stop* violence from occurring. Is that really the kind of chaotic warfare Ascanet and the ring desire?"

"Perhaps not," said Eliar, leaning his head back against the cliff. "But the physical result was exactly what they've always wanted. And in spite of all your arguments, there are hippogriffs circling the valley."

"True," she said, "but look at them! They're not landing; they're not striking; they're just . . . observing. Surely, if Damon had died differently—if you'd pushed him off, say—they'd swoop down and do whatever damage they wished."

Eliar looked at the hippogriffs a moment. "That's . . . possible . . ."

"Of course it is," she said eagerly. "And if nothing else, it means . . . well, it might mean . . . that Ascanet isn't sure whether the violence frees him to conquer the valley, but since there *was* violence, he can send his minions to see if the situation justifies an attempt."

Eliar sighed. "That's all very intelligent, Tania. But what good does it do?"

"All the good in the world!" she said indignantly. "Don't you see? If he isn't sure he can take the valley, if he has to wait until he is sure—that gives me time to get to the Waste before he decides." She scrambled to her feet. "So mourn for Damon, but don't mourn for the valley before you're sure that's necessary. And let's start over the pass as quickly as we can."

She strapped on her pack and picked up her cloak, then looked at him. He was still sitting with his head against the cliff, and his eyes were closed. "Eliar? Eliar! Are you all right?"

"Yes, yes," he said, opening his eyes. "I was just a little dizzy." He stood up, balancing himself against the cliff. "Are you ready?"

She stared at him, then rushed forward, supporting him as he fell to the ground. Anxiously, she felt his forehead; it was ice-cold, and he was shaking. Had he merely fainted, or was this something more serious? She had no idea, but she certainly couldn't leave him untended. Quickly, she covered him with her cloak, edged carefully to the path, and started downhill as fast as the rocky terrain would let her.

She hadn't gone more than a quarter of a mile when she saw someone bounding up the path below her at an impossible speed. She ran to meet whoever it might be, calling frantically. In a fraction of a minute, Kylian swept around the corner of a switchback and caught her up in his arms.

"Tania!" His voice was so relieved she hardly recognized it, and when she looked up, she saw a most un-Kylianlike expression on his face. "When I saw the landslide from the ledge," he panted, "I remembered you'd said you'd wait for Eliar there, and I thought you'd . . ." He released her, then looked at her carefully. All the light went out of his face. "What happened?"

She told him, watching his face grow pale and grave.

When she'd finished, he looked out over the valley, now almost empty of mist. "How will I ever be able to tell Sena and Bellanca?" he said softly.

Tania put one hand on either side of her face. "I . . . do they have to know?"

"If the valley is no longer protected from Ascanet, they'll soon learn I've deceived them; that would only add to their pain."

"But, Kylian, do you really think the valley is open to Ascanet?"

"I don't know," he said. "You've made an eloquent case for its safety, but I'm not the person you have to convince. You're right about one thing, though: it's absolutely essential that you get to the Waste as fast as you can. So come—we've left Eliar too long already. I'll carry him to the hermit's cave while you go on."

He leapt up the trail with his usual lithe grace; when he looked back at her, she waved him on. "Go ahead," she said. "He may need care—I'll come as fast as I can."

He disappeared, and she tried to follow at twice the pace she'd held earlier; but after a few minutes, she stopped, gasping for breath, and looked out over the valley. As she'd expected, she saw the hippogriffs, but they seemed to be going back to the Waste. Shading her eyes against the sun, she watched as they flew toward the mountains with long, purposeful wing strokes and disappeared over the horizon. She hurried up the trail again, wondering what they had seen that had made them decide to report to their master.

She arrived at the ledge a few minutes later and found Kylian waiting for her. "I thought you said you left him here, wrapped in your cloak," he said.

"Why, I did!" She looked beyond him. Her pack lay where she had left it, but Eliar and her cloak were nowhere to be seen. Mystified, she looked up the trail. "Do you suppose he came to, thought I'd gone on alone, and tried to follow me?"

"I thought of that," said Kylian, "and I ran ahead as far as he could possibly have gotten in his condition. But I saw no sign that anyone had been that way." He cleared his throat. "You . . . said he was terribly upset . . . ?"

"No!" she cried as he looked eloquently at the crumbling lip of the ledge. "He never would have done such a thing, even if he'd wanted to! Think what that would do to Dacaria!"

"But if he thought Dacaria was doomed in any case . . ."

"He still wouldn't have done it," she insisted. But this time, it took some strength to push away her knowledge of his black moods. Suddenly, she looked up with greater confidence. "And besides, if he had, he'd have left my cloak. You *know* he would have!"

A smile tugged at the corner of Kylian's mouth. "You know him very well. I submit to your logic. But"—he looked about them—"he couldn't possibly have left the ledge without leaving any trace, unless he flew."

Flew. Their eyes met; neither of them dared speak. After a few frozen seconds, Kylian dropped to his knees and began to examine the floor of the ledge, but Tania stared on at the place he had been. *Eliar, Eliar* . . . As if in answer to her thoughts, the sound of a flute wound its way up to the ledge from the pastures on her left, sweet and melancholy. She shuddered and hid her face in her hands.

Behind her, Kylian gave a low whistle. Half in a dream, Tania turned and looked at the spot before him: it was sharply, newly scored.

"Talon marks," he said.

She stared and stared, unable to move. Kylian stood up

quickly and put an arm around her, but she hardly felt it. The only thing that seemed real was the peaceful melody of the flute, joined now by another . . . "Oh, how can they bear to play?"

"They have no knowledge of what has happened," he said gently. "Landslides are common here, and the mist has just cleared. Very few people could have seen the hippogriffs."

She turned her face to the side, shaking as he held her. "What will the hippogriffs do with him?" she sobbed. "Drop him, play with him—oh, I can't even bear to *think* of it!"

"I doubt it."

He spoke with such certainty that she pulled away and looked at him through her tears. "You do?"

He nodded. "If they were going to torture him, they'd have done it right away; they don't postpone their pleasures. No, I think they're under instructions to take whoever they can find directly to the Waste."

She stared out over the valley. *If Ascanet were to discover that you loved the man who refused to betray Dacaria to him, he would take Eliar hostage and use him to weaken your resolve. And he would have no mercy.* Had he known? Had he sent the hippogriffs to find Eliar, or had the monsters simply seen Eliar and borne him off? In the final analysis, it didn't matter. In her desire to see Eliar once more before she left Dacaria, she'd agreed to meet him—in spite of Melibe's warning that for both her sake and his, she must travel by herself.

She turned to Kylian. "Do you think I have any hope of freeing him?"

"You have infinitely more hope than anyone else does," he said.

"An infinite amount of nothing is still nothing." She

looked down at the panpipe that hung from her belt, squared her shoulders, and looked up the path. "But then, I never undertook this journey because there was a mathematical chance of success."

"That's true," he said softly. In a changed tone, he added, "I'll walk across the pass with you. The hippogriffs may come back in two or three hours, looking for other Dacarians to abduct."

"That's very kind of you," she said, "but there would be little you could do for me against two hippogriffs. And after all, if they swoop down and pick me up, think how much they'll shorten my journey." She tried to smile at him, but her mouth twitched out of control. "What you can do for me, though, is find Sena and Bellanca, and tell them whatever you think will hurt them least. They will have missed Damon by now and perhaps have guessed that he followed me."

"Very well," he said, his voice thick. "And after that, I'll tell the hermit."

Tania sighed. "He probably knows already."

"That's true," said Kylian. "But he may be able to tell me if there's anything I can do to help you and Eliar." His yellow eyes dimmed as he looked at her. "And if there is, I will do it. The two of you are very dear to me."

She pressed his hand and started up the trail, not daring to speak.

The climb seemed interminable, and when Tania finally reached the edge of the chasm where she and Eliar had withstood the hippogriff, she looked across the pass and was shocked by how long and exposed it was. If the hippogriffs returned after two or three hours, as Kylian had said they might, they would certainly see her. Well, there was nothing to do but make what time she could. She started out, running as long as she could endure the weight of her pack, walking fast until she'd gotten her breath, then running again. Slowly, the mountains in front of her inched nearer and the gray clouds that hovered over them grew thicker.

Walk, jog, walk, jog. The straps of her pack dug into her shoulders, but she kept up her pace until she finally reached the mountains and plunged down the steep path, sliding on shale, crossing the railless bridge Eliar had warned her about on their way up, inching along the inside of cliffs, and looking up at the sky whenever she paused to catch her breath. After two hours of tumbling descent, she thought she saw something move several switchbacks below her. She slid to a stop, listening breathlessly—and heard hoofbeats.

Who could be riding up the pass? Shaking with dread, she slid down the steep slope to the stand of rocks at the next corner. The hoofbeats came closer as she slipped between the two largest rocks; cautiously, she edged herself into a position that let her see the open trail below her.

Around the corner scrambled an exhausted black mare, drenched with sweat and flecked with foam. On her back, a man in a Dacarian cloak slumped in the saddle, his hands clutching her mane. As they reached the turn, the mare sniffed the air, looked in Tania's direction, and stopped, her sides heaving. Tania hesitated, then left her hiding place and walked slowly toward them.

When she reached the black mare, she patted her soothingly before she forced the man's fingers open and half lifted, half dragged him to the ground. Pushing back his hood, she saw graying dark hair and a sunburned face that looked vaguely familiar. She frowned, trying to think of who it could be, but there was no time to puzzle over the matter. She pulled the flask Elissa had given her from her pack, remembering how quickly its sweetish black contents had revived her as she lay wounded on the pass when she first ar-

198

rived in Dacaria. Why hadn't she remembered she had it earlier? If she'd only given some to Eliar! She shook away the useless regret, poured a few drops into the man's mouth, then unsaddled the steaming mare and walked her, gazing periodically at the sky. She shouldn't be doing this; she should go on . . . but how could she?

When the mare was cool enough to let stand, Tania ran back to her rider and knelt by his side. He opened his eyes and looked at her, dully at first, then in bewilderment.

"Marinda," he murmured. "No . . . can't be . . . mad . . ."

"You're not mad," she said. "I'm Marinda's daughter, Tania. I know I look very like her. Can you tell me who you are and how you came here?"

"Sylvio . . . son of Sena," he said, struggling over each phrase. "I was . . . riding back from Theda with ten horses . . . two outriders. Silver Souls attacked us at the way station . . . scattered the horses . . . killed the outriders. Hit me, but . . . the black mare is very fast . . . don't remember anything more."

Tania gave him a few more drops of the black liquid and a little water. She left him then, climbing up some rocks to get a better view of the sky. It was clear; at least it was clear of hippogriffs. But the clouds she'd seen as she crossed the pass towered above the mountains. She pursed her lips; once she got through the strange tunnel-like entrance to the trail, she would find herself in the midst of a blizzard.

When she returned to Sylvio, his eyes were open and he spoke clearly. "I'm very grateful to you; if you hadn't found me, I suppose the mare and I would both have wandered here until we'd gone mad or died."

"Here!" said Tania, smiling. "Look about you! You're not in the forest."

He stared at her, lifting himself up on one elbow. "It's

199

impossible," he whispered as he looked. "No, I see you're right. But the mare was bred in Theda. How could she have found her way? Even experienced Dacarians have difficulty finding the tunnel."

Tania shook her head. "Strange things happen in the forest."

He sat up, looking about him uncomfortably. When his eyes fell on the mare, they widened in consternation. "She's exhausted!" He struggled to his feet.

"She'll be all right, I think," said Tania, steadying him. "I cooled her out, and she's breathing well."

Sylvio shook his head and walked stiffly toward the mare. As he approached her, he seemed to take on new energy; he stroked her, ran his hands down her legs, examined her eyes and nostrils, and finally sighed with relief. "She will be all right, and I don't know how to thank you enough for caring for her. I've only seen one or two horses of her quality in my whole lifetime. She was bred by a young man we used to trade with regularly, the only horseman I've ever met who could rival Father."

Tania looked at the mare, suddenly realizing why she had seemed familiar. "Not . . . Colin Lucot?"

Sylvio nodded. "You know him, then?" His face became grave. "I suppose I should say, 'knew him.' The traders said he'd had a falling out with Ascanet a month or so ago and had disappeared—either imprisoned or killed, nobody dared ask which. And his uncles have been carefully getting rid of everything that could possibly remind Ascanet of their association with him; they put his whole stable up for sale last week."

So Colin was dead. Tania looked sorrowfully at the black mare. She hadn't really thought he could survive after what he'd done for her, but she'd hoped . . . She sighed and slipped her hand in her pocket to warm it. The ring was still there, as little disturbed by Colin's death as it was by Eliar's abduction, waiting eagerly for Dacaria to fall. Her thoughts surged angrily as she picked up her pack and swung it over her shoulders.

Sylvio stopped patting the mare and looked at her. "You're not thinking of traveling Outside, are you?"

"I'm afraid I am," she said. "And if you can manage, I should go now."

"That's madness!" he said. "The whole order of things has changed. There are Silver Souls in the forest, where they've never been before; this morning, before we were attacked, we heard two hippogriffs shrieking the way they do when they've caught their prey . . . you should stay in Dacaria."

"There's little more safety there than there is Outside," she said. Briefly, and as gently as she could, she told him all that had happened.

He listened, his eyes closed in pain. "I always felt the lad would come to grief," he said softly. "Though, like Father, I hoped he would change as he grew older. And as for the valley—when I saw the Silver Souls in the forest, I should have known it was no longer . . ." He choked back the end of his sentence. "And you—where are you going?"

"To the Waste, to do what I can to help us all," she said, thinking how conceited the words sounded. "I haven't time to explain, but your father will tell you. And he'll be very glad to see you back. He needs you sorely."

Sylvio picked up his saddle. "I'll go at once," he said. "I'll have to lead the mare, and neither of us is fit for the climb, but I should be home by evening."

Tania handed him his girth, reminding him about the broken ledge. "I hope you'll have no trouble," she said as she finished.

He looked at her grimly. "That's a hope I wish I could return," he said. "I don't know what to tell you about the changes Outside, but stay far from the way station, and, if you have the courage, stay off the paths. The Silver Souls are still afraid of the forest; when they scattered our horses, I saw they let them go rather than stir one step into the trees. But here! you have no cloak!"

"I . . . lost it."

"Well, I'll have no need for mine," he said, sweeping it off. "No, don't think of thanking me; I'm deeply in your debt." He held out his hand. "Goodbye," he said. "I'll tell Father you got this far safely."

"I will thank you, in spite of your plea," she said, taking his hand. "Both for your cloak and your advice. I would probably have walked into the arms of the Silver Souls if I hadn't met you."

She wrapped his cloak around her and started off at a jog to make up for the time she'd lost. But when she emerged from the narrow, hidden tunnel that was the beginning of the trail to Dacaria, she found the clouds that had loomed over the mountains hadn't lied: it was snowing so heavily she could hardly see. She took a few steps forward, noticing deep indentations from the mare's hooves, now covered thickly, and a host of smaller indentations, covered beyond recognition. Eliar's words came back to her: *It's a peculiar place . . . I've felt . . . escorted.* Some forest creatures had "escorted" the mare to the tunnel—no wonder she'd run far beyond her strength. And what would those creatures do to her? She decided to keep on the trail for the first mile. After that, she'd have to hope for the best.

Snow stung her face as she started out, and within a few paces she wasn't sure if she was still on the path or had wandered into spaces between the trees. Well, at least she was heading in the right direction—winds like this one blew straight from the Waste. She plunged on, soon able to measure time only by the increasing depth of the snow. In spite of the labor of walking, the wind chilled her, and as she grew colder, she began to feel drowsy. She wrapped the cloak more tightly around her again and stopped, panting and trying to see what lay ahead. Even as she looked, the wind rose and the snow fell thicker; looking at it, she realized if she kept going, she would collapse and freeze only a few miles into her journey.

Something hummed in her ears—something entirely different from the howling wind. As she looked about her, she felt a peculiar warmth wrap itself about her and urge her to her left. She fought it, panicked, but in spite of her struggling, it pushed her off the path and rolled her into a patch of needle-covered ground under an uprooted fir. She sat up, dazed, and found she had rolled next to a boulder on which the huge tree had fallen. The wind roared over the top of the trunk, but where she sat it was quiet, warm—and utterly unmagical. Gradually, she stopped shivering and found she was hungry. She dug into her pack and ate some of the bread and cheese she'd brought, listening to the wind howl through the forest. There was no sense in continuing in such weather; it would be better to rest now and go on when it cleared. She curled up under Sylvio's cloak and felt her tense muscles relax.

She was awakened by the jingle of bridles and the sound of muffled hoofbeats. As her eyes flew open, she realized the snow and wind had died down and that it was almost dark. How long had she slept? And who . . . ?

"Halt!" The voice that cracked the cold air was only a few feet from her. "We'll camp here."

Tania peered out from under the log, then ducked back. Two Silver Souls sat stirrup to stirrup on the path. Behind them, she could see the silent, unmoving company of their followers.

"Did you hear me? I said we'd camp here!"

None of the men stirred, but the rider next to the man who had spoken touched his arm. "Captain Talus, may I talk to you privately?"

Talus turned his faceless visage toward him. "Are you questioning orders, Lieutenant Cern?"

"No, sir. But I wish to talk to you."

Talus wheeled his horse and rode a little apart from the men. Cern followed him. They halted three feet from Tania's shelter.

"Now. What is it?" Talus's voice was filled with irritation.

"It's the forest, sir," said Cern. "It weakens his lordship's influence on the men. At present, they no longer obey, but they haven't the wit to question; by tomorrow, they'll ask to be consulted in all decisions."

"Come, lieutenant, you can't expect me to believe that. You've never campaigned in the forest before!"

"With respect, sir, that's not the case. Before you were one of us, Captain Redurm, I, and ten others undertook a small mission in this very forest, by his lordship's orders. We were here only two days, but on the second, the men threatened mutiny, and we had to leave before we had learned all his lordship wished us to."

"And what mission was that?" Talus sounded skeptical.

"We were to watch the Dacarian who trades horses at the fair at Theda; when he had finished his business, we were to carry his lordship's newborn son into the forest and leave him in some spot where the old man was sure to find him."

Tania covered her mouth so they wouldn't hear her gasp of surprise. Damon—Ascanet's . . . !

"A newborn son?" said Talus. "Why, I never knew his lordship was a ladies' man!"

"He isn't, sir; this was business. He paid the girl hand-somely—I took her the purse myself. His lordship wanted to get his own flesh and blood into Dacaria; that was our duty."

"And the girl's," chuckled Talus. "But what does that have to do with the men and mutiny?"

"Only this, sir; we were supposed to wait until the old man left with the baby, then follow him to the path to Dacaria. But the forest was very strange, sir, the way it was this morning before the snow began, and after we'd spent one night here, the men were no longer . . . as they usually are. They spoke; they argued; they refused to go on. And Captain Redurm saw that if discipline were to be maintained, we would have to leave the forest without completing our task. So we left the baby in the shed where we found the Dacarians this morning, and we rode to the Waste. But the moment we rode out of the forest, the men became as they had been before."

"Was his lordship angry?"

"Not as angry as Redurm had feared, sir. We weren't punished; he said it was likely the old man would find the baby—and that he'd send no more troops into the forest until the boy had grown up and done his work. Apparently, he thought the forest would be safe once Dacaria had fallen."

"Did he indeed?" said Talus. "Well, then, we have nothing to fear."

"Perhaps, sir. But to me, the forest seems the same now as it was when I rode in it before. Which makes me wonder, sir, if his lordship *knows* Dacaria has fallen or whether he only *thinks* it may have. It sticks in my mind that he may have sent us out here to see what happens to us. If, instead of finding the entrance to Dacaria and invading it, as we're supposed to, we go mad in the forest, or the men mutiny and kill us . . . well, he'll have learned what he wished to—but at our expense."

"I think the forest has worked on *you*, Cern. But if that's so, it may also have worked on the men. Well, I'll be careful with them. We'll camp at the shed where we found those Dacarians this morning; that should please them. But his lordship's judgment is not to be doubted. If he didn't think Dacaria had fallen, why would have he sent only ten of us to find the path that leads to it and invade?"

"You could argue, sir, that he sent only ten men because he wished to risk only that many on a mission that might fail."

"I'll hear no more, Cern. You're weary, and that has sapped your courage. We'll rest tonight, and tomorrow, you'll see the men are more obedient. So. In the morning, we'll go on to Dacaria."

Cern sighed. "Very well, sir."

The two men rode away, and in a minute the whole band cantered off, leaving Tania huddled in her hole.

Her mind whirled. There was at least a possibility that things were as she'd hoped: if Cern's fears had any validity, Ascanet knew no better than she did whether his years of planning and waiting had borne fruit. But if he were gambling with the lives of ten men, he'd been careful to maximize his chances of success. Talus seemed immune to the fears that plagued his men; if he could lead them to Dacaria, their arrival in the valley would be its undoing, even if it weren't undone now. Clearly, she must stop them—and stop them in such a way that Ascanet would think the forest had foiled his plans.

She nibbled at some bread and cheese, trying to think how one girl could delay ten soldiers who would have no mercy if they discovered her. She could fill the entrance of the tunnel with snow—no, she might not be able to manage it quickly enough, and besides, her tracks would reveal her presence. Whatever she did must be more direct, and she must do it tonight.

She stuffed the remaining food in her pack, then sat with her chin in her hand. Suddenly, she nodded, crawled out of her shelter, and looked around cautiously. No mysterious hum enveloped her; she saw no shadows. The forest, in fact, seemed almost friendly. She waded to the well-packed trail the Silver Souls had left her, then slung on her pack and started toward the way station, smiling in the darkness.

CHAPTER
XV

TANIA STOPPED at the edge of the clearing that surrounded the way station, looking at it as the thin moon appeared between the clouds. The scene was exactly as she'd envisioned it: ten horses stood tied at the edge of the forest closest to the shed; inside, everything seemed still. She slipped toward the shed through the trees, looking for the guard that she was sure would be posted near its door. But though she stopped several times, certain that she was being observed, she saw nothing outside the shed but the horses. Puzzled, she crept to the shed and peered through a knothole in its wall. Inside, the Silver Souls lounged in the hay, some sleeping, some shoving food hungrily into their mouth slits. Tania shuddered and forced herself to count them. Ten. They hadn't posted a guard, then; that was strange, but it was certainly to her advantage.

She slipped to the place the horses were tied, bracing herself for a series of nickers. But none came: the horses merely pinned their ears back. Quickly, she unhitched them, then bridled Talus's horse and vaulted on, ignoring the ugly look he gave her. Settling her pack and cloak as comfortably as she could, she urged him along the path that led north. The others followed two by two, trotting in step as if they were on parade. It was almost too easy: she'd expected the loose horses to whinny or canter on ahead of her, making Talus's horse frantic—but no, they followed her as they'd followed Talus, an orderly subdivision of cavalry marching along the path. And when the distant shouts of the Silver Souls told her they'd discovered their loss, only Talus's horse turned his head.

She trotted on for several hours, apologizing mentally to Talus's horse, who had to break out the deep snow in the trail in addition to carrying her. Not wanting to tire him, she tried to drive the other horses in front of her, but they milled about aimlessly without his leadership and finally stopped in confusion. *Poor things,* she thought, *does Ascanet own your souls, too?* Well, there seemed no help for it; she rode in front of the line until the sky turned from black to gray.

By dawn, she was sure she'd put enough miles between her and the Silver Souls to warrant a brief rest, so when she saw a small clearing to her left, she turned Talus's horse toward it. He stopped short, shook his head, and backed up. She peered into the clearing, but all looked well. She stroked the horse's neck, then tried again. Flicking back his ears, he half reared; puzzled, she slipped to the ground and stepped off the path, leading him gently forward.

The reins snapped tight in her hand. Whirling around, she saw the horse rear high into the air, his ears flat back. Years of watching Campion train war-horses told her what was coming next; without stopping to think, she jerked him off balance, then dodged the hammer strokes of his front feet. He lunged at her as he landed; she dove sideways, rolled several times, then struggled to get up. He was at her before she was on her feet, and his bared teeth sank into her pack, pulling her backward. She squirmed out of the straps, unbalancing him just long enough to let her sweep off her cloak; the next time he dove at her, she threw it over his head. As he plunged away, she glanced at the other horses, who were

209

watching the unequal duel before them with white-ringed eyes. Their control would soon break, and they'd join their leader's attack . . . *Why? Why now, after they'd obeyed her so docilely all night?*

She plunged off the trail, floundering through the snow toward a tree. As she reached it, she heard her cloak rip; Talus's horse had shaken himself free and was snaking his head back and forth, looking for her. She ducked behind the huge trunk, but he'd seen her; he lunged at the tree, whirled around as she stepped behind it, then came at her from a different angle, his eyes red with fury. She jumped back, and he tripped over a sunken log as he attacked. Snorting, he thrashed to his feet and shook himself, looking for her once more. She picked up a stout branch, but as she straightened up, the horse plunged toward her. She struck at him, but something flashed by her shoulder from behind, making the blow miscarry and knocking her to the side. She felt a terrific crack as her head slammed against the tree, then slid downward, listening hopelessly to the snow-muffled thunder of oncoming hooves.

Something poked her, gently at first, then harder. Moaning, she pushed it away with her hand, then realized she was alive and cold, with a terrible headache.

Whatever it was poked her again, more insistently this time. She pushed herself into a sitting position and looked around dizzily. It was very strange: Talus's horse had become a dog, and it was looking at her from only a few feet away. Behind it, the other horses had also turned into dogs. She rubbed her throbbing head and looked at them more carefully. Perhaps twenty of the creatures sat around her in a circle, panting, their yellow eyes fastened on her. No, not dogs; dogs' eyes were brown. Wolves.

She felt a paw scrape her leg, none too gently. Looking to

the side, she saw the wolf next to her was rooting at the snow under her with its nose, forcing her to move. As she struggled to her feet, the other wolves got up, still panting. Tania looked around, feeling fear make her breath come short as her senses returned. Forty pricked-up ears moved closer to her; the smell of damp fur and wolf-breath filled her nostrils —it wasn't a vision.

Taking a frightened step backward, she almost fell over her torn cloak and her pack. She stared at them in surprise. Surely, she'd thrown the cloak at Talus's horse when she was still on the path! Thoroughly confused, she flung the cloak around her shoulders and sorted through the trampled pack, looking for the flask. It was there, and it was only cracked, not broken. She drank a few drops of the sweetish fluid, then leaned back against the tree. As she put the flask down, her hand touched something hard that poked out of the snow. She explored it with her fingers: reeds, fastened together. The panpipe must have come unhooked from her belt when she'd fallen. She brushed the snow off it and saw to her relief that it was undamaged.

She felt a paw scratch her leg again and saw that the silver wolf that had waked her was looking at the panpipe intently. Tania shrank back, clutching the little instrument. *It would protect you from your fears in the forest* . . . She brought it closer to her mouth, trembling. The other wolves leapt to their feet and edged closer to her, their white teeth gleaming. Tania closed her eyes and bleated out a stumbling version of a tune.

She felt the rush of paws as she played, and when she finished her melody, she opened her eyes eagerly, hoping to see an empty clearing. What she saw instead made her forget her aching head: the wolves had arranged themselves into four circles, and they were all looking at her impatiently. What they wanted was very clear, but . . . Watching them incredulously, Tania began to play one of the songs Eliar had taught her. The wolves faced each other, their tongues lolling in excitement. And then they began to dance.

There was nothing clumsy about their movements; their paws stepped delicately in time to the slow beat of the panpipe's tune, and they wove in and out between each other in complicated sequences, never losing the tension of their perfectly controlled power. When Tania reached a cadence, they bowed to each other, then turned and looked at her expectantly. Smiling, she played the liveliest tune she knew.

Their burst of energy made the clearing seem half the size it was: leaping high in the air, twisting as they landed, they whirled around each other in circles, ellipses, and squares that burst apart into stars. Carried away by their vigor, Tania piped faster, and her dancers responded, spinning through their patterns with a speed that made her dizzy. Suddenly, she realized they were no longer dancing on all fours—they leapt with their hind legs alone, and their forelegs stretched out to meet each other. As they danced faster to her ever-increasing pace, their noses shortened and blurred into faces, their ears folded back and became flowing hair, their coats dissolved into tunics and breeches—and finally, reaching out for each other's hands, they joined their four sets into a single star with a tall, dark-haired woman in its center, then changed their pattern so they formed a ring around her. Left alone, the woman danced with faultless grace, spinning in perfect time to the increasing beat, her dark hair flowing about her. As Tania piped the final cadence, the woman leapt almost to the level of her companions' heads—and landed in a deep bow, laughing.

The sound of her laughter rang across the clearing, chasing away the echoes of the panpipe. And then all became perfectly still. One by one, the dancers turned to Tania; at last, the dark-haired woman left the center of the circle, walked toward her across the trodden snow, and bowed. "You are welcome in our forest," she said. "We are greatly in your debt."

Tania looked at the majestic face before her and saw that it had no age, though the dark hair that framed it was touched with gray. Every one of its features showed its owner to be master of herself and of her followers, afraid of nobody, obedient to none but Theon and her own understanding. Tania gazed into the darkening yellow-green eyes and bowed. "I am honored to be of service to you," she said. "I have long revered your name."

The wolf queen looked at her in surprise. "And the name you have revered?"

"Asphodel."

"You do not think of Asphodel as a figure long dead, then?"

Tania shook her head. "Asphodel has always been alive to me," she said. "Not, perhaps, as other people are alive, but as the person who reminds those who suffer under Ascanet that he can someday be defeated. It's impossible for such a person to die." She looked past Asphodel at her subjects. "And I think," she added, "that I am in your debt, not the reverse. It can have been nobody but you who drove away the horses that went mad and attacked me."

"We drove away the horses," said Asphodel, "but they weren't mad."

"Not mad? But why else would a horse attack a person without provocation?"

Asphodel looked at her gravely. "The horse of the Captain of the Silver Souls is trained to kill any mortal who comes near him, the moment that mortal is defenseless and on foot. When we saw you bridling him, we feared he would kill you before you mounted; nobody but his master and Ascanet dares even approach him."

"I . . . I could see he had an ugly disposition when I mounted him," said Tania, "but I've seen such things before in horses who are overworked. I assumed he'd respond to kindness."

"That would have been a wise assumption if the horse served anyone other than whom he does," said Asphodel. "But the core of goodness you sought instinctively in him is not to be found in Ascanet's servants—man or beast. It's the first thing he extinguishes in them."

"And yet," said one of the wolf men, "you were no more at fault for your innocence than we. Your tact almost convinced us that you had found that core and hence had some power that would overcome both the horse and his master. Our faith would have been your undoing if our lady hadn't insisted that we follow you."

He stepped forward as he spoke, and when she could see him clearly, Tania stared at him with a shock she hadn't felt at all when she'd first seen Asphodel. "Colin!" She backed away a step. "Are you . . . real?"

Asphodel looked at her, half smiling. "Can he not be real in the same sense you allowed me to be?"

"I suppose . . . I mean . . . of course . . ." Tania stammered. "But he's . . . well, you see . . . younger . . ."

Laughter rang through the clearing, and the other wolf people trotted through the snow and formed a circle around Tania. As she looked at them now, she could see they were dressed, as the portraits in the Gallery had been dressed, in clothes of all different generations, some dating to the time of Asphodel, some much more recent. But their faces were as unlike those in the Gallery as any she'd ever seen: instead of being formal masks that hid both thought and feeling, each one was defenselessly open to all who viewed it and, in some way she couldn't quite identify, intensely sad.

Asphodel looked at them, then turned to Tania. "These are people of the Golden Age," she said, "but they were born in less fortunate times, and thus were aliens in the island Elyssonne had become. When they were forced to live by the laws of Ascanet's world, their bewilderment drove them to despair and the temptation to take their own lives. And yet, they were unable to do violence even to themselves, so they fled to the forest, where they found me and chose to share my form and my fate." She sighed. "Until a few weeks ago, I had thought it would be our fate to keep the forests of the Golden Age free from the influence of Ascanet and to protect the single entrance to Dacaria. But recently, I've felt that Dacaria was being corrupted from within, and that it is in as much danger now as it was five hundred years ago. This week, I sent two of my people to help the Dacarians, but I fear I acted too late. The Silver Souls have braved the forests; I can only guess how long it will be before Dacaria falls."

"If you sent two of your people to the valley," said Tania, "I'm more deeply in debt to you than I knew. One of them saved me from being harmed by a youth who followed me last night as I walked home, hoping to take something from me."

"That was I," said a broad-shouldered man who wore a tunic styled in the first century of Ascanet's reign. "I stepped between you and that same youth another time, too—after the dance, when he slipped into the grove where you had tied your pony. You were in great danger."

"So I have since learned," she said. "And I thank you."

"Cadwal tells me the youth was the one Sena of Dacaria found in the forest," said Asphodel. "What did he want of you?"

Tania looked up and found there was something in Asphodel's face that made equivocation impossible. "Ascanet's ring," she said. "And that's why I'm in the forest. If I reach Ascanet's castle, and if I can spend a day and a night in his company without wearing the ring, all he has done to the valley and the island will be undone."

Asphodel frowned. "If you cross the Waste, you will have to go alone, and if you reach the castle, you will have to face Ascanet alone also. Do you fully understand the risk you're taking? You are very young, and Ascanet is very powerful. Thus far, you have escaped death with the help of my people, but in Ascanet's castle, who will protect you from his guile?"

"I do understand the risk," said Tania. "But Dacaria's safety is threatened, and a dear friend of mine is imprisoned in Ascanet's castle, undergoing pain I cannot bear to think of. The ring has come, by accident, to me, so although I am young and have no wisdom to draw on in my own defense, I must go."

Asphodel gave her a wolflike stare. "If you are determined to continue," she said, "we'll go with you as far as we can. We know ways through the forest far more direct than the one you were following, so we can lead you to the Waste by late afternoon. That will enable you to cross to the castle in the dark, avoiding the hippogriffs that might be guarding it."

"If your help puts you in no danger, I'd be most grateful for it," said Tania. Her thanks sounded thin and graceless in her ears, her voice thinner still. For all her fine words, she thought sadly, the idea of facing Ascanet tomorrow—as opposed to some day in the distant future—made her shake with fear.

Asphodel nodded, then whirled around and gave a series of orders; in an instant, men and women bounded off in different directions with incredible speed and agility, returning before Tania had fully wrapped herself in her cloak. Seeing she was ready to go, Asphodel spoke to Colin, who nodded and walked to the place where she stood.

"We generally travel in pairs, even when we're all together," he said. "Asphodel has asked me to stay with you."

"I'll be glad of your company," she said, smiling at him. "I was very sad when I saw your black mare on the trail to Dacaria and learned that you'd disappeared."

"You saw her?" He looked at her anxiously. "Was she all right? It made me weep to drive her so, but her rider was unconscious, and there was no way of telling her that we were concerned for her safety."

"She was tired, but she'll be none the worse for wear after a week. And she'll be in very good hands in Dacaria."

"I'm sure she will," he said. But Tania noticed the sadness in his face.

Asphodel whistled, and the company set out along a trail that ran perpendicular to the one Tania and the horses had followed. After they'd trotted for a mile at what Tania found a punishing speed, they walked again.

"I'm afraid you owe the loss of your mare and your existence as a wolf to me," she said. "And I am deeply sorry. I know that if you hadn't let us escape from your manor, your future comfort would have been assured."

"I couldn't possibly have been comfortable knowing I'd let two innocent people be taken by Ascanet," he said. "And you shouldn't blame yourself for what happened to me; I told you I had no political sense." He smiled at her. "But I do have sense in other ways. I gave your lute to a master instrument maker in Theda who owes his training to my father's generosity. He admired it greatly and said he would be sure it never came to harm."

"Oh, thank you!" she said. "When I heard you'd disappeared, I thought it must surely have perished."

The company trotted for several miles; when they finally

walked, Colin spoke again. "The man who has your lute asked me—in confidence, of course—who it was that owned such a magnificent instrument. I'm not sure I would have told him if I'd known, but I was saved a struggle with my conscience. I knew you only by the name you gave in Theda. And that is still true."

"I'm sorry—I forgot I'd never told you what it was," she said. "I'm Tania, daughter of Marinda."

He looked at her oddly. "And no more?"

"How could I possibly be more than what I am?" she said, smiling.

"When Ascanet came to my manor and found you'd escaped, he was furious with me for having let the Prince of Mazion go free," said Colin. "I was able to assure him truthfully that you were not Prince Paran, having seen you at close range—but even while I denied his charges, I thought he was at least partly right."

"He was," she said. "It was I, not my brother, who escaped from the castle when it fell."

"I see," he said. "And what has happened to your master, who played your lute so beautifully?"

Tania looked ahead of her down the path. "He's the friend I hope to release from Ascanet's castle."

"I feared it might be so," he said, sighing. "But perhaps you'll find your love to be a source of the courage you'll need. Such things have happened."

She looked at him, startled. "You knew . . . ?"

"How could I help but know? Before he played in my music room, he looked for you, and you smiled at him—and I thought how I would envy you both, if what was promised came to pass. When I saw you here in the forest, I could see . . . well, I could say you've changed, but you haven't, in essence. It's some extra dimension . . ."

He stopped suddenly; ahead of them Asphodel had halted, motioning for silence. Tania looked questioningly at Colin and saw that like the other wolf people, he was sniffing the air uneasily. Something skulked in the trees to her right. Asphodel looked at it, sniffed some more, then threw back her head and sent a soft, longing howl echoing through the forest. For a moment everything was quiet; then a man slipped out of the shadows onto the narrow path. He looked quickly from person to person, pausing briefly as his yellow eyes met Tania's, but then skimming over the rest until they rested on Asphodel.

As she and he looked at each other, the air between them throbbed in the silence. At last, he strode across the snowy ground and knelt at her feet. As he looked up at her, she bent over; her hair fell about them both, hiding their faces and their words . . . if, indeed, they spoke at all. The wolf people glanced at each other; then, one by one, they slipped into the forest. Colin touched Tania's elbow and stepped off the path himself.

Cadwal met them as they rejoined the other wolf people; his eyes were shining with excitement. "You've just witnessed a strange and wondrous meeting," he said to Tania. "But you would have no way of knowing that if you didn't know the tale behind it."

"I think I know some of the tale," said Tania. "At least, enough to share your wonder."

Colin made a little gesture of surprise, but Cadwal smiled. "That's possible, since you have come from Dacaria. What do you know of the man who stepped from the forest?"

"I know that his name is Kylian, and that he once left the valley and traveled Outside. I have occasionally thought he might have found love there. And that's all I know, except . . ." As she hunted for words, she found herself sitting on the doorstep of a Dacarian cottage, seeing Anrican's perceptive face. *Kylian has an extraordinary . . . curiosity, I suppose I'd call it—not just about things of the mind, but about things the mind alone can't comprehend.* The vision faded; she was looking at Cadwal, not Anrican. But Cadwal was nodding.

"Yes," he said. "Comprehension like his is very rare—and not, finally, as conducive to happiness as it may seem to be."

"That's true," said Tania softly. "In Dacaria, Kylian is respected, even loved—but he is always restless."

"That's a matter of history as well as one of temperament," said Cadwal. "Ten years ago, Kylian traveled through the forest, as all Dacarians must when they leave the valley; and, as always, we escorted him to ensure his safety. But unlike other Dacarians, who felt our presence and feared that feeling as madness, Kylian stepped off the paths so he could see us—not in a brief moment of vision like the one that so terrified you, my lady—but steadily." Cadwal gazed into the trees. "I'm not sure, but I always suspected he saw Asphodel in her human form, even when the rest of us could see only the result of her metamorphosis." He smiled. "In any case, his admiration brought him to the forest frequently, and as their affection deepened into love, he became what she had become.

"For five years, he and she never hunted or lay apart. But one day when we were hunting, we scared up a deer that fled straight toward the Waste. It was particularly fleet, and we were all excited with the chase. Kylian was afraid we would lose it, and he outstripped the rest of us, even Asphodel, in his eagerness. The deer led him along the edge of the forest, then, just as he jumped for it, it leaped out into the Waste itself. Without thinking, he followed it . . . but before he had taken three bounds, he fell, writhing in pain, and when he had at last struggled to his feet, he had become a man again.

Beyond him, the deer ran toward Ascanet's castle, and we realized it had led us to the Waste, hoping for our destruction.

"Kylian was sorely punished for foiling Ascanet's scheme: when he staggered back into the forest, he could no longer see us—even Asphodel—or understand what we said; nor could the rest of us understand his words, though we could see him. We hoped he would change, but day after day passed, and he remained a man, searching the forest for the love who trotted unseen at his side. At last, weary and nearly starved, he returned to Dacaria. Asphodel accompanied him to the tunnel, but I'm not sure he knew even that." Cadwal sighed.

"But now," said Colin, "she has become what she once was . . ."

"But he is mortal," said Cadwal sadly, "while by the terms of her enchantment, she, like the rest of us, is not. What will happen is beyond my comprehension." He looked at Tania. "Perhaps if your mission succeeds, all such strange threads will become untangled and the two of them will be to each other what they once were."

And if she were not successful, she thought, how much would be lost! She looked up at Cadwal. "I should go on, dearly as I would like to wait for Kylian and Asphodel. But if you tell me the way, I can go by myself."

"We'll all go," said Cadwal. "They travel quickly, and despite their joy in each other, they'll soon join us." He turned to the others and spoke a few words Tania didn't understand; in less than a minute, they found the path again and trotted steadily through the forest. Late in the afternoon, Cadwal led the way up a little rise, then halted.

"There lies the Waste," he said, pointing. "And there, just on the horizon, lies the castle."

Tania looked out and saw a vast, empty plain of silver

snow that stretched to a horizon entirely featureless except for four gleaming towers. Ascanet's Waste. When she'd thought of it, she'd imagined plains like those in Mazion, not this fierce, gleaming void. Awed, she shivered as she looked across it. "How will I be able to see the castle if I go in the darkness?" she asked. "There are no landmarks."

"You'll have no trouble," said Cadwal. "The castle is made of ice, cut by a master craftsman so that it catches light like a jewel. You can see it glisten now; at night, it shines with a peculiar blue light it seems to draw from the stars. I've sat here many nights and looked at it."

"It must be very beautiful," she said.

"It is," he said. "And all the more dangerous because of that." He looked up at the sun, then back at her. "You have about three hours before it's dark, and there's shelter on the far side of this rise. Do you think you can sleep?"

"I doubt it," said Tania. "But I suppose it would be wise to try."

She let Colin lead her to a needle-filled indentation and curled up there, wrapping her torn cloak around her. As she'd suspected, her thoughts kept her awake—thoughts of Eliar in the crystal castle across the vast, empty Waste; thoughts of Melibe, who had warned her that Ascanet would use her love against her; thoughts of Dacaria . . . But as she thought of the green-and-gold valley, she heard the sounds of listening trees, of the brook that ran by the cottage, of the music that rose from the fields. Comforted and strangely peaceful, she drifted off to sleep.

CHAPTER
XVI

IT WAS DARK when someone woke her—so dark that it took her a moment to see the blond hair and gentle face that bent over her.

"Colin?" she murmured, sitting up groggily.

"Yes. It's after midnight. You should go."

Hastily, Tania unwrapped her cloak and stood up. "So late?"

She could feel his smile in the darkness. "It is only three miles, and the moon has just risen; you'll be at the gates at dawn if you leave now. Since you could sleep, Asphodel said not to wake you until we had to."

"Asphodel? Is she here?"

"Yes. And she wants to see you."

Tania nodded and followed him to the top of the rise. Asphodel stood at its center; around its edges sat the wolf people, gazing silently at the moon. She looked from face to face. "Where is Kylian?"

"He has gone with Cadwal and some of the others to find the Silver Souls whose horses you stole," said Asphodel. "We want to be sure you don't meet them as you cross the Waste." She beckoned, and as Tania joined her in the circle's center, she smiled. "He said to tell you a man he calls the hermit told him to seek me here—though he did not tell him in what form. We're to wait for you here, where we can see the castle; when it falls, we'll come to your aid as quickly as we can."

When it falls. What if it didn't fall? What if she . . . ?

Asphodel glanced at her. "It's better not to think such thoughts. Remember instead that you have allies whose debt to you can never be repaid, and whose love follows you on your journey." She looked across the Waste at the shimmering castle. "And think also about Ascanet himself. He's a man of tremendous intelligence, but he cannot see beyond words; he's blind to the very things Colin sees easily and Kylian understands without effort. If you can manage not to let his rhetoric convince you that what you know to be true is false, you will do what you hope to."

She shook her long hair back, and for a moment, Tania looked enviously at her intense face. "It is you who should be doing this, not I," she said. "You're much better suited to it than I am."

"Not I," said Asphodel. "I've seen too much injustice and felt it too deeply—and even if I had not, I would be unfitted for the task. If I faced Ascanet, I would try to tear him to pieces—thus succumbing to all I hate in him. No, it is you who must go, and I who must watch. But all my thoughts go with you." She turned to Tania, her eyes glowing in the moonlight. "Go now, Daughter of Marinda," she said softly. "And be brave."

She turned away. Tania watched her leave the silent circle, then walked down the rise and stepped out of the forest onto the plain.

From the forest, the Waste's silver snow had seemed to be hundreds of feet deep, and Tania had feared she would sink into it helplessly as she would sink into water. But to her surprise, she found it had no depth at all; she walked on it as she would have walked into the textureless landscape of a painting, feeling nothing beneath her feet and leaving no tracks. In fact, as she moved farther from the forest, she began to wonder if she hadn't stepped through some invisible frame into a world as deceiving in its perspective as Melibe's room of memories: about her, there was nothing but silence, before her, nothing but the immense, glowing walls that soared out of a moonlit void.

But when she neared the castle gates at dawn, watching the first rays of the rising sun touch its octagonal towers, she stopped, staring in awe. As the light touched its polished angles, the castle lost its silhouetted flatness and blazed in all the splendor of its true form. Perfect in its symmetry, shimmering blue-gray in the Waste's silver foil, it was a replica, a thousand times enlarged, of the ring.

The call of trumpets rose from the walls. Before the sound had died away, the gates swung open and eight silver riders encircled her, their faceless heads uncovered and their swords drawn. Their leader halted his horse a foot from where she stood. "Who are you that has dared to come to his lordship's castle unannounced?"

Tania drew herself up. "I would have announced myself if you had given me time to do so peaceably," she said. "I am Tania, daughter of Marinda, and I have crossed the Waste to talk to his lordship about a ring that he has lost."

"You have come here willingly?" A faint overtone of surprise made the leader's voice rise.

"I have."

The leader paused, then looked at his followers. "Take her to the hanging stone," he said. "I must talk to his lordship."

He wheeled his horse and galloped back to the castle. Si-

225

lently, the riders who encircled Tania rode a few hundred yards to the east and stopped at a large, slanting rock that leaned toward the castle as it rose out of the snow. Tania looked at it in curiosity. "How did this rock come here?" she asked the men.

None of them moved; they gazed at her with such blankness that she wondered if their leader had taken some essential part of them with him. She stepped toward one of them to repeat her question; instantly, he raised his sword, but as she backed away, he became motionless once more. Tania leaned against the rock, thinking of the horses she'd led through the forest. Apparently, Ascanet's minions could do only what they were told to.

After a half hour, the leader of the guards cantered out to the rock; at his approach, the horses began to prance, and the men opened their eye slits wide in anticipation. But a gesture from him stilled them immediately.

"His lordship welcomes you to his castle," said the leader, bowing to Tania. "If you will follow us, we'll put you in the care of someone who will show where you may rest and refresh yourself. Tonight, his lordship wishes you to join him at supper."

Tania bowed in return. "Tell his lordship I will be honored."

The leader wheeled his horse, and his followers wheeled theirs, seven versions of his reflection. They led her into a massive courtyard, gleaming blue in the light that shone through its high walls. The leader whistled; a faceless page slipped out of a side door and ran toward him.

"This is Tania, Princess of Mazion," said the leader. "Has his lordship given you instructions concerning her welfare?"

"Yes, Sir Rollin," said the boy, bowing.

"Then follow them," said Sir Rollin. "And don't forget;

226

she may go anyplace she wishes—except the place his lord-ship indicated."

"Yes, Sir Rollin." The boy backed slowly away, then turned to Tania and bowed again. "Will you follow me to your chamber, my lady?"

She nodded, thanked Sir Rollin for his service, and fol-lowed the boy through an arched door. Inside, she was met by a damp, still air that was far colder than the Waste; she wrapped her cloak about her as she walked through vast cor-ridors and rooms, each lit by the sunlight that filtered through the walls. In the eerie blue light, she could see there were no windows, no candles, and no portraits; the castle's only ornaments were its enormous Gothic arches. And though the rooms were beautifully furnished, no courtiers lounged in them and no attendants hurried to and fro. She and the boy seemed to have the frozen splendors to themselves.

At last, the boy turned and began to climb a double stair-case that soared up two hundred feet in elaborate concentric spirals. She followed him, looking about her in fascination. In contrast to the blank walls of the corridors, the sides of the staircases were lined with faces: not full heads, but bas-reliefs of eyes, ears, cheeks, noses, and mouths that stood out from the ice that backed them. Some of the faces were plain, some handsome, some intelligent, some arrogant, but all of them wore expressions of assurance and youth. She longed to ask the boy what such strange, lifelike faces were doing in a cas-tle in which there seemed to be neither life nor decoration, but as she hurried to catch up with him, she saw that every line of his back revealed fear, so she held her peace.

At the top of the first flight, he turned into a corridor filled with identical doors. Opening one of them, he ushered Tania into a carpeted chamber furnished with embroidered silver cushions and quilts. It was deliciously warm, and as she looked wonderingly for the source of the heat, she saw a flameless blue fire in a marble fireplace. The boy edged toward it, and Tania saw he was shivering.

"It is cold in the castle, isn't it?" she said. "Why don't you sit down and warm yourself?"

The boy turned his eye slits toward her, and she felt a little wave of surprise.

"Don't be afraid," she said. "Go ahead."

He walked uncertainly to the fire. She surveyed the room until she heard him curl up with a sigh on the cushion nearest the fireplace. Looking at him, she saw his eye slits droop; he was obviously exhausted. Poor child, she thought. Perhaps she should go look at the peculiar bas-reliefs and let him sleep undisturbed. She walked to the door and lifted the latch.

Instantly, the boy leapt to his feet with a wordless, animal snarl.

"I'll come right back," she said. "Sleep, if you're tired."

He shook his head and moved to the door. As he passed through it, she thought she heard someone say, "Orders; follow her everywhere."

She stopped dead. Had he spoken? "Wait!" she called. "I'll look at the reliefs later." Beckoning to him, she walked back into the room and sat down by the fire. He slunk back and curled up a few feet away from her, gazing at her out of the corners of his lidless eyes.

"Can you talk when Sir Rollin isn't here?" she asked.

His mouth slit remained shut; his thoughts, if he had any, remained equally so. She leaned back against the cushions, sighing, but as he turned away from her, someone said, "Mustn't know can think."

She stared at him, realizing she could hear his thoughts

when his empty face was turned from her. Could he hear hers?

He spun around, his eye slits wide open and his hands shaking. She smiled; he certainly could. But could he hear her thoughts when he faced her? She couldn't hear his. She tapped her fingers thoughtfully on her cushion, then gazed into his eye slits.

"I'm going to sleep," she said. "Will you wake me at noon?"

The boy nodded.

"After that, will you show me the rest of the castle?"

He nodded again.

You may sleep until noon, then, she thought, looking at him. *You're very tired, aren't you?*

He nodded wearily. Then suddenly, his eye slits opened to their fullest extent and he cowered from her.

Ah. Then Ascanet had given her a guide and servant who could tell him everything that passed through her mind. She lay back on her cushion and refrained from further reflection until the boy's panicked breathing calmed. Poor child, she thought again as she looked at his blank visage. He seemed to have retained a fraction of his soul; if that made him dangerous to her, it also made him more pitiable than the men who served their master without being able to see what they were doing.

Whatever his capacity for betrayal, the boy was obedient; he woke her promptly at noon and offered her sumptuous food on a silver platter. She was too nervous to be hungry, so she gave most of it to him, watching with amusement and awe as he devoured his portion in a quarter of the time it took her to eat hers. When they'd finished, she stood up. "Now," she said, "show me everything you can."

He led her through huge rooms whose echoing hammer-beamed ceilings rose a hundred feet above her head, all of them filled with beautifully wrought furniture. She followed him, looking for places where Eliar might be imprisoned, and realizing miserably that she could search for a year and never find him in this vast, frigid emptiness.

"Does your master have no courtiers?" she asked as the boy passed ahead of her through a magnificently carved door.

"Only souls." The answer drifted back to her as she'd hoped it would, but it was hardly satisfactory. Souls? Were the rooms filled with invisible knights and ladies?

"No—souls," came the reply. "Staircase."

She stared at his back, baffled. But as he opened another door, she found he had led her in a full circle to the double staircase. He started down the steps without looking back and pointed at the walls. "Souls."

Slowly, she looked at the bas-reliefs. Now that she had time to study them, she realized each face was set into a separate recess, locked behind a transparent door with minute hinges and a tiny catch. All at once, she understood. Stunned, she looked at the recesses that circled the stairwell. There were hundreds of them. "And their . . . owners live in the rooms we've seen?" she whispered.

The boy shook his head and led her back up the few steps she'd descended, then up two more circling flights. At the top, he flung open a wide door, ran along the windswept ramparts to a smaller door, and led her up twisting steps to the top of an octagonal tower. When she caught up with him, panting from the climb, he was leaning against the battlements, his hair blowing in the icy breeze. She stepped to his side; below her stretched the Waste, seeming very small from her great height. To her left were the courtyard and the castle gates; to her far right . . . she stepped back, her hands over her mouth.

The boy's lipless mouth stretched into a grin. "Don't worry. Chained."

Gingerly, she tiptoed back to the battlements and looked down. Below her, four hippogriffs trotted out to the end of their silver chains, reared and whirled as they reached the ends, then trotted back in the other direction. She watched them, surprised by her pity. "Do they trot up and down like that all day?" she asked.

The boy nodded.

"It's amazing they come back at all when he lets them loose."

He shook his head. "Die if can't see castle for a day."

"Then why does he chain them?"

He pointed to one of the guards below him, then stalked across the tower in a perfect imitation of a hippogriff's gait. Suddenly, he stopped, tensed his muscles, and pounced. Holding down an imaginary guard with his hands, he made little growling sounds in his throat and gnashed his teeth.

"I see," she said.

Below them trumpets sounded. The boy jumped up and touched Tania's arm, pointing to the gates. Two hundred yards in front of the castle, the ground slid silently open and fifty silver horsemen rode out of the gaping hole. As they formed ranks and saluted their leader, trumpets sounded again, and fifty different riders trotted from the castle gate, saluted the others, and trotted into the passage from which they'd emerged. The ground closed over them without a sound, and the new riders wheeled their horses in the circle Tania had seen at the demonstration, then trotted into the courtyard.

"Souls," said the boy's thoughts.

She glanced at him. "You mean they and their horses live underground, not in the rooms we've seen?"

He nodded.

"Can they not enter the castle?"

He looked out over the Waste. "No . . . staircase."

They were prisoners, then, shut away from light and air except when they were on guard, and carefully kept away from the souls with which they'd bought their captivity. She shivered, then looked curiously at the boy. Why was he allowed free run of the castle while they were not? Stepping in back of him, she listened for a reply—but felt instead a wave of fear, so clearly she thought for an instant it was her own. Then she heard the sound of a lute.

It wasn't close, but it was certainly not separated from her by hundreds of feet of ice walls. And while the wind blew the music to her in snatches, she could tell it was a fugue, filled with difficult turns and runs that only the finest lutenist could play. She looked quickly at the boy and saw he was staring at the tower diagonally across from her. Trembling with excitement, she asked casually, "Do the other towers have as fine a view as this?"

The boy nodded.

She pointed to the one directly across from her. "May I see that one?"

He nodded.

"Perhaps that one is too close to this," she said. "I think I'd rather go to the one on the diagonal."

He shook his head.

"Really?" She tried to look surprised. "I'd think you could see the channel from there. Well, take me down to my room. It's growing late, and you must soon take me to his lordship."

He led the way willingly; as she followed him, she studied the corridors and thought she could tell which one would lead to the tower. A renewed surge of fear from the boy told her she'd guessed correctly—and that he would suffer terribly for her discovery if it were known. *Have no fear,* she assured him as they neared her room. *You followed your instructions to the letter; I would never betray you.*

The boy stopped at her door, hesitated, then opened it and left her to herself. Somehow the simple gesture connoted thanks, and as she entered the room and found a tunic, breeches, and bathing water prepared for her, she wondered what—if anything—his gesture meant.

She spent some time readying herself for her encounter with Ascanet, though she knew she was doing it only for her own morale and not for any effect she could hope to have on him. When she was fully dressed, she pulled the ring out of her pocket and looked at it. As always, she was stirred by its beauty, and she noticed that it matched her elegant tunic perfectly. How clever of Ascanet, she thought; if she hadn't known the ring's powers, she would have been tempted to put it on. Shaking her head, she slipped it back into her pocket and called the boy.

He led her down the double staircase and through twelve empty halls she hadn't seen before. At the end of the last hall, he slipped behind a velvet hanging, then led her up a flight of stairs and through an open door. She found herself in a room filled with music: manuscripts that lay scattered on tables, chairs, and shelves, bound volumes that lay open on carved wooden stands, and stacks of sheet music that leaned precariously against the walls. In the midst of the confusion, a silver-haired man sat tuning a lute. He looked up, and Tania saw the sensitive, scholarly face she'd seen in Theda, illuminated by gray-blue eyes that looked like Damon's. The eyes studied her a moment, then the lutenist stood up and bowed.

"Good evening, Princess Tania," he whispered.

"Good evening, my lord," she said, bowing in return.

Ascanet put his lute in its case. "I hope you don't think I've been remiss; I would have called you this afternoon, but Sir Rollin told me Lorn was showing you the castle." He glanced at the boy. "I hope he showed you everything you wished to see."

"He did indeed, my lord. And everything I saw was magnificent."

Ascanet smiled at the boy, then dismissed him from the room. "He is the most simple—and therefore the most reliable—of my servants," he said. "He has accepted his duties here without the slightest attempt to remain an independent being. I trust him as I trust few others."

Tania looked at him in surprise, wondering that he had not detected Lorn's capacity to understand thought. It flashed across her mind that his lack of understanding might be useful to her. "Who is he, my lord? He can't be above twelve years old; that's very young for the kind of contract your lordship's servants usually make with you." As she spoke, she felt, rather than saw, a little movement on the stairs outside the room.

"Boys his age serve me for five years; then, if they wish to go, they may, upon making certain . . . payments. So far, none has wished to."

"I'm sure none has," she said courteously. "But tell me— can he talk only when he is with you? He showed me around the castle without a single word, though he understood what I said."

"None of my servants can talk, except in the presence of a captain, a knight, or myself. Nor can they think of anything beyond what they are told to do." He looked at her keenly. "It would be a mistake to try any of them; they are well trained."

"I wouldn't think of it," she said. But as she met his gaze, she was puzzled by what she saw. For all the cruelty she knew he was capable of, he seemed to have little in common with other men who had no conscience. His sensitive face had none of Radnor's hardness, Damon's hypocrisy, or Sir Harlan and Sir Dolan's dull complacence; every feature was cultured, thoughtful, and intelligent.

Ascanet smiled. "I see you are perplexed. You had thought, of course, that Ascanet was a man like those who served him."

"Perhaps . . ."

"A common misapprehension, I fear," he said. "But come—this isn't a place for conversation. You have had an arduous day. I trust you have come to join me for supper?"

"I have, my lord; and I am honored to be asked."

He gave her his arm, led her to another small, heated chamber, and seated her with her back to the fire. Sitting down himself, he clapped his hands twice. Lorn and nine faceless pages stepped from a door Tania hadn't seen, each one carrying a silver dish. While the pages served them, Lorn poured wine out of one of the many decanters on the sideboard.

"To your health," said Ascanet, touching her glass with his. The ring of fine crystal shimmered in the room, and as it died away, all the pages but Lorn bowed and left them.

Their master sipped his wine thoughtfully. "Yes," he said, "there are several misapprehensions that have driven men to set me apart from them. Not that the conditions in which I live are unpleasant, of course."

"And what are the misapprehensions?" she asked.

"I've mentioned one already—that Ascanet is a man like those who serve him. But you've already seen that I am not, so there's no need to address the matter. There is another, however, which I find equally annoying: the story of Elyssonne's perpetual winter, which historians attribute to my presence. The fiction has done my reputation great damage." He looked up from his glass. "I see you're skeptical. No doubt you've been raised on the tale yourself: Ascanet comes to Elyssonne, there is a great blizzard, and Elyssonne huddles under a burden of snow for five hundred years. Am I correct?"

"Yes," she said.

"So I feared," he sighed. "It's a fantasy, you know—a myth constructed by historians in the pay of patrons who benefit from it. But exposing it for what it is involves making the people of Elyssonne give up the illusion that their island is the last refuge of the Creation. And that they are most reluctant to do." He smiled sadly. "I can sympathize, of course. Don't we all glorify our ancestors in order to make ourselves look more impressive to our contemporaries? Still, facts are facts. And in this case, the facts are that Theon was displeased with the people of Elyssonne many years before I came; he expressed his displeasure by inflicting a change of climate upon the island."

He glanced at her shocked face. "Oh, yes—Elyssonne fell from its early purity long before the so-called Golden Age ended. I came to a land in which winter had been growing increasingly severe for several decades. But of course, the people of Elyssonne would rather blame me for their misfortunes than accuse their ancestors of irresponsibility. Thus, the history they have constructed has made me into Elyssonne's destroyer."

Tania looked thoughtfully at her plate. She could almost believe Ascanet's words, knowing what she did of human nature. And yet, accepting his version of Elyssonne's fall entailed believing that Melibe, who refused to rearrange the rooms in his cave to suit his convenience, had falsified the progress of history in order to explain the island's present condition. That seemed more than unlikely . . .

"And then," said Ascanet, signaling for more wine, "we have the case of Dacaria. Now there is a matter of simple geography that has been turned into a full-blown legend. The center of Elyssonne is protected by rings of mountains, sheltered from the cold winds from the sea; therefore, it isn't subject to the same extremes of temperature as the rest of the island. Yet out of this geographical accident has come the story that Dacaria is sacred to Theon, and—in some versions —that if Dacaria falls into my hands, Elyssonne will sink into the sea."

Tania thought of the green-and-gold valley, of the trees that whispered when she walked between them, of the shepherds' pipes. "Are you implying that Dacaria *isn't* sacred to Theon?" she said, lifting one eyebrow.

Ascanet smiled. "There are few places that are truly sacred; in fact, I sometimes suspect there are none at all. But there are many that men *call* sacred because their presence evokes historical fallacies that society has decided to deem true. Dacaria is one of those places—to Elyssonne's great misfortune. Think of the harm its false sanctity has caused!"

"Harm!"

As she spoke, Tania heard the whisper of footsteps outside the room. She felt a flash of fear, but Ascanet's obvious irritation assured her that he had laid no trap for her. He jerked his head at Lorn, who was standing next to the sideboard. Without a word, the boy bowed and left the room.

Ascanet leaned back in his chair. "Yes, harm," he said. "Lay aside what you've been taught, my lady, and think of Elyssonne as if it were a stranger's home, not your own. Think of a people, isolated from the Mainland for centuries, who believe that their island was created perfect but has become less so. Then think of the few scholars and kings who know of Dacaria (for it's so sacred, few people are permitted to know of its existence—an idea whose implications would make one weep if one were inclined to tears). When they look for truth and inspiration, where will they look but to the valley which is their present replica of past perfection? Doesn't the idealization of Dacaria force them to look backward and inward for knowledge, instead of forward and outward?"

Tania set down her wineglass. "Do you wish to argue that a country can prosper only if its people look forward and outward?"

"No. I wish to argue that failure to look beyond oneself inevitably leads to the restriction of progress." He leaned forward. "You're a musician, are you not? Consider what a restricted instrument the lute is: only the very finest musicians can play complicated music on it. On the Mainland, there are instruments beside which the lute looks as primitive as the panpipe that hangs from your belt: instruments whose strings can be bowed as well as plucked, instruments with keys that, when pressed, pluck strings so quickly that one can play scales and turns with twice the speed the lute allows. Yet in Elyssonne, such instruments are unknown; thus, its people play the same music now as they played fifteen hundred years ago. Doesn't that impoverish the very people who boast of their musical heritage?"

"Not necessarily," she said. "To every generation in Elyssonne, the lute is a new instrument, calling for new refinements of technique and construction; in the same way, every generation that plays the rebec designs it in a more sophisticated fashion. Furthermore, my lord, every child who learns a song from his father has memorized a theme on which he can compose variations. You have been here five hundred

238

years. Tell me—is the music you hear played now identical with that you heard when you first came?"

Ascanet tapped his fingers on the table. "Perhaps not," he admitted. "But the progress of its music and instruments could have been greatly accelerated if its craftsmen knew the instruments and music of the Mainland."

"That may be true, but the people of Elyssonne cannot be blamed for that."

His eyebrows rose. "No? Who can, then?"

Tania smiled. "Lay aside your assumptions, my lord, and think of Elyssonne as if it were a stranger's dominion, not your own. Think of a people, isolated from the Mainland for centuries, who are invaded by a man of your learning and skills. They can hardly be censured for insularity if their new ruler takes all the knowledge, virtue, and culture they have unto himself, but brings them none in return. My lord, Elyssonne would be filled with the finest music in the world if you had deigned to make that possible."

Ascanet was silent for a moment; then he looked up. "I have long wished to make it possible," he said. "But as you see, I'm limited by the men who serve me. To bring music and culture to Elyssonne, I would need somebody who understood both and who had, in addition, few moral flaws."

"Such a servant would no doubt be difficult to find," she said, somehow managing to keep all irony out of her voice.

"That is so, but there is an infallible test for the strength and intelligence I would need." His eyes glistened as he looked at her. "And I rather think you have passed it. Would you be so kind as to hold out your hands, my lady?"

She met his gaze, feeling her heart thump under her tunic. Then, slipping her hand hurriedly in and out of her pocket, she held both her fists out to him, their knuckles up. Ascanet sipped his wine. "And if you open them?"

Trembling inwardly, she turned her hands over and unflexed her fingers. The ring glistened in her right palm.

She'd expected him to explode with rage or perhaps sink helplessly to the floor, undone by his own weapon, but he simply nodded. "Have you never worn it, my lady?"

"Never."

"Why not? It's very beautiful."

"It is beautiful," she said, putting her hands on the table as they began to shake. "But . . . but I don't like jewelry."

"Not even this piece?" Ascanet stretched out his hand, displaying a magnificent collection of rings. "You can see, there is nothing here to compare with it."

"I can see how beautiful the ring is, my lord, but I don't wish to encumber my fingers—I love the lute too well."

Ascanet nodded. "You see? You have exactly the attributes I need to bring music to Elyssonne—you are not vain, you love the lute. And I suspect you are not ambitious. Is that correct?"

"Ambition would cause a woman little but unhappiness in Elyssonne, my lord," she said. "It is far easier to be obedient than to order the world according to one's wishes."

"That is true," he said, "if one has normal means at one's disposal. But what if I were to tell you that the ring would give you the power to do anything you liked, were you but to put it on?"

"Then I would tell you I could not believe your words, my lord. You wish to have an obedient servant who will bring music to Elyssonne for you; but if I had the power to do anything I liked, I could bring music to Elyssonne myself, without having to obey you."

Ascanet looked at her out of a face so like Damon's that she shuddered. "Ah—you have passed another test," he said, with a smile she knew was false. "You have shown me that you are not easily tempted."

240

His words thrummed in her ears. What was he thinking? What would he do? But as he began to speak again, the door opened and silken footsteps crossed the room. She turned and saw Lorn standing behind her, staring at the ring.

"You should not have interrupted us," whispered Ascanet in a tone she hadn't heard him use before.

"I am very sorry to do so, my lord," said Lorn. "But Sir Rollin said you were sorely needed in the northeast tower, and that I should fetch you, no matter how important your business."

Tania bit her lip—then realized Ascanet was looking at her with hooded eyes. "I apologize for this unseemly interruption," he said, rising. "I have a visitor at the castle—one of my pupils from many years ago—and he is ill." He turned to go, but suddenly whirled around with a smile that made her tremble. "Why—it just occurred to me that you know who my student is," he said. "Just yesterday, he told me he was with you at the demonstration at Theda."

She drew a deep breath. "Oh, do you mean Eliar? Yes, I know him—but not well."

Ascanet raised his eyebrows. "He didn't go to Dacaria with you?"

"No," she said, relieved that the question was so put that she could answer it truthfully. "He said he couldn't return there."

Ascanet's face creased in irritation. "I see," he said. "Well, I must go to him, it seems. When I am finished, I will have Lorn fetch you." He turned to the boy. "And you, my lad, must come to the tower as soon as you've taken Princess Tania to her room."

"Yes, my lord."

Ascanet bowed and left; Tania collapsed into her chair and dropped her forehead on her hands. A day and a night: she had to survive twelve more hours . . . and he had discovered that she knew Eliar. If only she'd kept her concern out of her face!

As she looked up, she saw that Lorn was waiting for her. Yes, he was to lead her to her chamber, then go to the tower. If she followed him, she could . . . She shut the thought away quickly, in case he could hear it, then leapt up. "Shall we go?"

He bowed and led the way through the door. No thoughts drifted back to her, but the air between them hummed with his desire to ask her a question. Following him, she wondered what it could possibly be.

CHAPTER
XVII

WHEN THEY REACHED HER CHAMBER, the hum Tania
had felt between herself and Lorn grew louder. She sat down
by the fire, not sure what to do. If she could answer his question, she would earn his gratitude; that might be wise, since
nobody needed an ally more than she did. On the other
hand, the lesson she'd learned from Talus's horse was sharp
in her mind. Lorn was Ascanet's creature; he might turn on
her when she least expected him to. As she thought the matter over, she heard a gentle thump. Looking around, she saw
the boy had shut the door and was leaning against it, looking
at her with as much intensity as his lidless eyes could muster.

Sympathy with his plight overcame her caution. "Do you
wish to ask me something?"

He nodded and stepped away from the door, looking over
his shoulder. His question was apparently too dangerous for
him to phrase, even in his elementary way. She thought back
over the evening and finally arrived at the small movement
she'd seen after Ascanet had dismissed Lorn from the music
room.

"Did you hear his lordship talking to me about boys your
age who can leave him after five years?" she asked.

His eager nod assured her she'd hit upon the right subject.

"I noticed you were taller than the other boys who served me. Is your time almost up?"

He nodded vigorously.

"Do you want to know what price you'll have to pay for that freedom—the price that no other boy has wanted to pay?"

He nodded and stepped closer, his hands clasped together.

"There is only one price Ascanet would be sure nobody would pay," she said. "That is, in return for your freedom, you leave the essential part of yourself that's imprisoned by the staircase and venture out into the world of ordinary men without a face."

The boy started, then leaned against the wall for support, staring at her with wide-open eye slits.

Looking at him compassionately, Tania wondered if he possibly could be like Talus's horse. He'd served Ascanet faithfully in the hope of reward, not because his soul had been cleared of every virtue but obedience. Could she . . . ? She shook her head; no, she couldn't afford to trust him. But she could help him. "Lorn," she said, "can the other boys hear thoughts, as you can?"

He shook his head.

"Do you think Ascanet knows you can?"

He shook his head violently.

"Then think of your position," she said. "Ascanet trusts most of his servants so little he won't even let them in the castle for fear they'll rescue their souls. But he trusts you so deeply and understands you so little that he gives you the free run of the castle. You could, if you had the courage, make your entire soul your own by simply opening its glass door."

Lorn stood transfixed, his mouth slit gaping open.

She smiled at him, then looked at the door behind him, thinking of Eliar. "But you're endangering yourself by staying here, Lorn. Your master wished you to go to him immediately after you'd brought me here. If you don't hurry, he'll be angry."

The boy gasped, then dashed from the room, forgetting even to bow. As she heard him run toward the staircase, she leapt to her feet and slipped out into the corridor after him.

It was so dark she could see almost nothing, but she could hear the whisper of footsteps on the stairs. Running softly to the staircase, she bounded up the long flight two steps at a time, ran across the landing, then dodged into the shadows as she caught sight of his dim form ahead of her. He was climbing slowly, looking at the wall. After a few steps, he stopped before a relief and gazed at it. A sob burst from his throat, and he slowly raised his hand.

"Where can the boy be?" Sir Rollin's voice boomed down the stairwell, amplified by the echoing walls.

Lorn started, then began to run up the stairs. Tania followed him, stopping for an instant before the relief he'd gazed at with such longing. A snub-nosed, intelligent face looked back at her out of eyes that begged for kindness. Quickly, she slipped the panpipe from her belt and laid it on the step directly under the relief, then ran up the stairs after its owner. In a minute she was forced to stop again, for he shrank against the wall as footsteps echoed in the hall above them.

"Lorn may have been delayed," hissed Ascanet's voice. "But there is no reason to wait for him. Please fetch me my lute."

"I, my lord?" Sir Rollin's voice was tinged with indignation.

"If you will." The words lowered the temperature of the

stairwell by several degrees. "It's important to begin quickly —the prisoner will soon be either mad or dead. I fear you've been too zealous."

"I did all that your lordship told me to do," said Sir Rollin sulkily.

"Yes, but you are still an apprentice. Real torture—torture of the mind, the heart, the soul—takes practice and insight. What's done is done, of course, and I am partly to blame, since it was I who assigned you a task for which you were unfit. I'm afraid you need a few more years in the ranks before you will be ready for the elevation I lately gave you. We can, however, discuss that later. At the moment, I need my lute, and I would be most grateful if you brought it to me."

"My lord . . . !" protested Sir Rollin.

"It would be unwise to cross me," whispered Ascanet. "I've had a trying evening, and I have much to attend to tonight."

"My lord," said Rollin, his voice rising. "I pray you, let me speak! The prisoner is no common mortal. Once you had done to him what you did, he seemed to welcome pain rather than fear it . . ."

"Did you not hear me say it would be unwise to cross me?"

"Please, my lord! I don't deserve to be demoted! What you asked me to do was impossible! You have no idea of the damage you do yourself in the eyes of your men in requiring them to do things that can't be done! Below the castle, they whisper that the loss of the ring has caused you to lose your judgment."

"Do they indeed?" Ascanet sounded only mildly interested. "Well, I thank you for your counsel; I had no idea things had reached such a state. It's nothing new, I assure you; every generation or so, some fool questions my judgment and encourages a rumor of my senility. Well, I'll deal with the rumor in the morning. But in the meantime, you've made me see that I have indeed lost my judgment where you are concerned; I hadn't thought you'd stoop to stirring up the men." He sighed. "Perhaps I was blinded by my fondness for you; you've served me well, and I regret the necessity of your extinction." His footsteps strode across the hall above Tania and Lorn, then ran down the staircase opposite the one in which they huddled.

"My lord!" Sir Rollin's voice rose to a scream, and his running footsteps followed Ascanet's. "My lord—I beg you!"

His voice was cut short by the crash of shattering glass. A shriek echoed up and down the stairwell, then something soft rolled down the steps with ever increasing speed. A breeze of sighs wafted softly from the reliefs on the wall; for a moment, there was no other sound. Then Ascanet's footsteps continued down the staircase, changed their rhythm as he reached the first floor, and disappeared into the corridors.

Shaking with horror, Tania forced herself to think quickly. Ascanet had left; Sir Rollin was dead—was Eliar perhaps unguarded? If he were . . . She glanced up to the place where Lorn lay weeping, and decided she would have to believe what his tears and his imprisoned face told her. Creeping up the stairs, she touched his shoulder, then put her finger to her lips as he started up in panic. *Listen to me.*

He settled back on the staircase, trembling.

"The prisoner they were arguing about is my friend," she whispered. "Will you lead me to him?"

He turned away from her. "Afraid."

"Of course. But listen. I have his lordship's ring—you saw it in my hand at supper. If I can spend the rest of the

247

night in the castle without wearing the ring, your master's power will be destroyed, and you will be free."

Lorn stared at her.

"All you have to do is lead me to the tower. If my friend can move, you and he can leave, and I'll wait for Ascanet by myself. He may discover you've gone, but he knows he has only a few hours left to make me wear the ring, so he won't be able to search for you. I've left my panpipe marking the place where your . . . er . . . face is, so you can find it quickly. Get it, then leave. The guards will let you by; say his lordship has forced the prisoner to reveal the entrance to Dacaria, and that you've been told to follow him there to make sure he hasn't lied. When you get to the forest, you'll find people waiting for me; they'll help you." She looked at him intently. "Will you do it?"

Lorn sat still for a long time; at last, he nodded and crept up the stairs, his blank face gleaming in the darkness as he turned to see that she was following him. When they reached the landing, he slipped through several corridors, then led her up a narrow circular staircase. After a climb that seemed to go on forever, he opened a door and stepped into a room tastefully furnished with chairs, a canopied bed, and a bookcase filled with music. Tania looked around it in perplexity; it hardly seemed to be a prison. But Lorn touched her arm and pointed past the bed. On its far side was a space empty of everything but a stool—and a man who slumped against the wall, his head dropped on his knees.

Tania darted across the room and embraced him. "Eliar!"

He started, then raised his head. "Tania," he muttered.

She took one of his thin hands in both of hers. "I've brought Lorn; he'll take you across the Waste while I talk to Ascanet. Do you think you can walk that far if he helps you?"

248

He leaned against her weakly. "You're talking," he said. "I can see that you are, but I can't understand your words."

"You can't understand . . . ?" She stared at him. "You can't *hear*?"

"He was very clever," said Eliar dully. "If he'd simply stricken me deaf, I would at least have been able to hear music of my own invention or remembrance. But he unstrung my ears so that every note I hear is a distortion of itself; what I hear isn't music, or even silence, but the perversion of music. Melody grates and shrieks in my ears; I've heard such dissonance, I can no longer imagine harmony. And when I hear music in my head now, it is simply noise, twenty times its proper volume, but devoid of pitch and meaning." He stared vacantly into the room. "They've taken my dagger, and when I tried to beat myself against the wall, I fainted before I died. But I can feel that I'm fading; soon there will be silence, blessed silence."

"No! No!" she cried. "Lorn will take you to the forest, and Melibe will help you . . . ."

"Don't speak to me," he begged. "Every word you say dodges from my senses. The kindest thing you can do is to say nothing."

Say nothing! But if she could say nothing, how could she tell him she'd come to help him? She looked at Lorn, hoping he would know something about Eliar's state that she did not—but the boy had turned and was facing the door. Listening, she heard Ascanet's footsteps climbing the twisting stairs.

Tania released Eliar and stood up. "Hide!" she whispered to Lorn. "He'll be so angry to find me here, he'll not bother to look for you."

Lorn hesitated for a moment, then took her arm with a strength she hadn't realized he possessed and pulled her into

249

the room's darkest corner. There was no time for her to resist; when the boy at last let her go, Ascanet was standing in
the doorway, his lute cradled under his arm. He looked
about the room, frowned, then sat down on the stool before
Eliar's slumped form.

"I trust you can still hear what I say to you, though you
can understand nobody else?" he whispered.

Eliar looked up; that was answer enough.

"I have come again to ask you a most important question.
If you answer it, I'll release you in a matter of hours."

"Ask whatever you wish," murmured Eliar.

"It's very simple," said Ascanet. "I want to know if the
daughter of Campion, King of Mazion, loves you."

Eliar was silent.

"Can you not understand me?" asked Ascanet, leaning
forward.

"I can understand you. But I don't know the answer."

Didn't know the answer! Tania stirred, but Lorn grasped
her arm.

"Are you stubborn still, despite all your trials?" asked
Ascanet. "Perhaps a little music will loosen your tongue."
He tuned his instrument, glancing at Eliar again. "Be sure to
listen attentively."

He began to play, and for several minutes, Tania sat
enthralled as the instrument spoke, rising and falling in liquid scales, pausing in full-throated chords, wandering on in
strange polyphony. As the piece progressed, however, she
recognized the strain that had wafted to her that afternoon;
and she remembered what Ascanet had said. Glancing at
Eliar, she saw he had drawn his knees up and buried his face
in them, his hands covering his ears. Through the brilliance
of the music, she could hear him sob.

Ascanet stopped in midphrase. "You aren't listening!"

Eliar sobbed on. Tania wasn't even sure he was aware the music had ceased.

Ascanet strode toward him and shook his shoulder. "If you won't listen to me, perhaps you'd rather play yourself," he hissed.

Eliar looked up and shook his head, but as Ascanet stared at him, he let his knees sink down and held out one arm. Ascanet handed him the lute and stepped back. "So—begin."

Shaking his unkempt hair out of his eyes, Eliar began to finger the strings. Tania felt tears rise in her throat as she recognized the fugue he'd played at Castle Mazion the first time she'd heard him. In spite of the fragility of his thin hands, he plaited the three strands of music together as carefully and as delicately now as he had then, forming them into a glorious braid of sound—but then his fingers faltered, lost the strands, and wandered on in tangled dissonance. The melodies rose in a crescendo so discordant that the instrument itself seemed to plead for resolution; yet Eliar played on, unaware of the cacophony, until he reached the final measures. Then he looked down at his hands, stumbled to a halt, and swept his fingers across the strings in a great, despairing chord.

Ascanet stood up. "You've forgotten the coda. Here—let me play it for you." Taking the instrument, he played the final bars and handed it back. "I'm sure you'll remember it now," he whispered. "Try it again."

Pushing Lorn aside, Tania flung herself across the room and snatched the lute out of Eliar's hands, then whirled to meet Ascanet's astonished gaze. "How *can* he finish? You've taken his hearing, you've taken his beauty, you've driven him nearly mad with despair—what more can you possibly want of him?"

Ascanet's surprise dissolved into a courteous smile. "If you have been here, you know what I want," he said. "But you've saved me a great deal of trouble by defending him."

"Is my defense a surprise?" she demanded. "Would you expect *anyone* to stand by and watch a fellow mortal suffer without coming to his aid?"

Ascanet shrugged. "Many people do so," he said. "But I'm interested not in what 'anyone' would do—only in what you've done. To come to Eliar's defense, you've had to search for this tower in a castle guarded by my servants. I can't think you'd take such risks for a man you cared little about."

"You're certainly free to assume that," she said evasively. "But I saw no risk in walking through rooms that were as open to me this evening as they were this afternoon."

Ascanet frowned. "When those rooms were open to you this afternoon, you had a guardian. Where is he now?"

"You told him to come to you, my lord; and since he left me in my room, I suppose that he did."

"Come, you can't expect me to believe you arrived here by accident!"

"You may believe whatever you choose to, my lord. But you must believe without evidence."

Ascanet's eyes narrowed as they looked at her; Tania turned around and set down the lute in order to escape his frightening gaze. As she did so, she forgot her own danger entirely, for Eliar had slipped down against the wall, his eyes closed. She touched first his forehead, then his chest, fearing that he'd fainted; but the flutter beneath her fingers told her what kind of loss of consciousness she was witnessing. Sobbing, she drew him into her arms. "He's dying!" she cried, looking up at Ascanet. "Are you going to watch without helping him?"

Ascanet's eyes glinted, but he shook his head sorrowfully.

"I can't help him—only you can do that. And if you revive him, you will also give him back everything his stubbornness has lost him over the years: his beauty, his hearing, his happiness."

"Tell me what I must do, then!" she cried, stroking Eliar's forehead. "I'll do it at once!"

Ascanet smiled. "Slide the ring onto your finger and say what you would like to have done—he'll revive in an instant."

She met his triumphant gaze and shuddered. "Is there no other way?"

"There may be," he said. "But there's no time to find what it is."

Tania held Eliar more tightly. "You *say* my putting on the ring will cure him. But how do I *know* it will?"

"You'll have to take my word, I'm afraid."

"And what have you done for Elyssonne, for Eliar, or for me that I should take your word?" she asked defiantly.

"You shouldn't think of what I have done, but of what the ring can do," he said. "Consider the pleasure in finding Eliar a whole man, perhaps king of Elyssonne. Consider Elyssonne, a realm filled with wondrous musical instruments, all at Eliar's command . . ."

"If the ring gives the power to make Elyssonne such a place, why have *you* not made it a justly ruled realm full of music?"

"Because the ring does not bring to one man what it brings to another."

"I don't believe you!" she cried.

"Ah," he said with a shrug. "Well, that's regrettable. If you'd believed me and put on the ring, Eliar would have lived, but because your doubt keeps you from wearing it, he will surely die."

253

Tania looked down at Eliar's scarred face. "Eliar," she whispered. "Eliar . . . look at me."

"I'm afraid he can't hear you," said Ascanet blandly. "He seems to be fading very quickly."

"No . . . he can't be!"

"You can easily stop it from happening," said Ascanet. "Slip the ring out of your pocket—you'll see how powerful it is."

Tania reached into her pocket and pulled out the ring. It shone gloriously, perfect in its loveliness. Ascanet stepped forward quietly and picked up the lute. Gently, gracefully, he began to play. "Do you really wish Eliar to die? Are his affections so easily replaced?" he whispered over the pensive melody that filled the room.

Easily replaced! She looked at the ring longingly, realizing that if she lost Eliar, what he was to her could never be replaced. And yet . . . She closed her fingers, shutting the glistening stone out of her sight. "No," she said. "It would be unutterably selfish to sacrifice Elyssonne to my desires."

"Selfish?" said Ascanet. "How can it be selfish to save a life that isn't yours? Come, my lady. If you truly loved him, you would save him, no matter what the cost. Your hesitation suggests you do not love him well enough to let him live. *That* is selfishness."

Could that possibly be true? Tania opened her hand, watching the ring glisten. She knew very little of love; her afternoon with Eliar had been sweet to her, but it had been short. Furthermore, in the rush of events that had followed those magical hours, there had been no time for her to learn what loving him would entail. In a way, she understood no more now than she had before she and Eliar had kissed; their embrace had simply enabled her to give a name to feelings that had gradually become clear to her. Perhaps those feel-

254

ings had not had time to deepen into real love. If that were the case, she was sacrificing Eliar's life to her own ignorance.

"Hurry," urged Ascanet's whisper through the halo of his music. "He is dying."

Eliar's breath was coming in uneven gasps; his face lost its tortured look and settled into a peaceful smile. He *was* dying; if she did nothing, she would lose him within the hour. And yet, and yet . . . she suddenly thought of Melibe and his deep understanding of the rooms he lived in. Putting on the ring, knowing it was what it was, would be a denial of every truth Melibe had ever shared with her. How could she do that? . . . On the other hand, how could she *not* do it? If she let Eliar die, she would have to live the rest of her life knowing that she could have saved him, could have become one person with him—and had not loved him enough to do it.

She kissed Eliar's peaceful face, then opened her palm. Slowly, she placed the ring in the grasp of her right hand, then moved it toward the ring finger of her left. For Eliar. Ascanet's sweet music wafted around her. For Eliar . . .

"No!" she sobbed suddenly. "I can't put it on! . . . Eliar, Eliar . . . forgive me, but I can't . . . Oh, Melibe . . ." She held Eliar to her, letting the ring roll back into her palm as she bent over him. And as she wept for her failure and her loss, her tears splashed down onto her half-open hand.

Ascanet's music stopped in midphrase, and he leapt up with a whispering cry. Tania raised her head quickly, fearing treachery—but he was standing motionless, staring at her hand. Before she could follow his gaze, she felt the ring shudder; looking down in terror, she saw the tear-drenched sapphire tremble, soften, then writhe out of its silver foil. With a cry, she jerked her hand away. The band dropped to the floor—but the stone hung suspended in the air, hissing and struggling until it lost its form completely and whirled toward Ascanet in a cloud of blue steam.

The room began to shake as if the earth under it were giving way. As Tania leaned over Eliar, trying to protect him from the pieces of crystal that fell from the ceiling, she saw Ascanet reel, his arms rising into the air. The lute fell from his hands and smashed to the trembling floor; but as he strove to look down, the blue cloud enveloped his knees, his chest, his shoulders, his head, his upraised arms—then spun around the room with him in its tumbling embrace, bored its way through the tower wall, and fled into the night with a shriek that filled the silent Waste.

The tower began to sway; an avalanche of rotten ice crashed from the ceiling, ripping the canopy off the bed and knocking over the bookcase. Tania hauled Eliar's unconscious body onto her shoulder and struggled to her feet, staggering under his weight.

"Lorn!" she called, looking at the corner where he was hiding. "Lorn—can you hear me?"

A small figure crawled out from under the torn canopy and reeled toward her. "Yes, I can hear you. Let me go first —if we can get to the walls, there's a way down from there!"

Tania stared at him, shocked at his sudden burst of language.

Lorn ran to the door, lurching as the floor moved beneath his feet. "Yes, I can speak now," he said, tugging at the door, "and move, too. When he asked you where I was, he looked around and saw me—and he froze me with his eyes. But I saw everything . . ." He wrenched the door open, jumping back as its frame crashed down into its opening. Kicking the rubble aside, he darted down the stairs, while Tania followed him more slowly, sliding her hand down the wall to keep her balance. As she descended, she felt the wall grow wet; by the time they reached the door to the corridor, the sound of cascading water echoed off every trembling arch.

"This way!" cried Lorn as she reached the bottom step.

She nodded breathlessly, and the two of them splashed through the roaring, icy currents that tumbled through the corridors, dodging chunks of sodden ice that crashed from the walls. Lorn rushed out onto the ramparts, then turned to her.

"Your way down lies there," he shouted over the noise, pointing to a door. "It's a chute that leads through the walls —it was made to enable his lordship to loose the hippogriffs if the castle were attacked."

Tania moved toward the door, then realized he hadn't moved. "Aren't you coming?"

He shook his head. "I've got to go to the double staircase," he shouted. "It's going to collapse soon, and when it does, the doors of the reliefs will break and I'll be lost, like Sir Rollin—do you see? You said you marked the place!"

She nodded. "All right! But look—you'll be crushed if you try to go out through the courtyard, and you'll run into the guards. Come back up here; I'll wait for you if I can."

He darted away. "Don't wait too long!" he called back over his shoulder.

Tania set Eliar down as gently as she could on the lurching parapet walk, then felt his chest anxiously. His heart was beating faintly—but no more faintly than it had been in the tower. Perhaps there was hope . . . She stood up, rubbing her aching shoulder, and looked out over the battlements. Far across the moonlit Waste, she could see a band of dark figures moving toward the castle, but as she watched them, an eerie light burst out from the ground below her. The light grew brighter—then the snow split open, and a surging mass of silver figures fled from the widening crack, followed by

257

panicked horses that trampled them as they ran toward the Waste. In the midst of the screaming crowd, one man vaulted onto a horse and began to lay about him with his sword.

"Back, back, you fools! To the castle! If it falls before we find what's ours, we'll all be dead men!" He spurred the horse toward the gate; the others hesitated, looked up at the swaying towers, then followed him, pushing each other aside as they reached the swaying arch. Deserted by their masters, the horses fled back to their subterranean stable, and the ground rumbled shut behind them.

Light footsteps ran across the walls; turning, Tania saw a boy with a snub nose and a smile that warmed the night. As she stared at him, he took her panpipe off his belt and handed it to her. "I never could have found it without this," he said. "The stairs are so sodden, they're impossible to count."

"I'm glad you found the right . . . place," she said awkwardly. "And I'm glad you missed the others. I saw them trying to get in."

He pursed his lips. "I heard them fighting in the corridors," he said. "But I . . . I'd rather not talk about it. Some of them were as kind to me as they were capable of being. Come, let's get out while we can." He helped her carry Eliar to the buckling door, then kicked it open. "Shall I go first?"

Tania looked down the icy incline and nodded, settling Eliar in her arms. Lorn disappeared into the darkness ahead of her; then she pushed herself off and slid down . . . down . . . down . . . whirling dizzily as the chute spun around, and whizzing out at last into the snow outside the walls. Breathless, she eased herself out from under Eliar and scrambled to her feet, then looked around for Lorn. He was lying a few feet from her, half covered by a pile of frozen rubble.

"Lorn!" she cried. And then she saw the hippogriffs. They were pecking at the walls with their beaks, backing away, pulling the huge staples that fastened their chains out of the rotting ice. Busy now with their project, they had no eyes for anything else, but they would soon be free.

Her cry of fear was covered by a tremendous roar as the castle gates collapsed. She dug furiously in the splintered ice and drew the boy out from under it. His eyes were open, but his face was contorted in pain. "There's something wrong with my ankle," he moaned. "You'd better go ahead."

"No!" she said fiercely. "Here—try to stand; maybe I can brace you. Hurry!" She eased Eliar over her shoulder and staggered back to Lorn. With sick fear, she saw he could barely walk.

"I'll take one of them!" shouted a voice behind her.

She turned and saw a man running toward her with a familiar, lithe stride. "Kylian!" she sobbed.

"Yes," he panted. "I came on ahead . . . great, merciful gods—is that Eliar? Here—let me take him. Hoist your little friend over your shoulder before these monsters escape. We haven't far to go, fortunately: there's a rock out on the plain that will give us shelter if we can reach it."

She boosted Lorn onto her back and ran past the crumbling walls, out onto the Waste. Ahead of her, she heard voices, then saw several people running toward them. "Get back!" shouted Kylian. "Leave room for us, and stay as close to the rock as you can." The people turned and ran back toward what Tania recognized as the rock the Silver Souls had taken her to the day before.

When they reached it, Kylian put Eliar down gently, and Colin lifted Lorn from Tania's back. Tania knelt at Eliar's side, anxiously feeling his weak pulse. Kylian bent over him, frowning.

Suddenly, Asphodel whistled a warning. Tania turned and saw the wolf people throw themselves to the ground near the rock. As she slipped down into its shadow next to Eliar, Kylian touched her arm. "Look!"

Tania crawled forward and looked where he pointed. Four gigantic black shadows rose into the sky, their broken chains glistening in the moonlight. They kited above the castle, shrieking in bewilderment as blazes of blue light shot up its swaying walls and towers. For a moment, the whole castle shone brilliantly across the Waste; then its shining mass tottered, collapsed, and began to spin, slowly at first, then faster and faster, brighter and brighter . . . until the ground beneath it opened, and the shining liquid poured into it like molten silver. Screaming in anguish, the hippogriffs dove frantically into the abyss, their wings aloft, their talons outstretched. As the last monster shot below the surface of the ground, it closed over them with a crash that echoed across all Elyssonne.

CHAPTER
XVIII

THE SILENCE THAT FOLLOWED seemed to suck the moon out of the sky; the Waste faded in its dwindling rays, then became one with the darkness. After a long time, Tania heard the scratch of flint, then blinked as Kylian lit a candle. Around her, the wolf people stared as if they'd awakened from a dream and slowly began to stir. A few of them helped Cadwal bind Lorn's ankle; the others looked at Eliar's still form, talking to each other in hushed voices.

Asphodel bent over Eliar, then looked up at Tania, shaking her head.

Tania bit her lower lip. "I hoped he'd revive when the castle fell."

"So did I," Asphodel said, "for I think there's little we can do. There's no injury to bind, no fever to lower, no illness to cure. He's simply fading, as if some essential part of him were lost."

"Yes," whispered Tania. "Ascanet took his hearing—or, rather, distorted it, so he could hear only dissonance and Ascanet himself."

"Took his hearing?" Kylian knelt next to Tania. "Then *the* essential part of him is lost. There can be no Eliar if there's no music." He slipped his arm around her shoulders.

Tania closed her eyes. "Ascanet said I could save his hearing—and his life—if I put the ring on. But I couldn't bring myself to do it."

"And you were right!" Asphodel's eyes blazed in the wan light. "If Ascanet told you to sacrifice Elyssonne for your love for Eliar, what he called love was no more love than the dissonance he made Eliar hear was music."

Tania looked at Eliar's still face. "Perhaps, perhaps—but some of what Ascanet said about my love was true . . ."

"Some of what he said was always true," said Asphodel. "Accomplished liars mix truth and falsehood so carefully that one accepts their whole concoction. If the truth in what Ascanet said struck some responsive chord in you, that's because you saw it apart from its false context and respected it for what it was."

"Maybe . . . but what I saw when he spoke was that I could refuse to wear the ring for all the right reasons—and still, my refusal might be a way of admitting that what I felt for Eliar was a dream of what I wished it to be, not a true feeling for what and who he was. And to sacrifice his life because I had deluded myself seemed . . ."

Asphodel looked at Tania's tear-streaked face, then took her hand. "I hadn't realized what pain your victory must have cost you," she said in a gentle voice Tania had never heard her use before. "Remember: Ascanet's most effective tactic was to confuse his opponents by making them doubt what they knew to be true."

"But I *don't* know it's true," sobbed Tania. "How can it be? He couldn't possibly be dying if I truly loved him!"

Kylian tightened his arm around her. "He doesn't need love; he needs wisdom none of us has," he said. "Tania, let me go find the hermit—Melibe, as you call him—and tell him of Eliar's state. He may be able to do what the rest of us cannot."

"Oh!" breathed Tania. "Oh, yes . . . but, Kylian—it's so far to Dacaria . . ."

"It is," said Kylian, "but I don't think Melibe is in Dacaria. When he sent me to find Asphodel, he said he'd soon follow himself. If I start now, I should be able to find him in the forest at daybreak tomorrow."

"The forest! But the Silver Souls are still there, aren't they?"

"In a manner of speaking," said Kylian dryly. "But they'll be no danger to him. When we found them, the captain, the lieutenant, and several of the men were dead, and the others were badly wounded. There must have been some kind of mutiny." He got to his knees and pressed Asphodel's hand. "I'll come back as quickly as I can," he said, and slipped out onto the Waste. They heard him take a few running steps— then stop. After a moment, his voice drifted back to them, strangely muffled but full of fear. "Asphodel . . ."

The wolf people glanced at each other and got up. Asphodel snatched a candle from the ledge and leapt out from under the stone. Tania followed her, but as she stood up, the tiny glimmer of the candle was almost invisible. All she could see was an immense white fog, so thick it parted around her as she moved. As she tried to peer through it, she heard a soft, musical hum that made her lose all sense of where she was. In panic, she stretched out a hand and felt the reassuring firmness of the rock under her fingers.

"Kylian! Asphodel!" she cried, her voice so stilled she felt as if she were speaking into a quilt.

"Tania—don't leave the rock!" called Asphodel's deadened voice.

"Stay where you are!" called Colin from behind her. "We can see your candle, and we'll make a chain. Cadwal?" Colin grasped Tania's hand. The fog whirled around her, and first he, then Cadwal edged past her out onto the Waste. For a few seconds, there was no other sound; then she heard a cry of welcome and pulled them toward her.

As she ducked back under the rock, she saw Kylian and Asphodel were trembling and the others were wide-eyed in the terror she'd felt before she'd touched the stone. "What is it?" she whispered.

Colin shook his head. "I don't know."

Asphodel swept her long hair back with unsteady hands. "There's music—or something like it." She smiled weakly at Kylian. "And I thought I'd grown used to that sort of thing . . ."

"So did I," he said, his voice shaking.

"Whatever it is, it's like nothing we've seen in the forest," said Cadwal.

Kylian drew a long breath and looked at Eliar. "I'm afraid I'll have to wait, Tania."

"Oh yes," she breathed. "What we saw and felt would terrify anybody—even Melibe."

"I wonder . . ." said Kylian.

"Melibe," said Cadwal. "I heard you say the name before, but I just realized . . . Is he—can he possibly be—the hermit who used to wander about Elyssonne?"

"Why, yes," said Tania, surprised. "And he still does wander, though I discovered that only recently. While I was growing up, he was my tutor at Castle Mazion, and I never thought to ask where he'd come from or why he sometimes left for a few days. Do you know him?"

"I knew him many years ago, when Ascanet had ruled Elyssonne only fifty years," he said. "He found me in my despair and told me to come to the forest. I wouldn't have thought he was still alive."

Tania thought of Melibe's old but ageless face. Perhaps it was no stranger than the faces about her. "He is alive," she said, "and he is . . . good."

"Yes," said Cadwal. "I was in no mood to appreciate that when I met him, but I've not forgotten it since."

Asphodel looked about her at the weary faces of the wolf people and at Lorn, who had crawled to Tania's side and was falling asleep with his head on her shoulder. "We should all sleep, if we can," she said. "It's only a few hours until dawn; we seem to be safe here—and who knows what lies before us?"

The wolf people murmured in assent and curled up where they sat. Kylian and Asphodel offered to stay with Eliar, but Tania looked at their exhausted eyes and insisted that they rest. Soon all was quiet, and the candles burned out one by one. Tania moved Lorn gently, settled herself against the rock, and drew Eliar into her arms.

For the rest of the night, she sat with her cheek pillowed in Eliar's hair and her fingers laced through his, her eyes wide-open as she thought of him, of Ascanet, of Melibe, and of the strange music that had swept about her in the fog. Gradually, the darkness turned gray, then brightened. Looking out from under the rock, she saw the fog had dispersed, leaving the air clear and strangely warm. Quietly, wonderingly, she slid Eliar to the ground and crept out onto the Waste to greet the dawn.

What she saw made her stare and rub her eyes. To her right, where the castle had been, a deep blue lake reflected the gray morning sky through a haze of rising silver mist. On its east side, great oak trees leaned toward each other in solemn silence; on its west, willow trees examined their images, their delicate branches trailing in the water. Somewhere in the groves, a thrush sang a long, ascending melody, and the sun rose, spilling its first rays across the luminous green meadow that had once been Ascanet's Waste. Looking toward the forest, Tania saw that the landscape was no longer featureless and flat; it rose and fell gently, its hills covered with sweet-smelling trees, its grass everywhere dotted with flowers. And as she looked at it, smiling in awe and wonder, a single rider on a gray horse crested one of the hills and cantered toward her.

For a moment, she was lost in time: the rider became Campion, the horse, Pandosto—and behind them was not the forest, but the great allied army of Elyssonne, marching toward Ascanet's castle to defeat the island's conquerer and restore the Golden Age. She blinked away the vision and her tears together, but as her eyes cleared, she saw what was before her was no fantasy. With a cry, she ran forward. "Melibe!"

Melibe swung off the gray horse and took her in his arms. "You have done well, child," he said.

Tania embraced him, then looked up and saw something unfamiliar in the face she'd always known. "You've . . . changed."

"Perhaps," he said. "But you also have changed, so you see me differently." He smiled. "Your work has wrought many changes."

She took his reins from him and looked toward the rock and the silent, marveling wolf people who had emerged from its shelter and grouped themselves behind Asphodel and Kylian. "Melibe, Eliar is very ill."

"I know; that's why I've come. Take me to him quickly."

She led him through the flowers. As they reached the rock, Asphodel and Kylian embraced him, and each of the wolf people dropped down upon one knee. Melibe looked at them all and smiled. "I will talk to each of you soon, for the island's changes have thrust new choices upon you. But before I do that, I must see Eliar. Will you bring him out here? The sun will do him good."

Colin and Cadwal bore Eliar gently out. Melibe bent over

the still form, his face serious. "He has been driven deep into the realm of Orcus," he said. "Since he refused to betray Dacaria, he has wandered back and forth between that realm and the world of men. When Ascanet took all the harmony that remained from him, he was lost indeed."

Tania looked at him through a haze of tears. "Is there nothing you can do? Is there nothing *I* can do?" She dropped on her knees and took Eliar's hand. "Oh, Eliar . . . please, Eliar . . . live."

Melibe laid his hand on her shoulder. "Tania, you're the daughter of a beautiful, joyful woman who never lived to see you. Do you think she would have died if your father's love —and Sena's and all Dacaria's—could have saved her?"

Slowly, Tania shook her head.

"And you are the daughter of a man whom you loved deeply, both for what he was and for what he strove to do. Could all your love, all your obedience, all your belief in him save him from destruction?"

"No," she whispered. Her eyes fell to Eliar's face. "Then . . . I must lose him?" she asked. "Lose him, just as I . . . as we . . . ?"

Melibe touched her wet cheek. "Not now. But you must love him knowing that your love can't preserve either of you from change and loss. To think otherwise is to demand of love a power it doesn't have." He smiled at her. "But it has powers of its own; if Eliar hadn't found you, there would be little I could do for him now. He'd grown weary of life itself."

"I've given him very little," she said, shaking her head.

"You've given him trust, loyalty, love—is that so little?"

"The words sound greater than the fact," she said. "I've been so clumsy and stupid . . . I know almost nothing . . ."

"You forget," he said, "that one needs time to learn. That

you have not had, and you'll find you both will need it; you are young, and he has been deeply damaged. Still''—he smiled—''many people would envy you what lies in your room of dreams.''

He bent over Eliar and blew gently on his forehead, then laid one hand on each of the scarred cheeks. Tania leaned forward, hardly daring to breathe. Beside her, Asphodel reached for Kylian's hand. For several seconds nothing changed; then Eliar stirred and opened his eyes.

Melibe took his hands away. "He has come back," he said quietly. "But be gentle. It will take him time to become accustomed to the world again."

Eliar sat up slowly and looked around him with dazed wonder. "Are we in Dacaria?"

He hadn't asked her, nor, when he looked at the people who stood silently around him, did he seem to recognize her. But she replied. "We're at Ascanet's castle—or rather, where the castle used to be. Don't you remember?"

"I remember . . ." Eliar raised his hands to his ears. "I remember dreaming that music was lost to me," he murmured. "And Tania . . ."

"I'm here," she said, taking his hand. "Can't you see me?"

His eyes seemed to look through her, but they gradually focused, and he smiled. "So you're not in the castle. I dreamed Ascanet had . . ."

Melibe touched Tania's arm. "Walk with him to the lake. He will soon remember all that has happened to him—and when he does, he'll be grateful for solitude."

Tania rose and offered Eliar her hand. "Will you come with me?" she asked, almost shyly.

He took it, and they walked toward the lake, looking at the grass and flowers that surrounded them. At the lake's edge, he sat down, and Tania sat beside him, waiting for him to speak. After a few minutes, he picked up a silver pebble and tossed it into the water. Waves rippled out in concentric circles, and as he watched them, a gentle turbulence stirred in his eyes.

"It wasn't a dream, then," he said faintly.

"No," she said. "Though it feels as if it must have been."

He threw another pebble; this time, a tremor rippled up and down his whole body. He dropped his head onto his knees, sitting as he had in the tower. "The sound, the sound . . . oh, Tania—each note was a horror . . . you can't possibly imagine . . ." Suddenly, he lifted his head and looked at her panpipe. "Play," he whispered.

Fear surged through her. "But, Eliar, if you can hear me speak . . ."

"Please," he begged. "There's nothing you can spare me now that I won't learn later."

She unhitched the panpipe with shaking hands. Unable to look at him, she raised the instrument to her lips and piped one of its wistful melodies. As she played, the willow trees sighed a sad accompaniment and the oaks rustled their leaves together, listening. She reached the cadence and stopped; a faint echo of the last bars drifted back to her across the lake.

As the last sounds died away, she turned to Eliar. His face was frozen, and his eyes looked at some point far in the distance. "Couldn't . . . couldn't you hear it?" she asked.

He didn't move; for a long time, he didn't speak. At last, his gaze came back from wherever it had gone and settled on the willows. "Yes," he said slowly. "Yes, I could hear it. And all that answered it." His voice shook, and he stopped.

Tania looked at him, then set the panpipe down on the grass. Gently, tenderly, she slipped one arm around him and stroked his scarred face with her hand. She felt a shudder as

269

cataclysmic as the shocks that had destroyed Ascanet's castle —then he turned to her and wept.

When they finally walked back to the others, hand in hand, Lorn came bouncing toward them on a pair of crutches. "Cadwal made me these," he said, beaming. "I'll only need them for a little while—it's just a sprain—but I'll keep them always. He's been good to me. He'll be near me, too; he's going to live in Theda and become a carpenter again, and Theda's where I used to live. Melibe said he has told my father I'm alive. I don't know how." A little shadow crossed his face. "You see, the Silver Souls heard my father supported King Campion, and they stole me away to punish him. And then, his lordship—I mean, Ascanet—told me Father had died of grief."

"All that's past now," Tania said. "You'll forget, in time."

"So Melibe said." He smiled. "Can you come visit me, my lady? And you, too, my lord. You'd like my father; he makes instruments. Maybe I'm old enough to help him now . . . Oh! but I forgot—I was supposed to tell you to hurry. Melibe has just finished talking to Colin, and only Kylian and Asphodel are left. You've been gone a long time."

"We had many things to say to each other," said Tania.

"When I see Father again, I suppose it will be the same." Lorn nodded. He rubbed his tunic sleeve across his eyes and looked away. "I'm going to sit by the lake awhile," he muttered.

Eliar watched him go. "Is that the boy who served me in the tower?"

"Yes," she said, waving to Colin as they started forward again. "I could never have gotten out of the castle without him."

"Are you talking about Lorn?" asked Colin as he joined

them. "He was just talking about his father, and I realized he was the instrument maker I gave your lute to. I knew he grieved for something, but I never used to ask people why they sorrowed. There was no reason to, and there was so little one could do . . . Well, the two of them will have each other now—and Lorn is already much changed." He smiled at them. "As, may I say, are you. It's good to see you both so happy."

Changed. Tania had just been about to apply that word to him, for his face had none of the sadness that had been in it before. "May we ask what Melibe has suggested that you do?"

Colin beamed. "He said the Dacarian herdsman I've been trading horses with all my life needs my help."

"Then you'll live in Dacaria?" said Tania joyfully. "Do you know, when I saw it and saw Sena's horses, I thought of what you said about there being no place in Elyssonne where you could live—and I wished I'd known about it."

"I'll live in Dacaria awhile," he said. "But from what Melibe says, Dacaria will no longer be as different from the rest of Elyssonne as it was. Apparently, it's not just the Waste that's seen all the changes that frightened us so last night, but the whole island."

"I wonder what the people of the island will think of that," said Tania.

"I think Melibe . . ." Colin broke off as they reached the rock. "Oh, there are Asphodel and Kylian. I must go." He slipped away, but as they turned to follow him, Melibe called to them.

"Wait where you are," he said. "These people have told me they have no secrets from you, and I wish to talk to you presently."

They sat down obediently, as Melibe put his hand on Asphodel's shoulder. "I am happy to see you in your proper form," he said. "As, I believe, is Kylian. He has sorrowed for the loss of his wolf's coat as deeply as you sorrowed for the loss of your humanity many years ago."

Asphodel took his hand. "I did grieve for my lost humanity," she said, "but I would happily have remained what I became if that had enabled me to be with Kylian. Tell me— are our enchantments past? Will we be able to live without further changes?"

Melibe looked at her seriously. "If you wish to be one with Kylian, you will have to shed the last of your enchantments and suffer the changes common to all mortals, including age and death. Is that your wish?"

"That would be my wish indeed," she said. "If . . . if in becoming mortal I didn't also become the age I truly am."

Melibe smiled. "So all your people have asked. And I've assured them that they will be released from their enchantment only a little older than they were when they first became subject to it, though infinitely more experienced."

"Then I would indeed like to be released, but it's not my choice alone." Asphodel turned to Kylian.

He shook his head. "It must be. How can I ask you to leave your subjects and become mortal for my sake?"

"My subjects, as you call them, are as free to leave me as they have always been, and I believe each of them has chosen to live in a different place. As for mortality, I'm no stranger to it: according to all reports, I have been dead for five hundred years, long enough to become accustomed to the idea of oblivion, if not the fact." She took his hand and looked at him more seriously. "And finally, how can you ask me to live after you have died? Was the pain of five years' separation so slight that you would wish me to suffer it permanently?"

Kylian kissed the hand that held his. "If I thought it were possible, I would wish that you never suffered again."

Melibe took their joined hands. "It shall be done, then. May you be as happy together in the world of man as you were in the forest—and now," he said in a different voice, "I wish to talk to all of you. Asphodel, will you draw your people together for the last time?"

Asphodel smiled sadly, then whistled. The wolf people rose from everywhere on the grass and trotted toward her, and Lorn bounced back swiftly from the lake. When they'd all assembled, Melibe looked at them affectionately, then held out his hand toward the rock that loomed behind him.

"This stone," he said, "is the stone on which Theon stood after he had set Elyssonne into the sea. From it, he addressed the first inhabitants of the island and blessed all their endeavors. That is why, of course, Ascanet chose to build his castle here; he wished to revel in Theon's defeat, and he wished to be sure that the defeat was permanent. But because Tania has undone Ascanet's victory, this is Theon's stone once more, and what Theon did then, I do now—bless you as the creators of a Golden Age.

"Your duties are more complex than those of your ancestors. When they settled the island, it was empty; you return to towns and cities whose inhabitants have forgotten what life was before there were kings, wars, and laws. If Elyssonne is to have another Golden Age, you will have to teach its people to recall the virtues of the first one. That may be difficult at the beginning, but you'll find you have willing students. The men whose lives depended upon Ascanet's commands perished when he did, for he had imprisoned their souls as securely—though less plainly—as he imprisoned those of his soldiers. And for the rest: when I journeyed here, the forest was filled with song; men and women had forgotten their fears and come there to renew the old friendship of man and nature. Hundreds of them stopped me, asking me if a new age were indeed dawning; and when I said it was, they hurried back to their homes to rejoice with their neighbors. Such pupils will need little instruction in theory; they will principally need to learn new ways of making the decisions that confront them daily."

The wolf people looked at each other and nodded. But Tania stepped forward. "Melibe—among us, only Kylian, Asphodel, and Eliar have experience with the way of life you wish us to teach. How can the rest of us teach what we haven't learned ourselves?"

"If I were you," said Melibe, "I would start by going to Dacaria and consulting Anrican, son of Aldar. Modest as he is, he is the man to whom all Dacarians turn as an example of living simply and well, as Elissa is the woman to whom they turn when they are ill. The two of them are the essence of all that was glorious in the Golden Age; their unassuming wisdom influences all who meet them." He smiled. "I doubt that they will ever leave Dacaria," he added. "But every time you return there, their presence will refresh you, and all who see you will learn what they know through your example."

Eliar, Tania, and Kylian exchanged glances of understanding.

"And now," said Melibe, "it is time for you to go to whatever places you have chosen. Remember, Dacaria is no longer cut off from the rest of Elyssonne; there are pathways to it all through the island, and it can be found easily by any who wish to travel there. Go there whenever you are weary; it will restore you."

"Can we come to you, too, Melibe?" asked Tania. "I'm sure we'll need your wisdom sorely."

Melibe looked across the meadow. "To those who don't

call me Melibe, I am known simply as the hermit," he said with a lightness his face did not reflect. "And the essence of being a hermit is being difficult to find. If you need wisdom, you may search for it in my library; there is plenty of it there, though you will have to sort through a certain amount of foolishness and ignorance to uncover it."

As she stared at him, she recognized the true meaning of his words. "You . . . you mean you are leaving us?" she stammered.

"In a manner of speaking."

"But where will you go?" she asked, bewildered.

"You will understand in time," he said. "For the present —come kiss me, child."

She ran to him and held him, sobbing in his arms. When she finally looked up at him, she saw his eyes were wet. "Think, sometimes, of how dearly I have loved you," he said softly, giving her hand to Eliar.

"Go now," he said, smiling at them all. "You will find your journeys shorter than the ones that brought you here. Farewell, sons and daughters of Elyssonne. May Theon grace your days."

One by one, they filed past him, kissing his hand; then they started across the rolling hills toward the mountains that ringed Dacaria. As they reached the top of the first rise, Tania turned and looked back. Melibe was still standing where he had been, his hair shining silver against the dark background of Theon's stone. She waved to him, then saw that Eliar, too, had looked back.

His eyes met hers as they turned toward Dacaria again, and she saw he understood what she did. Taking his hand, she smiled at him, and they followed the others across the meadow.